ADVANCED PRAISE

HURRICANE SEASON
BY MARK POWELL

"Brutal and poetic, Mark Powell's story will retune your heart strings, you'll begin with a triple-espresso and end with triple-shots of Kentucky bourbon and no chaser, it's a smooth burn."

— **Frank Bill,** author of ***Back to the Dirt***

"In ***Hurricane Season,*** Mark Powell writes about the places where America happens – its hospitals, prisons, fighting gyms, and roadside motels. This is an indispensable work of fiction about the contemporary South in all its tragic complexities. A book brimming with heart, as propulsive as it is wise."

— **Caleb Johnson**, author of ***Treeborne***

**OTHER WORKS
BY MARK POWELL**

Prodigals
Blood Kin
The Dark Corner
The Sheltering
Small Treasons
Firebird
Lioness

HURRICANE SEASON

a novel

MARK POWELL

SHOTGUN HONEY

2023

Published by **Shotgun Honey Books**

215 Loma Road
Charleston, WV 25314
www.ShotgunHoney.com

Cover Design by Ron Earl Phillips.

First Printing 2023.

ISBN-10: 1-956957-23-5
ISBN-13: 978-1-956957-23-5

9 8 7 6 5 4 3 2 1   23 22 21 20 19 18

for Dave and Reggie,
and in memory of Doc.
Hey Doc, I miss you, brother.

HURRICANE SEASON

That last day. I keep going back to it, back to Shy, back to the river.

Specifically: the way she comes out of it. The way Shy Walsh emerges from the St. Johns, long-limbed and silvered and streaming water so that the surface appears as merely the most recently shattered thing.

The way she wrings her hair.

The way she wipes her eyes.

Then I remind myself that was after, after the raid and after the fire.

So start there, I suppose.

Start with the two dozen FDLE agents working in coordination with the Marion County Sheriff's Department. The Cessna Skymaster the DEA kept overhead. Two arrests made at the scene. No resistance, just a moment of noise and surprise splintering an otherwise quiet evening. The whole thing over before it was clear what exactly was happening. At least that's how the Fox affiliate out of Ocala reported it. You can find it all online: photos of the three mobile homes stranded in a clearing of live oak and strangler vines. The man and woman perp-walked down the concrete steps, heads down, wrists flex-cuffed. A few kilos of Mexican Rail piled in an evidence locker by a few thousand Roxanol, labeled, for official purposes, Morphine Sulfate

(20 mg). That was the raid. As for the fire, you'll have to go to another website to learn that about an hour later, and some 45 miles to the southeast, the Church of Life More Abundant in Christ burned to its foundation.

Still, what I go back to is Shy.

How bursting from the river she must have thought of those moments before fights when she'd rise from her ice bath, her skin razored by the cold, by the sweat, by the rolling and sparring and battle ropes and box hops. By—I mean to say—the work: the day-after-day suffering that was neither more nor less than her life's project.

She was living on the houseboat then—living there with the light, with the honeysuckle and jasmine, that funk of mud—living there right up until the last day. But that sounds so needlessly dramatic. It sounds like the sort of thing I'm trying not to say.

Instead, imagine late morning, imagine May: Shy has just come back from her swim, alone on the deck, hair still damp, chest still panting. That her shoulders appear wider than you might remember is not simply a product of the way she stands: when you fight, you learn to crouch, to curl in on yourself; as a swimmer you lean out, you expand. So it's her, but not quite.

Nevertheless, she's there.

It's Doc who isn't.

It's Dr. Thomas Clayton who is disturbingly absent, having come in the day before with scabbed hands, the blood on them dried and flecking.

Shy must have noticed them, she must have asked.

I see him walking to the sink.

I see him shaking his head in that way he had, dismissive and superior, but honest too, always honest.

No, he must have told her, wiping them clean, it isn't my blood.

And it wasn't. Doc was many things, but he wasn't a liar.

Neither was Shy.

And neither am I.

So believe me when I tell you that sometime later Shy will wait on the bank until she sees it, and when she does, disappear into the St. John's River without so much as a second thought. And why not? She's already made the trip to Miami, back to the stucco ghetto that surrounds Hammerhead MMA, back to Doc alone in a hotel room. *You want to cry?* he told her. *I'll tell you when to cry.* So far as I know she never did.

She just stood there on the bank, alone with the honeysuckle and jasmine, that funk of mud.

And the water, of course.

Shy will slip into the water just as Doc slips into the Red Carpet Inn off 595 in Fort Lauderdale, puts on his Arvo Pärt, and pushes up the drop ceiling to find the floor joist. *Resourceful to the end,* his father will tell me. *The clever son of a bitch.* Meanwhile, Shy will slide into the deeper waters of the bay and then the ocean and then into whatever comes beyond that.

This is not the ending I intended.

This is not the ending I wished for.

But maybe to paraphrase Doc's precious Sartre *we all get the ending we deserve.*

Still, it makes you want to go back to before, back to the start.

Here's how it started for Doc.

As near as I can tell, here is his before:

Seventy-one days before he was sent up to Lawtey Correctional on a possession with intent to distribute charge—opioids being a schedule II drug, which, of course, he knew, but about which had simply failed to care—Dr. Thomas Clayton sat barefoot in his well-appointed study and fondled a first American edition of Ernest Hemingway's *A Farewell to Arms*. Full black morocco covers, marbled end papers, raised bands. Very Fine. He'd picked it up at auction in the spring, three-thousand pounds Sterling, and since then couldn't stop touching it. He had, in all, twenty-one different books, equating to a total investment of around one-hundred-ninety-five thousand US, none of which should be considered asset hiding. He was a collector, that was all. A connoisseur. The potential liquidity, the potential hide-ability of such being happenstance and having, obviously, nothing to do with the deterioration of his marriage of the last dozen years.

He put the book flat on his desk and ran a finger along the gilt spine while Arvo Pärt's *Da Pacem Domine* played softly from his desktop's speakers. He'd added the study in the last year: the mahogany bookshelves, the plush carpet, and little else. The room was narrow, just as he'd intended it. Room for nothing beyond Doc and his books and the small window overlooking the golf course where, over the last hour, he'd watched the sprinklers chug off and the sun come up, the gauzy half-light of dawn giving way to a Florida morning already impossibly bright. There were golfers out now, old men in Sanz-a-belt slacks with cigars and expensive Callaway clubs, and he was glad to see them, a little ordering to his world, a little arrangement.

His only regret was the noise: he should have soundproofed the room. He'd read up on it, the insulation, the acoustical caulk, but at the time he and his wife had been pretending to exist in a little meadow of sunlight, and the act had seemed if not aggressive certainly not embodying the "open channels of honest communication" to which they had committed in the presence of an Orlando marriage counselor.

But now he heard them, wife and daughter, hairdryer and Bluetooth speaker, and he regretted whatever naivety had allowed him to imagine the rotation of his world was somehow righting itself.

He turned the music up, but only slightly.

He'd worked the 7 PM to 7 AM shift in the ER of Bert Fish Medical, dusk to dawn, the nurses buzzing around while the charts piled and multiplied, and just after midnight had taken a bronchodilator in the fourth floor men's room in order to see it through. It was after nine now and though he could still feel the jangling of the Formoterol he could also feel it begin to wane. He yawned and tapped the mouse of his desktop: 9:13.

"Honey?" he could hear his wife calling.

He'd be asleep by 10 and brought up again the webpage of Hound's Ear Rare & Antique Books. His appointment was for 8 AM the following day. Today, he'd sleep, work his shift, and then drive straight from the hospital to sell a signed first edition of *In Our Time*, something he was loath to part with but, given the cash demands of his current situation, resigned too. His lawyer had advised against this. *Forget the books, you need to buckle down, Tommy. And maybe get your ass preemptively in rehab.* But his lawyer had only a layman's understanding of the extent to which Dr. Clayton had spent the last three years thoroughly wrecking his dopamine receptors. His lawyer failed to consider the depth and breadth of a habit that more and more induced bouts of aphasia, moments when Thomas Clayton absolutely could not find a name, a word, a procedure, a face. What was to be done with a habit of such magnitude? *Can you draw out Leviathan with a hook,* he asked himself. *Or snare his tongue with a line which you lower?* No, you can only feed it.

Which—after facing his wife, after facing his daughter, after facing the ever growing pile of financial commitments, bills, really, each overdue and screaming for assuagement—was exactly what Dr. Thomas Clayton intended to continue doing.

• • •

Bert Fish Medical was seven stories of pastel stucco and hurricane-grade glass built too close to the highway off-ramp but overlooking the Intracoastal Waterway. If it was an ugly building, that was its saving grace: proximity to water. That he could stand on the roof nine hours into his shift and watch the shorebirds disappear over the mangroves as the shrimpers motored out, minor constellations that worked the horizon left to right—there was a certain grace in such. That you could stand there at all, breathing the tidal air that came and went with the breeze—he was grateful. He never hid there, of course—*hiding* was certainly not the word. He just seemed to disappear there more and more often.

It was fine: the ER was calm.

The ER was mostly retirees with cardiac events or immigrants without insurance though there was the occasional overflow from Daytona Beach to the north or Cocoa to the south, the multiple gunshot wounds in the Popeye's parking lot, the biker finding the I-4 highway divider at 107 mph. You'd hear the Life Flight, feel the hush of the automatic doors and the industrial jets of the air conditioning. You'd walk into the triage room and find the stretcher littered with a confetti of denim or leather or the cheap Walmart poly-cotton the EMTs had scissored away.

He walked down to visit a Baker Act off her antipsychotics: a woman had bitten her husband's face. He walked down to write a script for Doxycycline: a capuchin monkey had bitten its owner's face. He walked and walked and it was in this walking that he had slowly discovered that his problems weren't that interesting. That was the first revelation. This was second: no one's were.

A monkey bite? Clean the wound, administer antibiotics, follow up with a rabies test.

A opioid addiction? Rehab.

A failing marriage? Counseling.

Maybe counseling, or maybe not.

Doc had left medical school at Tulane for a residency in Jacksonville where he met his wife Shawn. She was in her second year at Palmer's School of Chiropractic Medicine, posing outside GMC dealerships and ribbon-cuttings on Saturdays, cheering on Sundays for the Jaguars, but had given it all up when Tommy had been offered a job two hours south. They'd moved, bought the house, had a daughter, and for a long time they'd been happy, or at least too busy to realize they weren't. Lately, they'd been fighting. There'd been a fight that morning, in fact, and she certainly had cause: he was sleeping around and making little effort to hide it; there were the aforementioned unpaid bills; there were tantalizing clues of an addiction to which she had so far feigned ignorance. But they had also spent the summer in marriage counseling. They were to attend a political fundraiser Saturday night, the candidate's wife, whoever he was, a friend of Shawn's.

Doc didn't give a fuck.

He'd used those words.

You don't give a fuck about anything anymore.

Shawn had used those. It devolved, just as they knew it would: fighting had become the thing they shared, the thing they could work on together. So that was exactly what they did: they fought. Mostly verbally, attacking each other at the fine joinery of ego and fear. Twice physically. Though in both cases he had simply held her off, even when she came at him with the pizza wheel.

Standing alone on the roof, smoking a Macanudo and waiting for sunrise, he thought that spoke well of him, that there remained this reservoir of decency, that while he would lie and emotionally torture and conceivably abandon his wife he would never lay a hand on her. Yes, there was that. Maybe only that, but still.

Attending the fundraiser was a peace offering.

He would go with her, he would smile, he would laugh, and the following weekend Shawn would accompany Doc and their daughter Samantha to the Orlando City Ballet, something he and Samantha found mesmerizing and Shawn found boring. Their daughter was a dancer, an aspiring dancer, he supposed, though gifted, focused in a way no eleven-year-old should be. The way she moved, the way she jumped, like her body was a single roped muscle.

Dr. Clayton—

Like—

Dr. Clayton to the—

He put out his cigar when he was paged to the ER. The *turgid introspection*—his wife's judgment, delivered during counseling—would have to wait.

• ● •

The woman was sitting up in an examination room, late-twenties, long-legged in cut-off jean shorts and an RVCA tank top, good-looking with sandy blonde hair spilled down a shoulder. Doc paused by the curtain, her chart in his hand. She looked so much like Shawn a decade ago it scared him. But then she didn't. She was simply young and attractive while he was maudlin and exhausted. The attraction wasn't sexual; the attraction was nostalgic. She smelled of cocoa butter and was complaining of abdominal pain.

"Good morning, Mrs. Dahl," he said, and knew immediately it wasn't her real name, something about the way it was scribbled on her admittance form, something about the way she pulled her lips to the side, caught between disdain and amusement. "Tell me what we have happening here."

"I'm dying here, doctor." She had one hand pressed to her side. "My left ovary."

"Is this something new?"

"No. God. It's ongoing."

"Tell me what's happening?"

"Just—Jesus—just this endless pain."

"Was there any sort of trauma? Maybe you fell?"

"I'm not going to lie to you."

"Ran into something?"

"I'm not going to lie to you," she said. "I had a script for ten Percocets and I ate them all last night."

"You took ten Percocets last night?"

"I told you. I'm dying here."

"And you haven't fallen? No sort of injury?"

"No."

He crossed his arms, chart to his chest.

"You aren't pregnant are you?"

"Jesus no, I'm not pregnant. I have Persistent Abdominal Constriction Syndrome."

"You have what?"

"PACS. Persistent—"

He stopped her with a hand.

"Who gave you that diagnosis?"

"Pretty much everyone." She numbered them on her fingers. "First my GP then an internist who sent me to an OB/GYN who did an ultrasound and then—"

"There's no such thing."

"Excuse me?"

"I said there's no such thing. I'm sorry but persistent whatever—it doesn't exist."

"So what, I'm making this up?"

"I'm not saying that."

"Imagining this pain that pretty much has me doubled up 24/7? Look at this," she said, and slid down her shorts to reveal a narrow Laparoscopic scar. "Did I make this up?"

"I'm not saying that at all."

"Did I dream this, doctor?" She leaned forward on the examination table, caught herself. When she spoke again her voice had softened. "Look. I'm sorry. I just really, really need like twenty Oxys."

"No way."

"Doctor."

"Where do I know you from?"

"What makes you think you know me?"

"I don't know," he said. "You look familiar."

"Maybe your last wet dream."

"You know what, I think we're finished here."

"I just—Doctor, please. Twenty Oxys."

"I'm sorry," he said, and wrote a prescription for ten Percocets. "Maybe try somebody else."

"Oh fuck you," she said, seeing the script, but taking it all the same.

"Pill grifter," he told the nurse in the hall.

"Yes, sirree," she said, shaking her head. "God's chosen few."

"God's refuse more like."

"Yes, sirree. That too."

He was walking to his car a half hour later when he saw her standing by the open door of a Benz, cell phone to her ear. She looked up just in time to flip him off.

He nodded and kept walking.

● ● ●

Hound's Ear Rare & Antique Books sat along West Ave in downtown Winter Park, the street a half mile of bistros and wine bars and art galleries, purveyors of yoga wear and boutique hotels, all facing a green expanse of benches and fountains and a single carousel built in 1911 and shipped south on Henry Flagler's railroad. Doc parked behind Kathmandu Tribal Gifts and walked past the Eileen Fischer and the Prado to where Hound's Ear sat beneath a burgundy awning. The owner was in his sixties and sufficiently eccentric with his ponytail and nicotine yellow teeth. He'd lived in Greece for a decade, something he never tired of repeating.

The Attic world is not as you think, doctor. That was his primary line.

The Bible is not what you think. That was his other. *You should read it in the original Koine and then come talk to me.*

Doc would have preferred to avoid him altogether but he was discreet and made reasonably generous cash offers. The agreed upon price was $2400 but as expected he balked.

"I'm sorry, doc. People are just less and less interested in Hemingway. I can do 1500."

MARK POWELL

"We're not talking about people."

"The misogyny. The antiquated masculine code."

"We're talking about dealers."

"He let Hadley sodomize him with a strap-on broomstick. I'm not making this up."

"2200."

"I can do 1700 but already you're robbing me blind."

They settled on an even two grand—below the book's market value—but the dealer thumbed over the cash and Doc walked out with twenty bills folded into his front pocket. His car was sweltering but he sat for a moment, windows up, engine off. Took out his phone and for the second time that morning called his dealer.

"I can't meet you this morning," the man—kid, really—said. "Maybe this evening."

"I've got a pocket full of money."

"Man, I'm sorry as all get out."

"Like a roll of cash."

"Doc, brother, I mean I'm sorry as shit, but I'm still tied up till like sevenish."

"Come on, Jared. I'm kind of hurting this morning."

"Look. I can give you a number. A lady I trust."

"Jesus—"

"I'm sorry, but look. You got something to write with?"

He had a prescription pad, of course. He'd used it in the past but last fall there'd been some questions from the hospital review board. Nothing formal, but enough to let him know someone somewhere was keeping watch. He wrote the number there.

She answered on the first ring. Oxy 80s, sure. And yeah, noon was fine. Out behind the old K-Mart in Orange City.

Which was where he was sitting when the woman from the ER loped across the parking lot to knock on his window.

"Well, well, well," she said, and leaned into his open window. "How the tables have turned, doctor."

"You again," he said. "What a coincidence."

"More like a cosmic radiance, I'd say. Let's hope I'm nicer to you than you were to me."

"So I guess you scored."

"You know, when it rains and all." She shook a brown paper sack. "Unlock your door, doc."

And he did, though not without a certain trepidation, a certain excitement too.

"It's burning up in here," she said when she was seated. She was in jeans and a white satin t-shirt, a thin necklace with a seahorse charm, the kind of thing a little girl might wear. "How do you even breathe?"

"I'm sweating it out," he said. "What do you have?"

"Sweating what out?"

"Life, mostly. What's in the bag?"

She gave it a shake and passed it over.

"This is way more than I'd ever need," he said. "This is what?"

"100 Oxy 80s. Some of us aren't scrupulous assholes, doctor."

"Call me Tommy."

"Some of us aren't absolute skinflints, Tommy. Refusing their brothers and sisters in need."

"Shouldn't you be in a yoga class somewhere?" he asked. "Or maybe at a wine bar?"

"Let's pretend I'm on my way."

"I really think I know you from somewhere."

"I doubt it."

He dropped the bag in her lap.

"I want ten."

"100. Take it or leave it."

He peeled off one of the bills. "I want ten."

"All right, fine. I'll sell you twenty if you promise to share."

• ● •

They wound up at an I-4 Econo Lodge where he swallowed a Cialis and sat on the bed to grate one of the Oxys. 2 ccs of Dasani and a Luer Lock syringe, medical tubing to tie off—it was a dance, a bit of artistry. He shot up on the bed, batted his eyes, and passed over the rig.

"This is new to me," she said.

"I somehow doubt that."

"Seriously. I've always had a needle thing."

But it must not have been much of one: she was already tying off.

The rest of the night went down some dark hole not to be exhumed.

He woke once in the late afternoon, disoriented, the room bisected by a watery sunlight falling through the curtain, stumbled to the bathroom where he pissed brown urine and what might have been flecks of dark blood. She was a shape, a leg extended beneath the sheets, hair and an angled arm. This is bad, he thought. Bad, bad, bad.

The next time he woke it was dark and he could hear the shower, the triangled light of the open bathroom door, the warm steam that came through it. He crossed his arms on his bare chest, watched her blurred shape pull on her jeans, her t-shirt over her bare chest. It was a devotion, really. To have such a habit, to make such an offering—it was like worshipping a small god, a minor deity. It took everything from you, body and soul, but it gave back too. She pulled on her flats. It gave back, he told himself, and heard the door shut.

The next thing he knew housekeeping was knocking.

He rose from the bed sectionally, an exploratory foot, right leg, left.

The roll in his pants was untouched. His phone was flashing.

He found her seahorse necklace by the sink and was slipping it into his pocket when the door opened onto the chain.

He handed the Hispanic woman with her rolling cart one of the hundreds, bowed repentantly, and drove home.

• ◉ •

Meanwhile, life went on.

Doc made his rounds while the heart attacks and concussions and stitches and the car wreck that piled up a box truck and two sedans on Highway 44 kept arriving, kept summoning him from the trips to the roof where the pelicans moved in low formation, as if keeping watch.

Wednesday his pill count stood at 14.

Thursday at 11.

Friday—Jesus Christ, Friday was hard—Friday at 5.

But hard or not, Saturday eventually came, and with it Shawn's friend's husband's fundraiser. She had bought him a new pair of cowboy boots, her peace offering. His offering was to put them on without complaint, his willingness a product not of goodwill so much as a can of Red Bull topped with Stoli and chasing another of the quickly dwindling Oxys. Shawn was in a good mood and when the Oxy hit so was he. She had turned on some of the music they'd both loved when they first met, The Cure, Depeche Mode, and they had actually danced around the kitchen. The old life—there was something of the old life in it, a sepia-tint so absent yet so immediately recognizable Samantha came out to take a photo of dear ole mom and dad spinning around across the Calacatta marble like happy fools. Sam was staying home alone, something they were experimenting with. Eleven years old which was too young but maybe not. "The important moments in my life," he'd told his wife while she sat putting on her earrings, "were all tied up with independence. The only ones I remember."

"Oh, honey," she said, "that's kind of sad."

He sat on the edge of the bed with his second Red Bull and vodka.

"Is it?"

"Mine are all tied up with love."

The fundraiser was at an Ormond Beach house, three stories of poured concrete and broad glass sufficiently right-angled to qualify as "interesting," if not the mid-century modern Shawn had gushed about. They parked on the street, passenger side wheels in the blown sand.

"Who is this again?" he asked.

"Dan Garnett. He's running for Attorney General."

"For like the state?"

"Yes, for like the state."

"A Republican?"

"Does it matter? He's Monica's husband."

He was also a former police lieutenant turned ambulance chasing lawyer now running on a law-and-order platform that seemed built around arming everyone white while locking up everyone brown, though not necessarily in that order. Doc learned this standing out by the pool beneath the strings of fairy lights. Food was coming around and he focused on the proteins, the Ahi tuna, the Kobe beef. They—*actually me, dammit,* he must have thought—had paid a thousand dollars for the privilege of mingling amid the tight assholes of the very nearly rich, around him pleated pants and pastel dresses, a passing tray of Veuve Cliquot.

On the edge of it all, a quartet of students from the Stetson School of Music played Schubert, or something approaching such. It was not unlike his childhood. For forty years, his father had been the great healer of the Faubourg Marigny, his New

Orleans offices occupying the top two floors of the defunct S.H. Kress department store that had once served the neighborhoods of Frenchmen Street. Doc had grown up in the radiance of such, his childhood a Tennessee Williams's play of masked balls and Pimm's Cups, of watching his parents mix Sazeracs on their way to this party on St. Charles or that ball on Prytania. They were lately retired to a mansion in Fort Lauderdale, three hours and one impossible leap south, their lives having reorganized as a circuit of gin and tonics and FOX News amid the retired jewelers and Rust Belt car dealers. For Doc, the associations were not pleasant.

Still, he was fine.

He took a vodka tonic from the bar and stood by the diving board.

He was having a second when Shawn found him. *There you are, baby!* She was barefoot and with one hand had pulled her dress up to her knees as if preparing to skip across a creek. With her other hand she took his. She was happy, glowing, maybe a little drunk, and for a moment, moving through the crowd and across the dewy grass he loved her, or at least some past version of her. A strand of the golden hair she had piled beautifully on her head had come loose. A single sequin adhered to her neck. He realized—this came to him by the broad steps that led up to the vast estate that was the veranda—that he had once loved her wholly and without reservation and wished badly he did again.

He followed her up the stairs.

He'd never wanted to love someone more, but then he'd never felt so helpless in his indifference either.

"A requiem," he said, and she turned.

"What, baby?"

"A requiem."

She tilted her still smiling face and he said, "The music, the Schubert."

"Come on. They're dying to meet you."

Dan Garnett and his lovely wife, she meant. They stood in a clutch of well-wishers that parted like magic at Shawn's approach. Garnett was square-jawed and maybe five-eight; he'd had work done around his eyes.

"Dr. Clayton," he said, and extended a hand, "such a pleasure to meet you. This is my lovely better half—"

"Monica," the woman from the ER, the woman from the hotel room said, and extended her own long braceleted arm. "I absolutely adore your wife."

● ● ●

He went wandering through the house. It would have been surreptitious had everyone not been doing the same. Garnett had made a short speech. There had been the quiet applause of approving Protestants holding mixed drinks. Some people seemed to have left but more seemed to have arrived, and while the pool deck was now dark the house gleamed, the windows pouring a brilliant light. People moved from room to room, lounging on furniture, congregating by family photographs and the arty black-and-white photography done—he over-heard this—by Dan's crazy talented wife. Moving through the house, he was trying not to think about Dan's crazy talented wife. There was actually enough alcohol in his system to make the goal plausible.

Yet, he thought.

Still, he thought.

He was in an upstairs hall when she pushed herself against him.

"I'm really lusting for those boots."

"Is that all?" he asked.

"Tevcos?"

"Ariats."

"Ariats, how lovely."

"There's no such thing as PACS, Mrs. Garnett."

"Sure there is. Let me show you."

● ● ●

He drove home too fast, the top down and Shawn dreamy beneath a blanket. Stars, so many stars. Central Florida had an impossible sky, wider than seemed prudent, a western sky inviting the contemplation of smallness. It was his favorite kind of night, the way she made a pillow out of his arm, the way he felt so damn defiant. He pushed the darkness and felt it close behind as he passed, the long straightaway of the nearly empty four-lane, opening his wife's BMW up to 90, 95 mph, jangly from the coke he and Monica Garnett had done off the glass shelf in an upstairs bathroom. A single line through a paper straw and then they groped each other—there was really no other word for it. He'd grabbed handfuls of her while she put her hands down the front of his pants. After, they arranged themselves into something like respectability and made plans to meet at a hotel in Maitland on Tuesday. He had no illusions about his powers of attraction. She was no doubt a refugee from various addiction counseling programs—substance, sex—and he was simply Mr. Right Place, Right Time.

Or wrong, he thought, looking at his wife, her head back and eyes lidded. She was actually smiling, serene, dreamily content, and he turned on the radio to cheesy Eric Clapton singing *you look wonderful tonight*.

Shawn roused herself enough to reach for the volume.

"Oh, Tommy, I love this song."

She reached for him but the effort was too great and her left hand came to rest on his thigh, fingers half-splayed, as if she was about to show him something, some secret. He placed it back in her lap.

Still, she was smiling as he pulled into the garage.

"Where are we?" she asked sleepily.

"Home. Sit still."

"I think I'm drunk."

"Sit."

He walked around the car and lifted her, carried her through the kitchen and living room and into their bedroom where he managed to pull back the covers and lower her almost gently.

When he went to stand she held onto his hand.

"Lay down with me," she said.

"I'll be right back."

"Kiss me."

"Let me check on Sam. I'll be right back."

Samantha was asleep and he sat on the edge of her bed and kissed her forehead, her walls covered with posters and an old pair of toe-shoes hung by a ribbon, all of it barely visible in the grainy dark.

Though the air conditioner was shuddering, her skin was damp and he sat for a moment absorbing her smell, something he hadn't thought about since she was a child, the apple shampoo and Dove soap. Something he'd thought lost, yet there it was. My girl, he thought, and was flooded with tenderness, the soggy weight so heavy he could barely stand.

He walked to the kitchen, opened a bottle of '02 Fumé Blanc, and carried it by the neck to his office where he pulled down his first editions, zipped them into a gym bag, and searched online for Monica Garnett. She was 33—he'd thought younger—married five years with two children and a BFA in photography from the Savannah College of Art and Design. There was nothing about arrests or rehab though he suspected there was money enough to make such things disappear. He stared into her pixelated eyes. He knew her kind of crazy, the wounds all self-inflicted, and while not yet mortal certainly trending. He knew to stay away, too.

He shut down the computer, deposited the gym bag in the trunk of his car, and carried the wine up to the bedroom.

"You came back," Shawn said.

"I'm right here."

"I thought you weren't coming."

He sat in the chair by the bed, close enough to prop his feet against the mattress.

"What is that?" she asked.

"Some wine."

"For me?"

She sounded more like a little girl than his little girl, and he helped her drink, two slow pulls before she pushed the bottle away and pulled her husband toward her. Excepting a drunken New Year's Eve months prior it was the first time they had touched in he couldn't remember how long, and he felt, perhaps, that it signaled a new beginning, some form of mutual forgiveness, even if neither could say for what exactly.

They slept late and had breakfast together out by the pool.

Later, she came into his study to wordlessly kiss the back of his neck.

Yet when Tuesday came he lied to her and drove to meet Monica Garnett, exactly as he'd promised himself he wouldn't.

● ● ●

He was turning into the parking lot of the Maitland Sheraton when she called.

"Pull around back, okay? I'm in the black Benz."

"I remember."

He spotted her car beneath three dying palms on the far edge of the parking lot and pulled beside it. Before he could cut the engine, she was sliding in beside him, breathless and excited.

"What's up?" he asked.

"This." She dropped a brown paper bag in his lap and he felt the contents shift. "Remember the hundred I had? Well, I got a hundred more."

"How?"

"A friend, a pharmacy. You really shouldn't ask. You want them?"

"Can we share?"

"I probably wouldn't say no."

"How much?"

"You still have that roll?"

"Yeah, some of it."

"Okay. Okay then, just…just." She flushed, the pink of her neck all the more evident against the white of the strappy sundress she wore. Espadrilles. No bra.

"You all right?"

"Yeah, I just…"

"What's going on, Monica?"

"So I got like way more than I want to hold," she said. "Not just this but like seriously way more. It makes me nervous. I'll sell you the bag for a hundred."

"Why not just give it to me?"

"That's three thousand dollars' worth the Oxys, Tommy."

"From a friend, from a pharmacy." He shrugged. "Why not give it to me?"

"They're right there," she said. "There in your lap."

"I'm just messing with you."

"You want them or not?"

"Yeah," he said, and reached into his pocket. "I want them."

He was digging out the roll of cash when she leaned forward and he saw it: no bra because a nearly translucent wire ran from her stomach up her ribcage where it was held with a tiny square of medical tape. There was a brief moment of incomprehension and then she looked at him and mouthed: *I'm sorry.* The rest was sensory: the pounding on the roof, both doors jerking open. She seemed to leap from the car while beside him a voice very loud and very near said *I want your hands on the wheel, sir. Your hands. Now exit the vehicle* and he thought 100 pills yes, well past whatever dividing line separated possession from possession with intent to distribute, *exit the vehicle, sir* well past whatever dividing line separated his old life from this new world inhabited not just by Dr. Thomas Clayton but also by the FDLE agent who was yelling *sir, can you hear me?* and he could, of course, he could, even if doing so *sir!* even if doing so meant taking that irrevocable step, the one he couldn't take back, the one that left behind this world and stranded him in the next.

* ● *

Two weeks later he met Shawn at a bistro in Winter Park. Three o'clock and the place was otherwise empty, just the bartender who told them yeah, wherever, take any of the patio seats, and the waiter who came out reluctantly to stand in the shadow of the zinc awning to stare down Shawn's dress. Doc ordered a gin and tonic. Shawn ordered a water with lemon and then, just as he turned to leave, oh to hell with it, the same, I guess. A G and T.

"Good choice," Tommy said.

"Why's that?"

"I guess a G & T, it always felt somehow celebratory."

"And are we celebrating?"

"Not exactly celebrating, no."

"No," she said with a bitterness he'd never heard, "not exactly." After the arraignment, Doc had been bonded back into world but only briefly. He was facing up to thirteen years and his lawyer was recommending a plea deal. *Three, four years,* he'd told Doc. *We get you in rehab. You serve a year and a day and then walk.*

A year and a day in prison?

Minimum security. You'll watch a lot of cable news, maybe make a billfold in leather shop.

And what about my license?

Your medical license? He'd shaken his head as if exhausted by not just the conversation but the larger planet on which it took place. *Your license is as good as gone. Jesus, your license is the least of your concerns.*

Among his chief concerns was his current financial situation. He was living in an Extended Stay America, $289 a week with kitchenette and stackable washer and dryer. Shawn had filed for divorce and wanted everything, including Sam who was in St. Augustine with her grandparents.

"I have two requests," Doc said.

"Oh, Jesus."

The waiter brought out their drinks.

"Two requests," he said again.

"Tommy, really. Let's take the wide view here."

"All right. What's the wide view?"

"The wide view is like, are you really in any position to make requests?"

"One, let me collect some things from the house."

She shook her head. "The thing about this is—"

"Just some clothes, books, minor things."

"The thing about this..." She put her chin down to her tan chest and raised her head suddenly enough for a single tear to track beneath her giant diamond-encrusted sunglasses. He thought it looked more like a DeBeers commercial than real life.

"There's like this whole universe of hurt," she said, "of embarrassment, of actually just total humiliation, all right? Put that aside."

"Shawn."

"Put aside all the legal and financial issues. We're going to lose the house, Tommy."

"Shawn—"

"Don't interrupt me, okay? I've just realized lately you've spent the last however many years interrupting me, cheating on me, just generally undermining me. From the very start."

"That's not true."

"From the very moment I met you. Like that was actually your field, undermining me. Not emergency medicine or whatever."

"There were a lot of good years."

"I don't believe that."

"There were good years, Shawn. A lot of them."

"I don't believe that anymore." She took a drink and fitted the glass back in its circle of condensation. "What I believed, what I used to believe…I mean I knew you fooled around. I knew that. I knew you—what would be the word? I knew you like to indulge a bit. Not that I ever thought it was anything approaching this. 100 pills."

"It was a set up."

"100 fucking pills, Tommy. You weren't set up. Or maybe you were, but you had it coming, didn't you? If not that day, the next."

"Let me get some things from the house."

"I heard some cop kicked the shit out of you."

"I wouldn't say kicked."

"That you got the Ray-Bans slapped right off your smug face for not getting out of the car quick enough."

"I failed to comply," he said, and took a drink, "in what they call a timely manner."

"Aw, shit, honey. You *did* get smacked, didn't you?"

"The house, Shawn."

She shook her head.

"The house is gone."

"Please."

"The house is gone, Tommy. Everything's gone. Everything." She lifted her drink and looked out at the park. It was impossibly hot, the day, the hour. "If that sounds dramatic," she said.

"The other thing—"

"And you know, she was my friend. I think that might actually be worst of it all."

"I'd like to see Samantha."

"I don't have many friends, okay? I have none, in fact. Zero."

"I want to see Samantha."

"No. Absolutely not."

"She's my daughter too."

"I won't put her through that."

"It's not your choice."

"It's not my choice? Did you seriously just say that?"

"Please."

"Want to know the last thing she said to me before I came to meet you?"

"Forget it," he said.

"Want to know?"

"I said forget it."

"She said please don't make me see that bastard, mama. That man who's ruined everything. That goddamn monster who—"

"All right," he said, and tipped his drink back until the ice hit his teeth.

She stopped at the sound of it. They both stopped. Just sat there in the lengthening day, the seemingly endless day. No breeze, no shade, just the palms browning and sagging over the brittle grass.

"Get whatever you want from the house," she said eventually. "I don't care."

"Thank you."

"Just don't call."

"All right."

"Just leave us alone, okay?"

He nodded. She finished her drink and stood a little unsteadily, straightened her dress and looked at him.

"I don't know what I came here expecting," she said.

"An apology maybe."

"No."

"For me to say I'm sorry."

"No," she said. "Not that."

"Well I am. For what it's worth."

"Which is nothing."

"I get it," he said.

"No you don't," she told him. "You never got a goddamn thing."

● ● ●

Everything was just as he'd left it which was its own form of incongruity. The bed unmade. The bottle of Fumé Blanc in the recycling bin. His wife's hair in the tangle of a brush, his daughter's. He put Pärt's *Für Anna Maria* on the speakers and moved like a ghost, picking things up only to put them down, moving but never quite settling. These were last things and that made them somehow holy. How ephemeral it had all been, and how he'd recognized it, but not quite. Now the world had been revealed as transient and he felt like a fool, having known as much without ever actually understanding.

Still, geography is its own form of memory and he let his body guide him out to the pool where he and Shawn would sit barefoot drinking Sangria while Sam swam. The mermaid's tail they'd gotten her the Christmas she was what? eight, he thought, splashing on the steps, smiling and iridescent. The living room where they'd watched the movie of whatever book she was reading for school, Narnia, Harry Potter. He'd been using back then but so much less, party drugs, a little cocaine, the occasional ecstasy—it had made him interesting to himself, the addictions, the secrets. He kept moving: the kitchen with the black coffee and croissants from the French Bakery out in New Smyrna. The evening meals.

It was only when he reached his daughter's bedroom that he paused. The old posters and new photographs, the stuffed animals layered in a strata of moments, a geology from which you might infer a life. The programs signed by the Orlando City Ballet, the toes shoes and ribbons. He could remember so much. It was stunning in its way, how much he could remember.

The bedroom was dark and unkempt, his and Shawn's. He kept the light off. There's a power in things that are going away, in things just before they fall apart, an electricity, an awareness. He sat on the bed and sensed it, smelled it. But that was too much, maybe, their mingled scent, and he stood and walked quickly out to the garage where he took the gym bag from the trunk. The books were still there. The now twenty first editions totaling roughly $193,000 in value. It wasn't perhaps the smartest investment, but it was the one he had made.

When he found the seahorse necklace he considered throwing it out but instead left it on his daughter's pillow for her to maybe, someday, find.

He was climbing into his rental car, the bag in the backseat, when his phone went off.

"You, motherfucker."

"Damian."

"You weren't straight with me."

The voice was the lawyer to whom Doc had already paid a twenty-thousand dollar retainer of borrowed money and thus far his voice had sounded like leather feels, expensive and authoritative. But here it was scratching a higher octave.

"What's wrong?"

"Goddamn it, Tommy. You were having an affair with Dan Garnett's wife and somehow failed to mention that."

"I wouldn't call it an affair exactly."

"Oh, you wouldn't, would you? Well that doesn't seem to be how the goddamn prosecutor's office sees it. Dan Garrett is almost certainly our next attorney general and he is mortally and intractably pissed. He put the word out. He wants you put away for a very long time."

"What's a very long time mean?"

"He wants you in that hole that comes out in China. Remember the one you were digging when you were a kid?"

"How long?"

"They're talking the full thirteen. You'd likely serve six or seven of that."

"Jesus. We can plea it down though, right?"

"Right now that's off the table. I'm talking to the solicitor but she doesn't think it'll happen."

"What do we do then?"

"I need to think a little, make some calls. This all just tsunamied me, you know."

Doc said nothing.

"All right, look," his lawyer said, "We'll figure it out. We let things settle, let Garrett blow off steam and then I get back in touch with the solicitor's office. Normally, they'd prefer not to go to trial but this isn't normally. Anything else you want to tell me in the meantime?"

"I can't think of anything."

"If anything, you know, comes up."

"Of course."

"Let me talk to some people. I'll be in touch."

Doc hung up the phone and drove straight to Wells Fargo on South Orange where he put the twenty books in the largest safe deposit box they had.

He paid for thirteen years.

This wasn't normal.

None of this was normal.

• • •

The trial did not go to plan. The federal government had just filed charges against Purdue Pharma and the news was filled with talk of pill mills and collaborating doctors. There was also the anger of Dan Garnett who sat stoically in court for the preliminary hearing. There would be no plea deal. After the first day, Doc bought a six-pack of Natural Light and went back to his room while outside the rain fell and the wind blew and the palms up and down Euclid Avenue bowed and whipped. He sat on the foldout couch and thought about turning up the volume on *American Idol*. He was sweating; he was always sweating, thirty-three days clean besides the Antabuse but still wet there on the rough fabric. Which is where he was when someone knocked. He opened it with no hesitation, no concern. Whether it was his wife, his father, the blonde court reporter from Channel 9—it made no difference.

He hadn't expected to see Dan Garnett, but that didn't matter either.

"I'm not here to kill you if that's what you're thinking." First thing he said, standing there soaking, the rain a gray veil just behind him. "I didn't even come armed."

"That's good, I guess."

"Can I come in?"

Doc stepped aside and Garrett stood just inside the door, dripping.

"I didn't come here to shoot you," he said again, as if reminding himself, "though to be honest it crossed my mind. Then I thought about the first time some big gang-banger from Broward County catches you in the shower room. You know the kind of anal trauma kits the Florida DOC stocks, Doctor? You know how they handle things?"

"You want to sit down?"

"They basically shove a tampon up your bleeding ass and give you two Advil."

Doc gestured at the couch.

"You want to sit?"

"I guess why not."

Four of the six beers sat sweating in their cardboard sleeves and following Garnett's eyes Doc asked if he wanted one.

"No. Or maybe yeah," he said, taking the beer. "I've had a few already." He popped the top, sank into the couch, and exhaled as if home at long last.

"What are you doing here?" Doc asked.

Garnett held the beer and stared at the blank wall.

"You aren't the first," he said finally. "You probably figured that. She's done two stints in rehab but rehab is for quitters, right? I've always dealt with these incidents quietly—she's my wife, the mother of my children. Then you go and make me put that wire on her. It wasn't the first time, having to use her like that either. To cut a deal, I mean. But I tell you this, doctor. I'll tell you why this is different: you were in my house. You think I can't smell you on everything now? My goddamn house. Not some skanky roadside motel with the ice bucket and the clerk behind bulletproof glass, no. That's a sacred thing you violated.

We live there. Our children live there. You understand where I'm coming from?"

"Yeah."

"I guess that's why I'm here. Just to make sure you knew it wasn't just your family you wrecked."

"I get it."

"I guess you do. I understand you have a daughter yourself so I guess you sure fucking do." He put the beer on the floor and stood. "All right. I've said my piece."

The entire encounter had taken no more than two minutes. The beer was untouched, *American Idol* still at commercial. Later, years into his time, he would recount that night to me, the visiting writer who taught a course every Monday, the sort of naïve if well-intentioned spirit who rumbled up and down the halls wearing a belt-clipped panic button and asking did you need help with GED-prep?

"You should write all this down," I told him that night.

"Why?"

And I remember my exaggerated shrug:

"Why the hell not? For posterity, for therapy. Just put it on the page."

But that was years in the future, years before I would burn those very pages on the beach in front of the Golden Lion. That night, Doc simply took up the bottle and sat in the wet outline Garnett had shaped on the couch. A week later he was sentenced to thirteen years confinement at the Lawtey Correctional Institute in Starke.

● ● ●

He arrived with the early summer heat.

The prison sat in the barren pinelands of northern Florida. You cut west off I-95 around St. Augustine, crossed the St. John's

River, passed the marinas and retirement homes and strip malls set down in fields like alien crop patterns, cows grazing in green fields, a few churches beneath the pecan trees. After that, nothing. After that, a narrowing two lane road and the occasional trailer. A National Guard artillery range and the rowed pines managed by Georgia Pacific. Nearer the prison, they'd planted fields of actual wheat, shocks of it. Soybeans, cotton, as if they were landlocked as much by circumstance as geography.

He was given an upper bunk in a long narrow barracks that resembled a chicken house right down to the giant ventilation fans on each end. Three hundred men, warehoused with no air conditioning in summer, no heat in winter. He'd had two months to get straight and he mostly had. The realization of Antabuse. The realization that his habit was the realer thing; he was just the appendage, the thing holding its hand. Still, he occasionally found himself freezing, would wake to the snores and farts and someone masturbating beneath the thin blue blanket they were issued to find his body absolutely shivering with some leftover shard of withdrawal, some remnant of his habit that had suddenly dislodged itself and now demanded attention.

The nights were bad.

Days were better. Somewhat better. He was put to work on a road crew where his face burned and peeled from the sun and then the laundry where his fingers burned and peeled from the chemicals and then finally, eight months after arriving when someone actually got around to reading his file, the infirmary where he was put to work taking care of their feet. *Their* being everyone. The blistered, the ingrown, the fungal.

That was better. That he was something approaching useful. He lanced boils and cleaned abrasions and smeared anti-bacterial cream. He also found the library. It was down a short hall, a room smaller than his living room had once been but filled floor-to-ceiling with books. The clerk was a giant near-silent

Guatemalan-American named Dante who had been chief of security for the Brown Street Mob, his sentence a blur of gun and drug charges. He was six-five and should have been playing defensive end for the Dolphins. Instead, he shelved books or sat at his desk and logged the comings and goings of mystery novels and How-To guides in his tiny leaning script. After breakfast and the morning headcount, Doc would walk to the infirmary where a line of the sick and lame already stretched out beneath the awning that connected one building to another like a community college campus. Technically, the prison had both a doctor and nurse, but they served throughout the corrections system, moving from prison to prison so that their visits were as unpredictable as they were rare. So by and large it was Dr. Thomas Clayton listening to lungs or checking testicles for lumps or removing splinters from hands.

He would finish by ten am. There would be another crowd after the noon meal and mid-day headcount, but mornings he had some time, and invariably walked down to the cool hush of the library where each day he wrote and erased a letter to his daughter. He'd heard nothing from her since his arrest. It was possible she was writing and erasing letters to him as well, though he doubted it. Eventually, he stopped writing and began reading. Not his precious Americans, his Hemingway and Fitzgerald, but whatever he could find. Books on finance, psychology, philosophy. Three times a day he tended to his patients, as he came to think of them, his flock with their denim slippers and chest infections, and three times a day, having attended to all, he was granted an hour, perhaps an hour and a half to simply read. Sartre. Camus. Dostoevsky and Nietzsche—they became part of his world, a bedrock thing no different from the toilet paper that came in brown stiff squares like fast food napkins, or the way they played chess with bottle caps.

He read Kierkegaard and Gabriel Marcel.

Discovered you could put Preparation H on anything.

He handed *The Stranger* to Dante, *The Fall, The Plague,* and when Dante failed to read them Doc simply sat and explained them to him. He was coming to see himself as having failed to respond to the exigencies of life. He was coming to see that life must be treated like an exercise in resistance, you go underground, you organize, you hold out not against hope but without even the possibility of hope's existence. One was thrown into the world and what was required of him was to accept such, to put himself in his own historicity. To understand that, per Wittgenstein, a depressed man lives in a depressed world.

Dante glancing up from his own book.

"Yeah, I hear you, doc."

Doc kept talking.

Doc was learning things.

When Palm Bay Correctional closed and three hundred prisoners were transferred in he learned to staunch bleeding with the cotton batting of a pillow, to remove a shiv manufactured in the machine shop using tweezers. It was a new world, but also an older one, more fundamental, the grass-earth-sky-cold-pain you understood as a child. The world as what you knew before you knew anything. It took him two more years to learn its navigation required not thought but action.

But he did learn it.

He felt himself excited in a way he hadn't been since he'd started medical school nearly two decades ago, and stood by the desk to discuss these ideas with Dante. It was a cafeteria school of thought, picking from Heidegger here, from Kierkegaard there, but he needed his own system, his own worldview. The evil genius? The likelihood that life was a computer simulation? There was the possibility this had all been arranged for him, the walls and headcounts and diarrhea. That he was the only living person here, the rest of the universe a construction born in a lab at Stanford or a star nursery in the Crab Nebula. But then he remembered the shame of his trial, of being watched. Was his daughter there, his parents, his brain-damaged brother? Surely not, but the mere possibility of their presence—their realness—had been enough to keep him from looking.

Dante would look up from the novel he was writing on yellow legal pads to nod.

"I hear you, doc. I hear what you saying."

Then one day Dante was gone.

Solitary, he heard out on the yard. Shit happens to Dante every time he has a court date, Doc was told. Some punk-ass CO shows up to take him to court, sees the sheer size of the man, and just tazes his ass out of pure fucking panic. But you taze somebody you better be prepared to explain that shit in triplicate. So they say the same thing: he came after me, big brown motherfucker tried to wring my neck. He got ten days, probably. He's used to it.

He came back even quieter, more contemplative.

"What did you do in there?" Doc wanted to know.

"I thought. I prayed. I even wrote a story."

Along with the tray of food that slid through a slot three times a day, he had been slipped a pencil from One Eyed Jack's Putt-Putt Experience and a pack of Big Red gum, and on the dull undersides of the sixteen wrappers he had written a story about a young man watching his father arrested. When his ten days were up, he'd wadded the wrappers into a single silver ball and packed it into the corner of his mouth. Back in the library, he laid it out in a four by four square, the handwriting so tiny as to be almost nonexistent. Yet there it was.

When a young novelist showed up to teach a writing course—when I showed up—Doc made sure Dante went, and then decided at the last minute to join him. Doc wrote his story down and entrusted it to me.

"Burn them like Kafka," he said, a bit theatrically, and walked back to the clinic.

He was always busy now, treating not just his fellow inmates but the correctional officers, the admin folks, even the warden who came in complaining of the gas pains Doc diagnosed (correctly) as acute appendicitis. After five years he could no longer believe in his previous existence. There were memories, of course; he would sometimes cut away to a moment he couldn't quite place, only to have it fit hours later, another piece in the larger jigsaw of being. He remembered it; but believe in it? No, not really. He'd found his calling in prison, his real life. He'd come in blandly handsome if somewhat bloated, but prison had sharpened his face. He was lean now, and though he appeared much older, he also appeared more as himself, elemental, gray-eyed and shaved to the bone. He no longer counted his days—with gain time he'd do seven or so years. He no longer fantasized about reuniting with his daughter. He simply woke, showered, shaved, put on the blue poly/cotton uniform that was so much like his old scrubs, and went to work. Everything beyond the double fencing and watchtowers was suspect, as real as vapor, which is certainly real. But try holding it; try making a life out of it. He saw to the needs of others with a saint-like devotion, read his philosophy, sat in companionable silence with Dante. Came to understand what Kafka meant when he wrote:

You do not need to leave your room. Remain sitting at your table and listen. Do not even listen, simply wait. Do not even wait, be still and solitary. The world will freely offer itself to you and be unmasked, it has no choice, it will roll in ecstasy at your feet.

Still and solitary, I imagine Doc thinking, yes, exactly.

His world was ordered and sealed and within it he was perfectly content.

So it came as a blow when early in Doc's sixth year Dante was released to a halfway house in Miami Gardens to become part of that greater imagined vapor that ghosted its way through the pines and out to the far edges of who could ever say. It came as a greater blow still when, in his seventh year, Doc was given back a brown envelope containing the possessions he had handed over in that previous lifetime, and put on a bus that deposited him at the Orlando station on the John Young Parkway. Seven years, but then it happened so suddenly—he was free. He was to see his parole officer every two weeks for the next six months but he was free. He was to find a job and a stable place to live. He was subject to random drug tests. Should he test positive, should he skip meeting his PO, should he leave the state without prior authorization—should he return to his old life he would be remanded to the proper authorities where he would serve out the remainder of his sentence.

There was a great lure in returning, in reassuming his old life, but he knew it was over. So instead he got a room at a motel on Colonial Drive and a job at a car wash. He took his meals at the 7-Eleven and a KFC near the intersection and one night watched Shy Walsh get knocked out on pay-per-view. The world had changed. The women in tights looking down at their phones, everyone looking at their phones—he watched them. The unfinished subdivisions, abandoned around the time he was marking off year one—he walked them. The weeds and poured footings, the cracked asphalt and fading graffiti. What appeared to be a robot with what appeared to be a dick extending from its robot ear, a Cy Twombly for the great recession.

He bought a phone with cash and a used Camry on credit.

The world had changed.

The Stand Your Ground laws and exhausted phosphate

mines. The I-4 Denny's and waterparks and folks making minimum wage selling $75 wands at Harry Potter World or Land or
whatever it was called. The world had changed, but he had too.
He saw his PO. He took the drug tests. He did everything that
was required of him and at the end of sixth months, his debt to
the state of Florida repaid in full, he dug back into the envelope
he'd been given on his release and found the small gold key that
opened the safe deposit box.

It was four miles to the bank.

He got in his car and drove over.

Took half an hour to find parking but he found it all the same.

● ● ●

The decision to visit his daughter was not so much made as
revealed.

Dostoevsky once wrote, "The most basic need of the Russian
people is the need for suffering, incessant and unslakeable suffering, everywhere and in everything." That wouldn't have been
lost on Doc. As for his daughter, he didn't want to hurt her, and
knew his contacting her carried with it the very real possibility
of pain. But if we are thrown into this world we are required to
face such throwness. *Dasein*, the realness of being alive—everything he'd read and come to believe demanded it. He had his
phone and his used car—he wasn't dead. Life went on, you had
to act like it. He got Shawn's new number from his lawyer. She
was remarried and living with a land developer in Ponte Verda
overlooking a tee box and two houses down from the Tebow
family.

"I'd heard you were getting out," she said.

"Hey, you kept up."

"How could I not? I kept getting these calls. 'Oh my god,
Shawn, Tommy is getting out. Oh my god, how will you ever

cope?' I guess I've been waiting to hear from you since then. To find out what you'd want."

But he just wanted Sam's number. She was a sophomore in college now, studying art in Gainesville. He just wanted to talk to her.

His ex-wife didn't think that was a good idea, getting back in touch.

He didn't think that was hers to decide.

"You know, Tommy. I'm experiencing actual impatience now talking to you. Like actual physical pressure on my skull and I'm realizing I haven't felt like this since they locked you up."

"I have the right to speak to her."

"And she has the right to ignore you."

"Then let her make the decision, Shawn. Let her decide. I'm still her father."

There was a sigh and the sort of long pause that had once defined their relationship.

"All right," she said eventually. "She won't talk to me anyway. Maybe she'll talk to you."

He'd already sold one of the books. $1600 for a signed first edition of William Carlos Williams's *In the American Grain*, black cloth over boards with gilt lettering on the spine. But not to the Grecophile in Winter Park. His shop was gone now, so too the tobacco shop next door, both gutted for a Lululemon retailer. He drove instead to a shop in New Smyrna Beach that specialized in the New Age and Occult, lots of treatises on Wicca and creative visualization. Not their sort of thing, William Carlos William. But the book was valued at $2500 and Doc wanted to see his daughter more than he wanted to get a fair price. He wanted to hurry. In that moment it seemed possible, going to see her, but if he delayed—he knew better than to delay.

Just get on the interstate, drive—anyone could drive.

When he saw the UF Ballet was doing Boléro it seemed like a sign.

He called her from the car and got her voicemail. *Hi Sam, yeah, it's dad. I don't know if your mom said anything, but I was hoping actually to maybe, you know, come up and see you, to visit. Call me back when you can. I love you.* He sat for another moment, arguing with himself, and then started the car, started north, if only because he was tired of his own voice.

• • •

He was pumping gas when she called back and didn't notice the light flashing on his phone until he was deep in the National Forest. By that time there were two messages, the first from his daughter, very angry—*how goddamn dare you just come back into my life like this*—and the second from his daughter's boyfriend, Dwayne speaking very calm—he should come, Sam wanted him too even if she didn't realize it. *Sam's actually taking a semester off and not doing so good, dad.* Doc pulled over and called from the shoulder of I-75.

The boyfriend Dwayne answered.

"How not well?" Doc asked.

"What do you mean, dad?" The *dad* came in a mocking glide *daaaaad.*

"You said she wasn't doing so well. How do you mean?"

"I just mean like generally lobotomized. Maybe paralyzed—I don't know. We just moved to this place that's like isolated you might want to say and she's not getting out much."

"She wants to see me?"

"Just come on as soon as you can. I think she's got some unresolved shit and sitting all day in a trailer ain't solving it."

He got the address but didn't put it into his phone yet, just wandered north on backroads, not a direct route but he wasn't hurrying anymore. He drove to Gainesville, bought two tickets for the evening performance, and typed in the address. It was to the south, outside Ocala, and he drove through the manicured suburbs and shopping centers with their Trader Joe's and ethnic restaurants and into the countryside, a dozen winding miles along the two-lane that threaded the horse farms and old homeplaces. He lost internet around the time he turned onto a gravel road that slipped through the pines but he had only to stay straight. Lake Jemike Road was washed out in places, cut by runoff with the occasional trailer or abandoned house off in the poke salad and kudzu. It ended in a cul-de-sac of three trailers *like isolated you might say*. On the block steps of one stood a young man in a dirty III Percenters t-shirt, porkpie hat, and a hipster mustache that blurred his lips when he smirked. A giant Dodge pickup was parked out front, new and gleaming.

"Hey, dad," Dwayne Robbins called from beneath a string of Christmas lights. "Nice of you to join us, dad."

"I'm Tommy." He extended his hand, which the boy took limply.

"Dr. Thomas Clayton, I know."

"Where's Sam?"

"Your daughters inside, dad. Come on in."

His daughter was barefoot on a couch, eyes fixed on the Manchester United flag that covered the window opposite her, a purple heart tattoo visible where her shirt had slid up. Doc stood in the door, hands clasped in front of him, and waited.

"Sam?" She seemed not to see him. "Hello, Sam."

She seemed not to hear him either.

The boy knelt in front of her and took her hands in his. She'd had a boob job; the realization stung him.

"Hey, baby. Daddy's here. Dear ole dad showed up after all."

"You can knock that off," Doc said.

"What?"

"The dad shit."

The boy blurred his lips and turned back to Sam.

"Dr. Clayton is here, darling. Dear Dr. Clayton has come to save us."

"What?" she asked, though it was more a gasp than a word.

"Hi, Sam," Doc said.

"Daddy?"

"I'm right here."

"She's a little," the boy said.

"Daddy?"

"Here I am, honey."

"She's just a little, you know."

They walked in the yard past a moped and through the high grass down to where a few plastic lawn chairs sat around a fire ring by the creek. She was on something, daddy's girl. Her eyes flat and glossy. He watched her track something with such slowness he knew whatever she was seeing couldn't possibly exist.

"Are you still dancing?" he asked.

"My heart's just flying right now."

"Are you?"

"Dancing? God, daddy, look at me."

He did and then tried not to. She was pale with a pink abscess on her left arm, round as a mouth, her hair tangled. Thin and slow in paisley pants and slip-on shoes that had faded to a dingy white. Skinny, too skinny. She kept looking at her phone without actually touching the screen.

"So you're taking a semester off school?" he asked.

"Who told you that? Mama said that, didn't she?"

"She said you were studying art."

"Art?" She looked at her phone. "I spent a semester at Santa Fe Community College, not even a semester. But I bet she told you I was at UF, didn't she?"

"She didn't actually say."

"I know, just let you draw the conclusion. Fuck her." She lowered herself into one of chairs and took out a pack of Marlboros. "I think I'll just rest a minute." It was only when she lit up and looked at him that he realized she was panting. "Why don't you walk on up, daddy."

"I can sit with you."

"No, why don't you go ahead." She put the cigarette between her lips. "Sometimes I see us on like a staircase."

"On a what?"

"Like...I don't know." She shrugged and for a moment appeared confused. Eventually she remembered the Marlboro and lit it. "Just go on up, daddy. Please."

Dwayne was waiting on the porch, one leg hooked over the rail.

"She's an addict, dad."

"I asked you to quit the dad shit."

"Oh forgive me please. Your daughter is an addict, Dr. Clayton."

"There are no addicts," Doc said. "Only people engaging in addictive behavior."

Dwayne smiled.

"No," he said. "She's pretty much an addict."

"I thought maybe I could take you two out. I have some tickets for the ballet."

"The ballet?"

"She used to love to dance. Ballet was her thing."

"Her thing? What was yours?"

"I could pick you both up."

"Just tell us where to meet you, doc. We've made it this long on our own."

● ● ●

He drove back to Gainesville to buy a third ticket and get a room at the Best Western out on 441, showered, changed. At a quarter to six he drove to the Outback Steakhouse where he sat by the door and waited. He called Sam at 6:15 but she didn't answer. When he called back at 6:30 and then 6:45 he knew she wasn't going to. He thought of his precious Sartre. *The woman does not weep because he is sad. She is sad because she weeps.* Or the man, or the goddamn man.

He watched Boléro alone and dry-eyed, managing not to cry until he was in his car and driving home.

To the extent that he had one.

A home, he meant, not bothering to wipe his eyes.

• • •

He stopped at a package store as soon as he entered Volusia County, got on a back road and drank a McDonald's Sprite topped with Stoli. It was after ten by the time he made it to the bookstore in New Smyrna.

"You again," the man said.

"I've got a couple more for you, some Fitzgerald."

"Who?"

"Francis Scott. Look here."

He walked out with thirty-one hundred dollars but nowhere to lay his head. It was Bike Week and the only room available was at a campground that backed onto the St. John's River. The campground had a cabin with a propane stove and single bed. $200 for the week which he paid in cash. He drove to Alvin's Island & Beachware and bought a pair of expensive Ray-Bans and some cheap Hawaiian shirts. Went out for groceries and a bag of McGriddles and another bottle of Stoli but nothing else. So here he was once again, laid up drunk with the scratchy skin and self-loathing.

Still, he tried to order his life.

The two pairs of jeans, one (why exactly?) acid washed. Three or four balls of socks. The board shorts and Hanes t-shirts that were cheap. The Ray Bans that cost him genuine American dollars. In the kitchen were boxes of Kraft Mac & Cheese. Bread and eggs. Butter and milk and the flimsy Tupperware he had yet to fill. Frozen pizzas of all variety—he'd indulged on the Margarita and Quattro Formagio. Sprite to mix with the vodka. Coffee to get up. Booze to come down. Eventually he sold enough of his books to buy a used houseboat he docked behind the campground. He made trips to see his daughter, tried to salvage something there, fed her, listened to her, went with her to the Dhammaram Temple where he watched her dance across the bamboo floor while a scrawny teenage boy watched from the wings. Doc met Craig, the shaman with his ponytail and bag of Mexican Rail. He met the kid named Twitch with his JESUS DIDN'T TAP t-shirt and worn-out moped, the seat sticky and silvered with duct tape. He met the kid named Alan Holman. The dope came from Craig and soon enough Craig and his buddy Dwayne had hired Twitch as a runner. Things got so big so fast Dwayne decided to call dear ole dad and enlist his help.

Doc took the call by the pool.

"You're a fascist, aren't you, dad?"

"It's very possible."

"Perfect. I've got a proposition for you then."

Doc fixed a drink, put on his glasses, and reclined his chair.

He'd been sitting there for months when the woman he came to know as Shy Walsh showed up and started swimming lap after lap.

"Look at you," he called from his chaise longue. "I see ribs!"

It would be months before they fell in love, months before he told her *you want to cry, I'll tell when to cry,* more months still before the church burned and the cops descended. Eventually,

Doc's father would call me, but by then Shy would be gone, having disappeared into the waters, Doc would be dead, and I would be sitting alone in Atlanta, waiting for something, even if I could never say exactly what.

Still, that's how it started for Doc.

Here is how it started for me:

In the fall of 2017, I received first an email and then a phone call, and it was as much their proximity as content that threw me back into a world and a time I had (unforgivably, it now seems) largely forgotten. The email came in late October from the Assistant Public Defender in Daytona Beach. He wrote to tell me that Dante Henry had been charged with Felony Battery after a fight in a nightclub and that if convicted would face a mandatory five-year sentence, it was even possible the State would amend the charges in an attempt to lock Dante up for the rest of his life. It was a raw deal, the defender wrote. Dante was a giant of a man and according to witnesses had been relentlessly provoked until finally, his patience exhausted, his sobriety compromised, Dante kicked the shit out of the guy. The defender conceded that Dante had indeed been intoxicated—he had an alcohol problem, there was no denying this. Nevertheless, five years for a man simply defending himself would be a grievous injustice. A life sentence under a three-strikes-and-you're-out provision would be a crime in and of itself.

Mr. Henry, he wrote, had spoken of the three years we had spent working together in the writing workshop I had taught at Lawtey Correctional Institute. Should I remember Mr. Henry, would I consider writing a letter on his behalf asserting to his character?

That afternoon I wrote a letter praising his kindness and intelligence, admitting that while I didn't know all the peculiarities of "the night in question," I did know that Dante was a good man. I trusted him. I considered him a friend. I sent the letter and immediately began working back through my phone looking for our last contact. In the years since his release, I'd left Florida for a teaching job a half hour outside Atlanta and we had stayed in semi-regular touch. I knew he'd spent six months in a halfway house, eventually moving out and getting a job in construction. But looking back through my phone I realized we hadn't spoken in almost three months. He had not responded to my last two texts. He had not answered my last call.

I had written it off at the time as circumstance. That September, Hurricane Maria had shattered Dominica, St. Croix, and much of Puerto Rico before skirting the Atlantic Seaboard. In the wake of the storm, power along Florida's Atlantic coast was sporadic, phone towers were down, and I assumed Dante's silence was owed to such. When things settled down, I'd no doubt hear from him.

I must have put my phone away then.

I must have forgotten about things.

A few weeks later, I received a second note from the Public Defender's Office: as feared, the State had amended the charges. Facing the possibility of life in prison, Dante had accepted a plea deal and would spend the next five years at Columbia Correctional in Lake City. He was sorry it had turned out that way, but appreciated the letter all the same. He wished me well.

I did not respond.

• ● •

It must have been December when I got the phone call. The voice was older, measured, the sort of cloying southern drawl that reveals not so much geography as wealth. He asked was this Jesse Powers? The Jesse Powers who had once taught at a prison in Florida?

"I'm calling because of my son, Thomas Clayton," he said. "You probably knew him as Doc back then. They tell me he went by Doc while he was locked up."

I was sitting in my office at the time, a cube of pale yellow cinder blocks that looked out onto the underside of a community college stairwell. The garden level some of my colleagues called it. But it felt like a dungeon, as if I was under some sort of confinement. I didn't mind. I felt, in fact, as if I deserved such. In the past year I'd lost my girlfriend, both my parents, and any sense of direction so that I was prone to spend days without leaving my apartment, too busy not being depressed, as I told myself, to actually do anything.

Listless was, perhaps, the word.

Whereas the three years I'd spent in Florida had seemed defined by energy and promise: besides the writing workshop I'd taught at Lawtey Correctional, I'd published a second slim novel that, like the first, had received a few good reviews before disappearing without so much as a ripple. That hadn't mattered at the time. I was young, precocious; I was "full of wild and rich promise" as a book critic (back when there were such things as book critics) had put it. I had a superstar agent who assured me I was on the rise. I'd left Florida and took the job outside Atlanta both to be nearer my aging parents who lived in the mountains of north Georgia and in order to finish the new book—a sprawling epic I imagined being breathlessly promoted as a southern *The Brothers Karamazov*—the book that would make me a household name, at least in those households that spoke of such.

The book had taken me five years to write and landed with a 900 page thud on the desk of my agent who suddenly started taking four or five days to respond to my increasingly fevered emails.

Eventually, I cut the it to 700 pages—my artistic integrity would allow for no less—and as the book was systematically rejected by every major publishing house felt myself shed the affectations and illusions I'd spent the last decade collecting with the same focus my mother had once acquired ceramic figurines of barnyard animals, cows, pigs, a throaty rooster she loved more than seemed wise. My agent disappeared—"ghosted me," my much younger girlfriend would tell me, just before she did the same.

So there I was in my corduroy pants and scratchy sweater, spending my days behind a veil of Klonopin and sleep, when Doc's father called. Thomas Clayton and I had once been as close as brothers, at least it had felt that way at the time. He'd told me about his habit, his divorce, his estranged daughter Sam. But he'd wanted a "clean start" when he'd been released and we hadn't spoken since. It had pained me at the time, though to be honest I'd hardly thought of him since. Holding the phone it all came back. His face: the ruined dignity of the well-read alcoholic. His voice: all self-effacing bullshit giving way to actual wisdom. That was Doc.

I assured his father I remembered his son, absolutely, though I was sorry to say I hadn't spoken with him since he'd been released. How was he?

"He's dead. I'm sorry to be so blunt but that's why I'm calling. He hanged himself back in the spring in the sort of shitty motel room you wouldn't want to park outside let alone die in."

"Oh, God," I said. "I'm so sorry."

"Used goddamn jumper cables if you can believe such. Went up through the drop ceiling to the joist. Had cranked up the classical music. Otherwise, who knows when they would have found him."

"I had no idea. I'm so sorry."

"Anyway, I'm not fishing for consolation here. Tommy and I had our problems, not least of which is the awful bullshit he put his daughter through. I saw him only once after he got out and he mentioned you. That's why I'm calling. Said you'd taught a class he was in."

"He was one of the most gifted writers I've ever met."

"Yeah. A smart boy, Thomas. Intelligence was never the problem. But when I saw him—he came down here last Thanksgiving it would have been, and he mentioned some stories he had written."

"I still have them."

"I figured from what he said you might. He was loaded that night which was no surprise to me or his mother but I knew when he mentioned those stories they were real."

"I have them right here. I could send them to you."

"No. No, I appreciate it but I have no desire to revisit what he did or didn't say. But you're a writer yourself, right?"

"A fiction writer, yes."

"But you surely do research now and then?"

"Of a sort, sometimes."

"All right," he said, "good. I don't want the stories, but I do have a favor to ask."

"Anything," I said, without really thinking.

"When he was down here last Christmas he had two people with him, his girlfriend and this absolutely enormous Guatemalan man. His girlfriend was some sort of ex-boxer or something. Siobhan Walsh. The Guatemalan, I don't know. Very polite. I'm not racist. He was certainly polite, but vaguely scary too. Anyway, Tommy shows up with both of them just loaded to the goddamn gills and proceeds—what else?—to make a scene.

That's the last we heard from him until the Sheriff's department called in May to say a cleaning lady had found his body out at the Red Carpet Inn by 595. This whole thing has just about killed his mother."

"What's the favor, Dr. Clayton?"

"What's that?"

"You said you had a favor to ask."

"Right, yeah. Well, that's pretty simple," he said. "You're a writer. I want you to find out what happened."

"I make up stories, sir."

"Then make this one up. I want something to tell my wife. I want something to help her sleep at night."

That night—unable to sleep myself—I took out the pages Doc had written, the same pages I would burn months later on the beach there in front of the Golden Lion, a gesture that would have been ceremonial had it not been for a wind that whipped away first the smoke and then the papers themselves, scattering them over the water.

I shuffled through them and tried to imagine Doc that last night. He was sarcastic and cynical, gentle and kind. But maybe not that night. That night it must have been all pity, an off-the-rack sadness he must have thought belonged to a lesser man. That must have been nearly impossible for Doc, the self-indulgence, the loneliness that was just beginning to sour into despair. He'd left his girlfriend by then.

Some sort of ex-boxer or something.

Siobhan Walsh. I knew the name. I have spent most of my adult life fascinated by fighting, by the how and why of it, the riddle at its center, and Shy Walsh was the biggest riddle of all. The most successful female mixed martial artist in history, she had drifted away after her single loss, a first-round knockout in Las Vegas in November of 2015, disappearing into obscurity, and then simply disappearing.

I'd even met her once. Around the time Shy was finishing high school I was living nearby, a young professor who spent one night a week teaching at a prison and the others training at a local gym. We moved in the same universe, though so far as I remember I saw her only the single time I attended a seminar at Rolly's Boxing & Fitness Emporium and there she was, the lone girl in the corner, pony-tailed and unsmiling while Rolly spoke of omoplatas and arm-bars. It was years later, when Shy Walsh had become something of a star, that I connected that frowning, intense young woman with the woman on my screen.

Professional fighting is a world of misogyny and expensive t-shirts, of collapsed sinus cavities and unhappy boys. But it is also a world of the occasional genius, someone who seems to have sprung from the skin of a Grecian Urn, nervous system as hair-triggered as a peregrine. That was Shy. When she fought, she seemed to rise steadily, the movement imperceptible until you judged it against her opponent, sinking like a child's balloon: deflating and forgotten and better left in the corner. She was a genius in the cage, but then she wasn't. She was just gone.

I straightened the pages, put them away, took them back out. I didn't know what to do with them and instead just sat there, thinking of Doc's father.

I want something to help her sleep at night.

It was weeks before I realized I did too.

That's how it started for me.

For Siobhan, we have to go back to November, 2015.

Seven months before she'd lose her mother to bone cancer; nine months before she would meet Doc by a Central Florida swimming pool; and nearly two years before the Church of Life More Abundant in Christ would burn to its foundations and she would follow whatever it was she followed into the tea-colored waters of the St. John's River, Shy Walsh would lie beneath the camper shell of her boyfriend Kenny's Tacoma and try to drink a Met-Rx shake through a silly straw. She was still sick from the Lortab they had given her in the emergency room, her left orbital still puffed with a green-glass brilliance, but at least she was finally sitting up, finally eating something, even if it meant sucking protein isolate through her wired jaw. All of this somewhere in East Texas. Uvalde or maybe Utopia. Some place where the wind was howling at dawn and Kenny was out stalking whitetail.

Kenny being the boyfriend.

Baby-hearted smug-ass Kenny.

But no, she didn't mean that, not really, and instead of thinking it brought the straw to her lips, drank as much as possible, and laid back against the inflatable mattress slowly bleeding air so that she felt the truck's ribbed bed beneath her. They had put two stitches in her tongue, dissolvable things scratching around the soft of her mouth, doing whatever damage they were doing.

She felt that too.

She felt everything.

She'd been in the truck since Vegas, having decided to drive. Eighteen hours and in hindsight what a stupid decision. But no one had thought she would end the night in the ER at Sunrise Medical. Certainly no one had thought she would lose the fight, least of all her. She was a 10 to 1 favorite but caught a left hook not thirty seconds in and her mouth started bleeding and there was something about that blood. Not the coppery taste of it— she knew the taste of blood—but the simple fact of it being there, pumping into her mouth with an arterial glee. It rattled her. Her feet never felt set. She kept drifting closer, and closer was the one thing she knew not to do. You keep your distance from a counter-puncher, you go to the mat, do the ground work. She was a grappler, after all.

Yet there she was: closer, closer still.

And then the roundhouse popped in her head, a little flash-bulb of surprise, a little afterthought of regret…stupid, stupid… and they were helping her up off the mat. Or not helping her, lifting her, and she could hear the crowd somewhere out there through the grainy darkness of concussion, the crowd totally losing its shit, cheering, booing. Someone asked could she wiggle her fingers. *Siobhan? Can you wiggle your fingers for me? Hey, Shy?* Her neck felt warm and it occurred to her that was her blood, spilling from the cave of her mouth.

Can you squeeze my hand?

The latexed fingers removing her mouthpiece.

The penlight in first one eye and then the other.

Hey, Shy?

They walked her after that, to the locker room and to the waiting ambulance and on to the hospital. She didn't shower until she got back to The Sands but by then the blood had dried and she came out of the shower thinking, *clean* thinking *sleep* until Kenny saw her and started crying and she was all *what?* and Kenny just sort of collapsing against her, crying right there in the master suite with its minibar and zebra curtains and the giant bouquet her agent Stu had sent over. But Kenny, Jesus. Something about it hurt her more than losing, the way he crumpled. As if she was no longer the person she had been, and Kenny crying like he was mourning her. Kenny crying like he was grieving their future which was ridiculous.

But then soon enough she was crying too.

They sat up all night, her head pounding, eyes dilated, adrenaline lingering. Then the Lortab settled over her like ground fog and it was *I'm so tired, Kenny.* And Kenny was all, *stay awake, babe. Hey, hon, look at me, okay?* Her coach Dominic arrived the next morning with a doctor from the Nevada State Athletic Commission who looked in her eyes with yet another tiny light. She made a fist for him, she touched her nose. She signed a photo for his daughter, and then something else, some sort of release, and they made their solemn nods and left.

She slept after that, she and Kenny both, slept the day away while outside the hotel the paparazzi had gathered, not that she wanted to know. She'd turned her phone off just before the fight and left it off. No Twitter, no Instagram. No reassurances to her fans or calls for the inevitable rematch. They slept and at dusk crept out to the parking garage. The paparazzi with their Vespas and telephoto lenses were gone. Everyone was gone. *Fuck them*, Kenny said, screamed actually, into the concrete cavern with its elevator and pale cancer light. *Fuck all y'all.* They left around seven and drove all night and part of the next day. Nevada to Texas, half the trip holding a Dairy Queen Oreo Blizzard that slowly melted against her face, the other half swallowing her own blood. Stupid but who could have seen it coming, the future, the left that opened her mouth, the roundhouse that shut it?

Now, alone in the camper shell, she arched her spine, feeling it open, the spasmed muscles of her back releasing. Above her was a generalized glow she saw as much through her eyelids as the pain medication. Goddamn November. The truck parked in a field of blue grama on the edge of the pines. Kenny was out there. She could yell for him if she needed to, she could bang one foot against the glass. But she wasn't going to do that. She was flat on her back, half-covered by the nylon of her sleeping bag, socked feet up on the cold metal of the tire well. One of the windows was propped open and despite the wind she smelled something. Despite the pain medicine she had a sneaking suspicion she might have shit her pants. Also—oh, please, Jesus— she was about to vomit again, which was its own manner of suffering what with the broken jaw.

She pulled herself onto hands and knees, and began the long crawl to the back of the truck just as it came through her clenched teeth, a stringy heartburn bile. On all fours, head hanging over the tailgate, eyes tearing, while a part of herself— maybe the realest self she had—began to wonder if this hadn't been what she'd wanted all along.

That realest self asking if just maybe she had let herself get kicked on purpose?

The thought was on the verge of articulating itself when another spasm pushed through her and—*oh shit oh shit oh shit...*

As if that had become her name.

And in a way, it had.

● ● ●

Her name before that, her real name, was Siobhan Rae Walsh,

and until she lost that night in Vegas she was the girl who could not lose. 27 and 0 here in her 27th year, which felt magical until it didn't. Not that she hadn't suffered before. She'd been raised poor, watched her daddy's burial by an East Tennessee cow pond and then rode south with her mama down GA-1 into Florida and a deeper understanding of the intricacies of poverty. She'd worked three jobs simultaneously. She'd been mocked, shunned, and just more or less shit on by any number of men.

Yet here she was.

She'd been to the Olympics—a screw up of colossal proportions—but had rebounded from it all, recovered, spiraled but pulled out of said spiral to reinvent herself as a mixed martial artist, to become relatively famous and moderately rich. By twenty-five, she had endorsements with an energy drink and a manufacturer of headgear. By twenty-six, she had her own protein bar, had fought in nine countries, flown in a hot air balloon, and been wooed by a Serbian count obsessed with Systema. Yet it felt like nothing. She had a trainer and a manager, a line of athleisure clothing and a boyfriend but she still felt alone. She had almost six hundred K in the bank but she still felt poor.

By twenty-seven, she knew she always would.

• ⊙ •

Kenny came back what time—seven-thirty, maybe. Eight if she was guessing.

He opened the back glass and instantly, despite the sleeping bag and blankets and Polar fleece, she was freezing. The morning hovered around thirty, the sun an area of uncertain light, white and heatless in the overcast sky. The wind gusting. He hadn't seen fuck all. Plenty of sign but he'd been all morning in a stand on the edge of a field of red clover and there'd been nothing but a big tom turkey easing through the sedge like he owned the place which, Kenny told her, he reckoned it did.

He mixed her another Met-Rx in the shaker cup even though she hadn't finished the first.

There was dried vomit on her chin and on the collar of her North Face jacket, clotted blood on one cheek, clotted protein on her shirt.

"The hell, girl." He used his sleeve to wipe her face. "You all right?"

He was sipping a RockStar, he was going back.

"There's a blind about a half mile away. Maybe I'll just give it another hour. Hey, Shy?"

He used his sleeve to touch her chin.

"That all right, babe?"

That was all right, sure, that was fine. Everything was fine because what else could she say? She nodded and for a moment he gently brushed the puff of her lower lip, purple and split, but then he looked like he might start crying again and she turned away, pulled the blankets back over her and he nodded, finished his RockStar, and was gone.

Eight, maybe nine o'clock in the morning but it all felt so indeterminate.

Herself, she meant. About the others, she knew what they were saying. 10 to 1 odds, which meant how much money had changed hands? Which meant how many pay-per-view subscribers in how many bars had stood there, drinks in hand, saying *oh, shit. Bitch just got knocked the fuck out?* A nine-hundred K purse which right about now—less the take for her agent and trainer and all the rest—was shifting into her account. They would be talking about that on sports radio ("I guess I'd let them break my jaw for that, Tom."). On ESPN they would be earnestly discussing her refusal to touch gloves ("It's hard not to see this as her comeuppance."). Every man everywhere—it would be all men, or mostly men—would be holding forth on whether or not that uppity bitch got what was coming.

She took her phone out, held it, put it away.

Her face hurt in a way that made her aware of its shape.

Which was a strange thing to be.

Where you are is a place, she told herself.

She lay back and shut her eyes.

Where you are is a place.

What is happening to you is your life.

That was the first day.

● ● ●

On the second day it occurred to her she had four more days to get through and then it occurred to her not only that she probably could, but that probably she deserved it: the cold truck, the stinging face, the diarrhea in the freezing woods.

They had planned it different.

The trip was meant to be celebratory, a sort of carnal asceticism, just the two of them and a Yeti full of good food and good Jack Daniels. They'd done the same a year ago. At the time, she was coming off eighteen dazzling months, seven knockouts in seven fights, a string of endorsements and with them the first intimations of celebrity. There was the lunch at Chateau Marmont, the congratulatory tweet from Beyoncé, her own line of yoga tights and poly-cotton t-shirts with KEEP FIGHTING in retro Bauhaus font. She and Kenny had spent six days camping alone, laughing and drinking, hunting in the morning and driving into town in the afternoon to have an early dinner of ribeyes and Shiner on draft. Then back to the deer camp where the sex was mind-boggling, some sort of ongoing wonderfuck, sometimes vigorous and exhausting. Sometimes slow and delicate, and sometimes—impossible as it seemed—both at once.

They had been together over a year by then, properly together, and it felt right, had begun, even, to feel permanent.

He had a Halon 32 compound bow and they both got a buck and rode into town with them tied to the front bumper, laughing and honking the horn. She put a shot on Instagram holding her deer tag like a prize, everybody's sweetheart, the grinning girl-next-door with her blue ribbon like she'd just won the spelling bee. They'd had a drink to celebrate, and when her agent texted that evening to say she had an endorsement offer from Bass Pro Shop and he was taking it to Cabela's to see if they would up it, they'd had another.

At the end of that week, they'd driven over to San Antonio and spent Thanksgiving with his parents, all piled into the living room with their turkey and stuffing and the Cowboys on the TV the way the good Lord intended.

The next morning they had gotten up early, the house still sleeping, and ran together through the warm pre-dawn streets, sprinklers flashing, streetlights flickering out. Three miles that turned into four and then five and then something happened—it was hard not to think of it like some rom-com moment turned into a cheesy gif, but okay, whatever, she knew she would never forget it—but something had happened and running along past a brake-and-tire place and then a McDonald's and then the turn lane to the Costco, they made eye contact and tacitly agreed to just keep going, to keep running, but also—she felt later—to keep going in some larger way.

They'd wound up running thirteen miles.

They'd wound up falling in love.

They had met at the Hammerhead MMA Gym in Miami. Kenny was a welterweight and she was new in town, straight off the nineteen dollar GoTo bus from Orlando which was its own form of sad, but again, whatever. She'd been a judoka growing up in Daytona Beach, a dojo kid taking the dojo bus from school to practice where her mother would pick her up, too exhausted to check her homework or her lunchbox.

The vocabulary words and the sevens table—that was Shy's business.

The apple, the yogurt, the whole wheat bread—that was hers and her alone.

When she was eighteen, she moved to Rolly's Boxing & Fitness Emporium in Daytona. Two hours of Jiu Jitsu and another hour of sparring. Mats closed with duct tape and mopped with Clorox and still you got the ringworm, you got the purple bruises where the skin pinched, the—what was the word?—the contusions. Rolly Peterson being the coach, this old-school white guy who had trouble taking her seriously. Woman, female, what the hell was she doing in his fight gym, this wannabe Million Dollar Baby? Here one had the company of men. One had the slim Cuban punchers it was impossible to get ahold of, the little Thai guys with shins like razors. The white kids with their Mohawks and acne pits. The black dudes with fades right out of 1986. You had the ex-mil, the cops, the former offensive lineman that had dropped out of whatever Division II program to hang sheetrock by day and work the door of the TomCat Klub by night. But women—there ain't no lady folk here, ma'am.

He put her to hitting twenty rounds on the heavy bag, a shits and giggles thing for the boys gassed after open mat. Then she went and did it. That night, next night, every night—twenty rounds. It was limitless, what she could endure. Broken fingers and floating ribs. The nail flipped off each big toe like the cap off a bottle. The burst capillaries appeared as red starbursts on her milky skin.

"She was working three jobs at the time," Rolly would tell me years later, sitting in his wood-paneled office, around him pages torn from magazines. Tyson chewing Holyfield in *Sports*

Illustrated. Ronnie Coleman at his most gigantic in *Muscular Development.* Ken Shamrock appearing to have stepped straight from the Troubles and into the pages of I didn't know what.

"Three goddamn jobs," Rolly said.

Bartending at Booth's Bowery. Dressing like a pirate at the shrimp place near Ormond. Something else Rolly couldn't remember. Putt-putt maybe, only it wasn't putt-putt. Go-cart attendant at the place you got the coupons for? It didn't matter. Twenty rounds and he wonders one night, when does she eat? Where does she eat? So he gets takeout from Golden Wok, orders extra everything, the Kung Pao, the Chow Mein. Rice, just mound after mound of white rice like you never seen. Thinks she'll refuse—she's too proud—and he can tell she's going to, can tell, too, that she's starving so he preemptively insists. This after twenty rounds, after sparring, after rolling, after how many jobs behind her and how many jobs to go?

"Eat, girl. Come on now. You think I got room in the fridge for this?"

That sort of drive, that sort of heart—Rolly had never seen it.

A year later she was at the Olympic Training Center in Boulder.

United States National Judo Team.

"There's a word for that sort of rise," Rolly would say. "I just can't damn remember it."

But Shy could.

That was how she spent the second day: remembering.

● ● ●

On the third day, they drove into town, or Kenny drove and she slumped in the passenger seat with her still-swollen face pressed into her balled coat. No radio, no conversation. She wanted just being out of the camper bed to feel like something but it didn't. She wanted a few other basic things as well. She wanted to shower and they got a room at the Best Western off Highway 90. She wanted to shit on a toilet except by now there seemed nothing left to pass. The Lortab made her skin itch. Her jaw ached. She kept not so much swallowing blood as feeling it slide down the back of her throat and decided she wanted Kenny to unwire her jaw.

"Like when?"

"Like now."

He sat on the corner of the motel bed staring at her, not quite believing.

"Are you serious?"

She nodded yes but Kenny just shook his head no.

"Baby, you been wired what? Like barely forty-eight hours."

"Take it off please."

"Doc said ten days minimum."

"Kenny…"

"Why don't we drive back to Vegas? Or we can fly even, leave the truck."

"Take it off or I will."

He argued but she made clear that she was serious and he had her sit on the lowered toilet seat in the overlit bathroom, head tipped back. There were horizontal arch bars, impressive spidery things, but only a single vertical wire connecting them.

"I'll have to get something." He leaned forward and canted his head, almost as if he intended to kiss her. "I've got pliers in the truck but I think like needle-nose."

"There's a hardware store back…"

"What's that?"

"I saw a hardware store driving in."

She started to get up but he put both hands on her thighs. She was in a robe, still wet from the shower, her blonde hair dark and swept back over the creamy bruises that had settled her face into something almost like its original incarnation.

"I'll go," he said. "Sit still, babe. I got this."

She waited until the door shut to move to the bed, took up her phone but put it down again. She'd turned it off twenty-four hours before the fight and it was off still. The longest she could ever remember going and what had started as a sort of nervousness—*what are they saying?*—had now passed into a sort of contempt—*I know good and goddamn well what they're saying*. She should at least call her mom, call her agent Stu, call her coach Dominic, but she knew Kenny had done that already, that Kenny was handling things, and she slipped her phone into one of zippered pockets on the big North Face bag. She was still sitting there when he came back in and took the needle-nose pliers from his pocket.

"Let's go in the bathroom," he said. "Better light."

He unwound it slowly, meticulously, the pressure enough to nearly turn her head, the ache dull and bone deep. When he pulled it from her mouth—it looked like a tangle of something, a failed art project—she sat there, rubbing her jaw but not yet sure if she should open it, or even how.

"I don't think you should," Kenny started to say, but then she did, as wide as possible, and the pain, even through the Lortab, the pain was like the greater part of her, like it was this corporeal thing to which her body was just an imagined appendage. Her eyes watered. She thought she would faint. She sat on the toilet seat with Kenny telling her to breathe through her nose, breathe through your nose, babe. Slow, slow.

"Your hands are shaking," he said, and he was right, only she hadn't noticed. "Your hands, Jesus, Shy."

Eventually, she showered a second time and they drove to a bar on Getty where she drank a pitcher of Coors. The beer so cold and her body so empty that for the first time since before the fight she felt nothing, and it was such a welcome thing, this nothingness. It was the same calmness she'd felt the night before the fight, the same calmness that only proximity to violence could induce. It was the thing maybe that made her great—past tense, she supposed, maybe past tense—and not just how the closer she got to fighting the calmer she became: though uncommon, this wasn't an unheard of trait. Ask any sociopath and he'll tell you of singing, say, the sweetest Sam Cooke while stalking his victim. The thing about Shy was that the closer she got to the fight, the better of a person she became.

Her mind cleared.

Her heart slowed.

She became so generous she could only describe it as feeling the edges of self fall away, very Buddhist, very Zen. Very *wow, there goes my posterior parietal cortex* and with it any sense of edges. Which meant, she told herself, that when she fought it wasn't an act of violence; it was an act of solidarity, a sisterhood formed in an octagonal cage.

Stupid.

She knew it sounded stupid, but that didn't make it any less real. All those people thinking fighting was savage, but fighting simply *is*. War, murder, life without health insurance—that was savage.

The children drowning in the Mediterranean.

The families dehydrating in the Sonoran Desert.

The disappearance of whales/bats/insects/gorillas/the black rhino.

The thirty-five thousand Congolese children who die every year to provide the coltan in your iPhone. That was savage. But fighting, think about this—and she thought about it there in the bar while Kenny went to refill the pitcher one more time before happy hour prices ran out—two people come together, agree to abide by a certain set of very specific rules, then attempt to kill each other by exploiting every weakness evolution had yet to attend to, but—and this was the important part—but stop the moment the referee tells them too. Stop and accept the judgment of a third party. Stop and hold no grudges, feel, in fact, a tremendous gratitude. That wasn't barbarity. That was a humane acknowledgment of the human condition, and it induced calmness.

She felt it now just as she'd felt it the night before the fight.

By then, twenty-seven fights into her professional life, she had the routine down. She moved into the Sands three days before, living in baggy sweats and weighing herself morning, noon, and night. She'd gone to the gym for some light sparring and stretching, to spend a half hour on the recumbent bike, but mostly she'd sat around eating pre-made meals and watching HGTV.

The day before the fight she weighed in at exactly 134 pounds, the precision being part of the awe she sought to project, standing on the stage in her KEEP FIGHTING bikini, her hair actually blow-dried for the event. (The promoters had sent over a stylist.)

They'd acted out the usual pre-fight routine—the staring and posing and angry headshakes. Shy knew the woman's weight and reach and how the way she kept her feet planted made her vulnerable to a quick takedown. She knew every in and out of her technique.

That was also part of the awe: the focus, the preparation.

That evening they'd gone to dinner at the Olive Garden on East Flamingo, a holdover from the days when eating there was not an ironic inside joke but a splurge. And she liked the food. It was plain and hearty and made her think of the best of her childhood, not just the times before her dad died, but those rare times after too. Times when her mama came down from whatever spiritual plane she occupied to turn on the *Golden Girls* and boil a pot of angel hair.

She went with Kenny and her agent Stu the Cuban, a former powerlifter with tattoos of Reagan and Nixon, with her coach Dominic the Dominican who'd busted both ear drums in his mid-twenties. Back in Miami, Shy also had a grappling coach and a strength and conditioning coach, a physical therapist and a nutritionist. But what she'd found was that in the lead up to a fight they all became needy. When they were supposed to be giving, they wound up taking: her assurances, her stillness. She had learned to then use a minimalist approach, flying out with just Kenny and Dominic who would be her seconds, Stu flying in later. There was a publicist who was supposed to be having dinner with them as well but they had ignored his pleas and left without returning any of his messages. It was a shame really because in a world of men who vacillated between treating her with absolute respect one minute, only to try to try to sleep with her in the next, it was the one time they treated her in the only way they felt fully comfortable: as a man, a fighter, a machine with a precise and violent agenda.

They brought out the bread.

They brought out the salad.

All was right in Shy's world, the meal calm, the company relaxed.

She hugged Stu in the parking lot and told him she'd see him tomorrow.

He took both her hands into his giant paws.

"Day of days, Shy."

She wanted to shrug away but couldn't quite do it.

"Day of days," he said again and shut his eyes. "Pray with me. Come on, girl. Oh, Immaculate Mary, Virgin most Powerful…"

Then she and Kenny and Dominic headed to The Sands basement where a trashcan filled with fifty pounds of ice waited.

"Babe," Kenny said.

He didn't care for the ice. Dominic thought it was some voodoo shit that would at best induce a head cold. But she'd done it before her first fight and done it ever since. The ice mounded waist deep and Kenny running water over it until it reached the brim. She stripped to her underwear and stood for a moment with a single fingertip hooked on the edge. Kenny and Dominic looked grim. It was the moment, they both knew, the flipping of the switch when the raison d'etre shifted from staying calm and loose to contemplating murder in a very specific fashion.

"All right," she said. "We ready?"

When Kenny went to steady her she brushed him away. You fought alone, you got into the ice alone, and if it was dramatic it was also necessary: you needed a clear demarcation between the old world of cooperation and friendship and the one to come, the one where you were revealed as what you'd always been: utterly and completely abandoned.

She locked her arms on the side, the rubber giving but holding, and lowered first her left leg and then her right. The feet—it felt good on the feet, good on the shins. But somewhere around the thighs it began to burn. By the time it touched her crotch it was splashing out and she was taking short quick hits of oxygen through her nose.

"Shy," Kenny said, as if uncertain of her name.

She slid down to her waist and then her navel and then in one sudden movement that always brought to mind a calving glacier, let her entire body go. The splash was tremendous. The shock a physical blow, like the big Seminole woman who'd once hit her just below her heart. But she'd stayed on her feet then and she stayed on her feet now, crouching, breath held, hair waving above her like the newly drowned.

She surfaced in an explosion, panting, her skin pink, underwear clinging.

"I'm ready," she'd said, when she'd collected her breath.
And she had been.

Only now was she beginning to wonder for what.

Kenny came back with the pitcher but she was already pleasantly drunk and simply sat attempting to smile while he refilled her glass. She could feel her face in that way that was becoming less strange and it didn't so much hurt as assert itself, its dull presence a very material thing as she allowed her tongue to search around the farther reaches of her mouth.

"We could drive on to my parents," Kenny said.

Three of her teeth were loose, one of them a molar.

"Hey, hon? You hear me?"

She did, but she didn't want to go to his parents. She didn't want to go anywhere. She shut her eyes and was circling again, back in the octagon, circling, hands up, hands out, not so much striking as pawing the air, and then—from nowhere—the left she doesn't see, and then the right she does. Yet she lets it come anyway.

She lets it come and then it's all penlight and latexed fingers and she is spitting out blood and saliva and two decades of work, spitting out her entire goddamn life.

"Hon?"

She was almost certain she had let herself get kicked on purpose.

Only she couldn't say why.

No one could.

Not you, and certainly not me.

Not Kenny either.

● ● ●

Kenny had come into her life the year after the Olympics, six months after Shy flamed out in the Rio semi-finals, an inexplicable and unforgiveable fuck up that was no more and no less than having purely and simply choked. You see Bob Costas over there by the NBC cameras, hear the national anthem, finger the expensive tracksuits they let you keep and you realize it's bigger than you, the expectations, the consequences.

You get dizzy and lose on points to a Russian, weep in the locker room.

It's not a joke.

Finish fourth—no podium, no medal—when here you'd been a favorite.

It's not a joke, Shy.

She'd gone back to Daytona after that, back to her mama's prayers, back to her own small dreams. Locked herself in her childhood bedroom and gorged on hard candy, looked at the photographs tacked to a corkboard, a collage she'd made back in high school. Photos from East Tennessee where she'd grown up working-class poor until her daddy stroked out one night sitting in the cab of his F-250 outside the gym he owned and operated in the dying heart of Elizabethton, his central nervous system preloaded with enough Dianobol and cocaine to float him through a dozen sets of heavy squats. He was junkyard mean and wide as a table, strutting his 6'3" 255 pound frame down East Elk from where it crossed the Doe River all the way past the pizza shop to Iron Mayhem, Walkman clipped to the running shorts into which he tucked a pressed wife-beater out of which flowed two giant hairless arms. Attached to the right one was an eight-year-old girl smacking her gum.

She loved him, her daddy.

He might have been a bastard—even at eight she'd understood this—but he was her bastard and she didn't care. Her daddy's side of the family were Scots-Irish, his own father part of the original SAS and said to have murdered Germans in North Africa with his bare hands. In France, he made a practice of defenestration—snipers, prisoners of war, rumored collaborators, it didn't matter. Though eventually it did, and when charges quietly materialized they were just as quietly dropped when he demonstrated a willingness to immigrate to the United States.

After her father died, her mother brought her to central Florida where they exchanged their working-class poverty for poverty of the unadulterated kind, a variety defined by good-hearted shoplifting at the Orange City K-Mart.

Still, Shy had always done the best she could.

She was a good child. Trusting and honest, if always on the move. Bold, incapable of stillness. Sometimes too defiant her mother would think, though it was an authentic defiance, a curiosity. She was ingenuous, and people recognized such, people were drawn to her. Her kindergarten teacher *such a kind heart.* The woman giving out Kool-Aid and Big Sixty cookies at Vacation Bible School *such a pure little thing.* Children too. They played detective on the case of her father's missing ring last seen in a change dish by the exhausted hand soap dispenser. Sang songs from *Annie.* Jumped on the nearly-but-not-quite busted trampoline. But mostly she went with her father to the gym and her mother to church or circle or gathering. So it was all God and the hundred pound concrete sphere her father hauled over his shoulder before racing the length of mirrors. It was the Universal Intelligence and the pull-up bars she began first hanging on and then swinging from until the local gymnastics teacher saw her and offered free tuition.

Her daddy's world: Everyone in a circle, cheering on the rubberized flooring, while Big Pete attempted to deadlift twelve plates. On the wall a sign that read *DON'T BE A LITTLE BITCH* beneath a muscular woman in lime green Lycra.

Her mama's: Everyone in a circle, kneeling on the carpet, jeans shiny at the knees. On the walls the Ten Commandants and a poster showing a great cartoon rising, people pulled from a stadium into clouds that read *Do not lay up your treasures on Earth.* Beside it, a hand-drawn Moses (white beard, bulbous eyes) parting the Red Sea as if the waters were a televangelist's pompadour.

That was how that life started.

It ended with her daddy in his truck, skin the color of pork, body slumped like a side of beef, like the dead meat he was in the process of becoming.

Bug, he'd always called her. Come here, bug.

But not anymore.

That was when they left. In the wake of her husband's death, in wake of his *abandonment* (as her mother came to call it), in the wake of the disaster that was probate (there was no will, but there were back taxes and two outstanding liens against Iron Mayhem), after the yard sale and the drive south, the I-95 traffic barrels and construction mesh and thirty-nine-dollars-a-night no-tell motels, Shy's mother experienced a sort of vision and who should stand before this once proud woman now reduced to widowhood and the ash of marriage but Jesus Himself, so blue-eyed and clear skinned he appeared to have emerged from swimming in a Norwegian fjord so recently he had yet to take up the sword or the flame or the serpents that surely laid in wait out back in the swamp of live oaks and retaining ponds behind their one-bedroom efficiency somewhere in the mire of Volusia County.

That was when her mother began to live at the Church of Life More Abundant in Christ. She was a lapsed Catholic of spiritualist bent, then, later, a Jehovah's Witness refugee with a Seventh Day Adventist fetish who eventually became a washed-in-the-blood Southern Baptist busy studying *A Course in Miracles* and opening her chakras.

You lived a life to be rid of it—that was the moral of her mother's story.

Her mama's method was to embrace that which couldn't be seen while ignoring that which could. Every moment save those she wasn't cleaning toilets or whisking the carpet at the Econolodge on LPGA Boulevard or plating strawberry crepes at the IHOP, her mother was at the Church of Life More Abundant in Christ, dopesick for any sort of love.

It was a pull that wasn't lost on her daughter.

Back home from the Olympics and eating Starbursts by the value-sized bag, Shy paced the confines of her room, a caged animal, restless, tireless. Eventually, her mama talked her out and whatever shit she carried against her mama she would always owe her for that. The prayers, the nagging, the anointed cloth her mama brought home from church, a handkerchief sopped in olive oil she dropped across Shy's sleeping face.

"God, mama, what is this?"

"That's the hand of the Lord, child. I ain't gonna let you die on me like your daddy did."

(Which is the sort of thing you can say when your husband actually has died on you.)

After weeks of cajoling and pleading and threatening, Shy finally puked Jolly Rancher and went online. Turns out the best fight gym in the eastern US was in Miami. Her mama bought the bus ticket.

She met Kenny on her third day though he told her later he had noticed her on her first. *Been watching you, girl.* It hadn't seemed so creepy at the time. *Had my eye on you.* It had seemed almost sweet. The gym was full of pros and would-be pros and there was a family-vibe of cookouts and surfing and trips down to Largo where they all snorkeled off a borrowed yacht. The gym was as large as a hangar, and situated in Kendale Lakes behind an apartment complex and a sprawling stucco ghetto of fifteen-hundred square foot ranchers with single-car garages and fenced pools: the American middle class constructed within easy walking distance of a Taco Bell and a Jiffy Lube. The gym itself was at least four times as large as Rolly's place in Daytona Beach and at least that many times nicer. At any one time, there were three dozen serious fighters, maybe eighty locals taking BJJ and Muay Thai classes, and a good five hundred moms and college kids and senior citizens using the weight room, the cardio room, the pool or Zumba classes.

But the fighters were the heart of the operation.

A spear, the owner Pitr Roque was fond of saying, his fighters being the tip. He was a Romanian real estate developer with a love for combat sports and a need to lessen his tax burden. The gym was the perfect shelter, run like a charity at a constant if immaterial loss. All the fighters accepted into the upper tier were given a stipend and a bed in one of the three communal houses, two for the men and one for the women.

Which was the other thing: there were women here.

Shy's first two friends were Romi, a compact Israeli fresh out of the IDF, all elbows and angles, and Sophia, a Brazilian with wild blonde hair to her waist who'd grown up wrestling three older brothers. One quiet, one magnificent, both decent and accepting, and for this, Shy was disproportionately grateful. She was a curiosity after all, an Olympian who'd had a sidebar in *Sports Illustrated* yet watch the match on YouTube and goddamn, girl got her ass beat, just flat out rolled over and died. But neither mentioned it, neither seemed even aware though Shy knew they were.

She moved into a three-bedroom house with them and a revolving door of other women: a red-haired flyweight who had gotten out of a women's correctional facility in Alabama for check kiting and was gone after a single sparring session, her bag stuffed with stolen gym merchandise. A bantamweight from "not anywhere a bitch like you ever been" (no elaboration offered, none requested) who refused to remove her press-on nails and hair extensions and was thus expelled. Some mean white girls who grew up fighting in trailers. A sweet white girl who grew up tumbling in a gymnastics center. A woman with a shaved head worthy of Sinead O'Connor. Two black sisters who claimed to be Venus and Serena but, like, pissed, you know? A forty-year old woman cut razor-sharp who had survived breast cancer but broke down crying "from gratitude" halfway through every cardio circuit (burpees, she explained, made her "take stock.") There was the occasional runaway (they called the sheriff's department), and the occasional psychotic (again with the sheriff). They cycled in and out, discovered that being a bad ass in their hometown or home gym maybe didn't amount to as much as they'd thought, or maybe just figured out they didn't like getting beaten up, as clarifying as it might be.

It was worse for the men: they didn't know when to quit. They'd come and sleep on the mats, desperate, living off Isopure and anger, waking up with Impetigo on a cheek, spend two weeks getting absolutely battered before someone convinced them to leave, that the concussion and two broken ribs were just the start.

Shy was different.

Shy had an upstairs room with a futon that folded into a bed and a TV/VCR combo from the 90s she never bothered to plug in. She bought a plastic wastebasket she flipped for a nightstand, a lamp to go on it. There was a sleeper sofa on the other end of the room and sometimes someone was on it, sometimes it was empty; Shy quit noticing, lying on her futon between sparring sessions or grappling classes or weight work with barely enough energy to eat, let alone read or think or notice.

Mondays, Wednesdays, and Fridays they ate oatmeal and eggs with black coffee and jogged to the gym where they ran hills and ground through a circuit of pushups and pull-ups and overhead presses and squats and box hops and toes-to-bar. One hundred twenty grueling minutes of strength and conditioning. They walked back after that, ate, napped, did was what was necessary to prepare for the afternoon because that was when they sparred. Tuesdays and Thursdays they grappled. Sprawls, chokes, passing guard. This was where Shy excelled and she quickly came to look forward to days on the mat, the smell of the Clorox wipes, the little skin contusions that appeared as henna.

Saturday was a long beach run and it was here she got to know the men she was always saw but never quite talked to around the gym. A dark-skinned Brazilian ju-jitsu master known as Mr. Wizard. A giant former NCAA champion heavyweight wrestler from Lehigh, six-four and two-sixty, whose massive body was topped with the too-small blonde head of a preteen, all downy peach fuzz and cratered acne. There were good old boys and mid-western farm boys. Guys who worked as security guards at Krome. Black kids from Little Haiti, corn-rowed and capable. An ex-marine whose back was a three-colored map of the Greater Levant, complete with a legend that depicted battles and troop movements. There was a Serbian kid (not a kid really, Shy's age, very bad ass), a French kid (cute), a black kid from Albany, Georgia, two Cuban brothers.

There was Kenny, of course.

In the tiered system of world-class (Mr. Wizard, the Lehigh Behemoth), up-and-coming (the bulks of the fighters, especially the Serbian kid), and serious-but-going-nowhere, Kenny was very decidedly in the third group. There was constant movement between two and three, the goal being to leap to the first, but about moving up Kenny had no illusions. He was tough but slow, dedicated but not maniacal, and, remarkably, okay with that.

He liked to train, wanted to become a coach.

"I know I'll never fight like for real fight," he told her on that first Saturday run when he simply materialized at her side. "Like go into that state where you lose it and just beat someone senseless. I mean I don't say this to people, you know? That's not like Jakob's eat-matches-shit-fire attitude."

Jakob was Jakob De Lomme, a white South African who in his early thirties had won three UFC titles at 170 pounds and now ran the gym. Before that, he'd been a commando in a counter-insurgency Recce unit. Before that, he had twice completed the Comrades Marathon, once on a fractured foot. He was not—to be clear—a weak man, but neither was he brutal. She could see him up at the front of the group, cropped head titled forward, listening. It was just after dawn and they were thirty or so fighters strung out along a stretch of sand. They'd started at South Pointe Park, headed for Mid-Beach where they'd cross boardwalks and highways and eventually loop back onto the sand. Ten slow miles.

The run wasn't so much physical as communal, the only time the entire team would gather as a group, the place where folks relaxed a little, where folks let up a little, laughed, made plans for the rest of the weekend. Which, turns out, is what Kenny was up to.

Which was why Shy and Sophia (the Brazilian with *all that hair!*) were in the gym parking lot two hours later, bathing suits beneath covers ups, bags packed with sunscreen and a change of clothes. Kenny picked them up in Mr. Wizard's tricked-out Jeep and they drove to the marina where he and three other fighters were scrambling around a giant white boat.

"Mr. Roque's yacht," Kenny said with a certain amount of disbelief. "One of, I should say."

The boat was a 33 meter Atlantic Endeavor that slept ten, a massive sleek thing of teak and radar mast, wet bar and Jacuzzi. Mr. Wizard had just successfully defended his world light heavyweight title and this was one of the fringe benefits.

"That's like a five million dollar toy right there," Kenny said.

Sophia leaned forward between the Jeep seats.

"And he lets you drive it?"

"Nah, shit, it's got like a crew. He don't trust nobody like that."

They motored out of the Miami River and south toward the Keys, all seven of them on the rear deck drinking Absolut which was fine—no one had a fight scheduled. By the time they were in the backwater of Biscayne Bay, Shy was drunk and maybe sunburned and most definitely happy. The boat was loaded with food and booze and they were all laughing, gnawing the carrot sticks in the plastic dish Sophia had picked up at Publix, tossing the broccoli (they ate too much broccoli in their normal lives) into the water. Mr. Wizard was very much the center of gravity, the alpha of alphas sprawled into a deck chair and telling stories of fighting in Japan and Russia, the women, the fans, the time he'd agreed on the spot to do a commercial for a Moscow Ferrari dealership and spent the rest of the night taking shots of Stoli beneath a strobe light while girls in heels and bikinis danced in the bed of an old Soviet military ambulance.

They laughed and laughed and then someone put on Rihanna.

Someone put on Nicki Minaj.

Someone put on Eminem (someone was always putting on Eminem).

Shy was sitting by Kenny and without really intending to found herself leaning into him, leaning onto him, looking up to see Sophia giving her a look that was both happy, like *all right, girl!* and concerned, like, *all right, girl?* But she was more than all right, she was fine, she was perfect. Kenny was talking to her, laughing with her, here was a man being nice to her, and God, when was the last time that had happened?

Her father, in his way.

Rolly, in his.

But not like this. Like this, never.

You weren't supposed to have relations within the team, of course. No hooking up, no one night stands. It was like a corporation was what everyone said: you get in a relationship you go declare it to Jakob, make sure everyone's on the same page, but this, Shy thought, this was something entirely different. This was something more, maybe.

It was afternoon by the time the captain came out to say they were anchored over the Biscayne Reef should anyone want to dive which, of course, they all did. Shy put on her snorkel and mask and the reflective vest the captain insisted on, and flopped across the deck in her fins. She was about to jump in, or simply fall in, maybe, when she felt Kenny pull at her vest.

"You done this before?" he asked.

"No. You?"

He slid a pink pool noodle beneath her vest.

"For flotation." He smiled beneath his mask. "And fun, of course."

She watched Sophia backflip off the deck and tumbled in after her, her mask popping off so that she had to surface to refit it. Kenny was beside her, water gleaming in his dark goatee.

"Let's stick together," he said, and smiled again.

And she meant to, she did. But it was one thing above the water and another below. Below was, perhaps, the word she'd been intended for. No wonder I've been unhappy, she thought, not realizing she had been until the thought bubbled up. But she was happy now, she realized that as well. Everything here felt slower, blurred, the hard edges erased by a sort of floating grace she saw around the bright fish just eight or ten feet below her, found in the grasses, in the staghorn and brain coral which though bleached still appeared exactly as it was: a living thing. And then there was that presence behind it all, whatever that was. It could almost be confused with simple pressure but she knew it wasn't just that, the way it pressed against her length, her ears, her hair, that living thing that made her think of her mother on her knees at church, that enveloping thing everywhere evident but nowhere seen.

She let the pool noodle slide out and began to dive deeper, flaring down expecting the fish to scatter but they didn't, they simply made space for her, they simply *allowed* her, whatever she meant by that. How long she did this she didn't know, only that eventually she looked up to see Kenny hovering near, watching her. She surfaced, smiling, laughing.

Kenny was holding the pool noodle she'd discarded.

"You a fish girl," he said.

"Maybe."

"Ain't no maybe. You should have told me."

They anchored that night forty or so feet off three acres of sand and scrub, a little brown atoll in the bluest stream. Most of the people were sleeping on the boat but she and Kenny waded ashore and made a small fire. She had sobered up, a slight headache giving way to a bone deep lethargy, and she sat there leaned back against his sprawled body, his arms around the old cable-knit sweater she'd pulled on against the sunburned cool of evening. It was dusk when he nudged her awake.

"Shy, wake up."

"I'm not asleep."

"Wake up. Look."

Following the line of his arm she saw nothing at first, and then she did, the silver sliver of its back, the wet gleam, and then another, and then a third.

"Dolphins," she said, and then they were both shedding clothes, wading out, and then she felt it. Magnificently, gloriously, she felt its slick body move against her open hand in a whisper of passing as if what she had almost touched just below the surface had manifested into this, just above, and what she felt was *finally, finally* because she was here, and she was happy, and she knew she was meant to be because what is a dolphin but a sign?

What is a dolphin but a blessing?

● ● ●

She didn't want to go to Kenny's parents, but the next day that was exactly where they went. Spent the night in the Best Western wondering if her teeth would fall out and maybe she'd just choke to death on a molar and how would that be any worse, any more humiliating than what had already happened? She'd come back from the bar happily buzzed, the cold beer having opened a sluice through her that had been closed for days. But then Kenny wanted to get on the phone, Kenny wanted to call his mom and Shy sat there straight-backed on the edge of the bed, running her tongue around the inside of her mouth and sensing the contours of her face, fingertips up by her still swollen cheeks, her brittle jawline, almost touching but not quite. Not quite doing anything really until Kenny was nudging her saying she wants to talk to you.

"What?"

"My mom." He held out his cell. "Shy?"

"No."

"Kenny," came the voice from the phone, "put her on, Kenny."

He gave her that pleading look, eyes bulging, brow wrinkled.

"No," she said.

"Please."

"No," she said, and walked into the bathroom to take another shower, slower this time, more steam.

When she came out he was in bed with the lights off, asleep or pretending to sleep. She lay beside him until she heard him snoring lightly and then crawled into the floor and did 500 sit-ups.

• ● •

The next morning they headed west toward San Antonio.

"They're worried about you." Kenny saying this, Kenny driving. "Lots of folks are."

But lots of folks didn't get it, lots of folks weren't capable of getting it. People talked about passion and commitment, but didn't meant it. They wanted you to be mediocre, just like them, and when you weren't it scared them. That you weren't well-rounded, that you didn't know when to quit. That enough was never enough—which was maybe why she'd let herself get kicked?

She put her forehead against the glass.

"Hey," Kenny was saying, "hey, babe?"

She didn't mean like intentional, like *yes, please kick me in the face.* More like this subconscious wondering, this desire to know how fragile it really was. You survived the building of this world but could you survive the taking apart?

It was the thing you were holding, but it was also the thing holding you.

Was that ridiculous to think? Was that the Lortab talking?

She watched the trees and the billboards and pasture giving way to tract houses, turned on the radio to 92.5 "The Bull Country" where Willie Nelson's blue eyes cried in the rain and Randy Travis sang *but on the other hand, there's a golden band.* The news came on. An airstrike in Syria. A shooting in New Orleans, another in Colorado Springs. Bobby Jindal—no longer a contender for the Republican nomination after disastrous polling numbers! Then commercials for Pet Smart and GrubHub and the Jersey Mike's Subs with three area locations and then John Anderson was describing yet another straight tequila night.

"Hey, hon?"

She spun the dial, found Mix 96, music for Now, goddamn it, not Then, she didn't need anymore *then*.

She heard Adele (boring), The Weekend (meh), Ellie Goulding (oddly moving). Drake. Fall Out Boy. More commercials. More news. Climate scientists disagreed on CO_2 levels but one thing was clear: there was no resurrecting Bobby Jindal.

"Hon, just listen to me for one second, all right?"

She spun the dial.

"About the fight," he said.

She spun the dial again.

The fight.

The fight.

Jesus, when would he stop talking?

• ● •

For my part, I hadn't watched and learned of her loss the next morning online. The clip of the roundhouse looked bad, and after I watched it for maybe the fifth time, I prayed for her, or tried to, at least. It seemed like enough at the time, the gesture.

But then again I hadn't seen the fight.

• ● •

Kenny's parents had. After the knockout, his mother had cried for two, three hours it must have been. *I was just scared so bad, you laying there like that, not moving.* They gave her space. Still, Shy didn't like it there. Everything a bad idea, an 'on second thought,' a misunderstood look. The cat no more to be trusted than the chain on the door. But she was cooling out on the Lortab, and there were moments of honest lucidity, or at least the possibility of such. Unwiring her jaw had been the right thing. It was still all Met-Rx and milk shakes but it felt like the right thing and they all collectively, silently—or maybe just behind Shy's still cramped back—decided on an outing, riding to the DQ with the cute walk-up window, the one where they'd shot that country music video back in the 90s that everybody talked about but no one quite remembered seeing.

They all got Blizzards and then Kenny's mother got back up to get another chilidog and his father said, "No, Delilah. Just sit," and went off to get it for her himself.

She lowered herself back to the molded plastic seat, smoothed the floral print of her Kmart blouse and said, "So…" Just let it hang there: *so…*

"So what?" Kenny finally said.

"So what's next, I guess I'm saying."

"What do you mean *next*?"

"I don't mean nothing."

"Well, you said it, didn't you? You must mean something."

She lifted the spoon of her blizzard, a fin of broken Oreo upright and jagged. Her pack of Kools untouched on the metal lattice of the table.

"I guess I mean the two of you been sitting around doing a bunch of nothing. Johnny don't want me to say it, but moping. I mean so what are you going to do next?"

"Mama," Kenny said.

She put her fat palms up as if surrendering. "Lord knows I ain't trying to pick or pry. You remember it was me was so upset. It was me crying for days seems like. So don't you sit there, Kenneth Wayne Chandler, and act like I'm trying to pick or pry. I'm just asking."

Kenny looked at Shy, though it seemed he saw everything but her.

"We just want a little breathing room is all," he said. "But if you want us to go."

"Want who to go?" his father asked, and slid the paper boat with its chilidog in front of his wife.

"Nothing," Kenny said.

His mother lifted the chilidog with her fingertips, delicately, as if it might otherwise wake.

"We're just talking is all," she said.

"Shy's in a dark place right now, okay?" Kenny said.

But she'd been in darker places, more broken ones too.

That was the fourth day.

• ● •

On the fifth day she was supposed to visit a neurologist out near Lackland Air Force Base, but decided instead to blow it off. She was starting to think about going home. Not Vegas or even Miami but Daytona. Getting back to training. Maybe getting back to training. Cardio, she guessed. The recumbent bike. She could swim at the Y. Training but training alone. She waited until Kenny got up and lay beneath the covers staring up at the poster of Troy Aikman he'd tacked two decades ago to the wood paneling. These were the times she would test her jaw, lie on the double bed and move it side to side so that it hurt.

The ache had the effect of grounding her.

There is a reason children cut themselves, the teenage girls who hate their thighs, the teenage boys whose dads like to flip their too long hair and ask if they have a boyfriend yet. She understood. Now and then a sleeve would slip up the thin wrist of some girl at some ju-jitsu clinic at a strip-mall dojo or middle school gym, and Shy would see the little sandbar of scar on which they had beached their hurt. Or the red lines, plowed furrows, so fresh and raw they appeared like ground beef on their otherwise perfect skin. She always wanted to touch them. If not the actual wounds, then at least the children who wore them. To say something to the effect of *yes, I get it, I understand.* But that was the very thing you couldn't say because the entire point of the cutting, the point of the pain, was that it expressed something that picked up past grammar. A language that found expression only in the act.

When she walked into the kitchen Kenny was on the phone.

"We'll get out there shortly," he was saying, referring to, she realized, the missed neurology appointment. "Yeah, I'll call em as soon as I hang up."

He looked at her and he mouthed Stu, Stu her agent who may or may not have been tied to the Cuban mafia but was most definitely tethered to Pitr Roque.

"Yeah," he was saying, "sure. I know, I'll call him…*the Rolling Stone*, yeah…I got his number in my phone. Yeah, the *ESPN* guy too…Stu, my brother, I know we do, I know we do…No, man, she's badass. You know Shy." Here he winked at her. Coffee, he mouthed, and chinned toward the machine. "He wants you to meet Pit Bull," he whispered.

"Hang up."

He turned back to the phone.

"I hear you, Stu…She's just like regrouping, you know?"

She poured a cup and burnt her tongue, and then burnt it again.

She'd been like this after the Olympics, but actually she had never been like this.

● ● ●

Her coaches had thought it would take her a year to be ready to fight, but two months after arriving in Miami she'd stepped into the ring—her first fight, all those lifetimes ago that was actually, God, barely five years in the past. No one had known. It was an unsanctioned event in a warehouse up in Liberty City, just a local thing, the fight sponsored by Pain & Wonder Tattoo & Piercing. A fifty-dollar entry fee for the fighters. Five-dollar Bud Lights for the fans. She entered under a fake name and went alone. Actually sparred at Hammerhead that Friday afternoon so no one would be suspicious, took an ice bath in private, showered and told Sophia and Romi she was going out to see a friend.

Sophia, floating through the house in a gauzy skirt and a mid-riff baring shirt that read MY FAVORITE SEASON IS THE FALL OF THE PATRIARCHY, wanted to know if she should come with?

"That's okay."

"Because if you're just like, you know."

She smiled, shook her head, asked Romi if it was still okay if she borrowed her car, got in the second-hand Camry with its menorah-and-doves air freshener (Fresh Laundry the scent), and drove up, alternating sips of a sugar-free Monster with a citrus Gatorade. She parked back by the Dumpsters and checked her gear a second time: water, Pedialyte, towel. Gloves, wraps, change of clothes. The place was packed with men and women, mostly men, and she checked in, handed over her medical form (no HIV, no Hep C), and finally weighed in which was a joke. She was 127. The girl she was fighting, a big Indian girl from Hendry County, was what? Shy had no idea but across the crowded room where men and women waited to step on a bathroom scale the woman appeared at least 150. Shy pulled up her hoodie and paced, went outside to shadowbox, and then got inexplicably nervous and puked in a drainage ditch.

The bathroom had no paper towels but she'd brought the towel.

Ridiculous, getting sick like that. She'd fought at bigger venues as a teenager, she'd been in the Olympics for god's sake. But this was different. She'd uprooted her life, was two months into training, possibly in love, and needed to know if she was actually any good before she got in any deeper.

Turned out she was.

She walked inside twenty minutes before her bell—filmed now in a light sweat, the crowd loud and suffocating—and knocked out the big Seminole woman in something like fourteen seconds. For it, she took home two hundred bucks which was nothing, but also very much something even it had felt accidental.

Her second fight was the real one.

Her second fight made her.

The fight was at the Volusia Fairgrounds fifteen minutes from her mama's house. It was an all-day event: Shy would weigh in Friday on arrival and fight Saturday at 2 PM. She rode up in the gym van with three of the second-tier fighters, including the new guy, the ex-Marine who'd turned up just a few weeks ago; Dominic, who would work everyone's corner; and Kenny who wasn't fighting but came along to second her corner. The ride up had been quiet, no one eating or drinking, just worried about making weight, tucked into their iPods and personal shit.

They hit the Wawa bathrooms and then the Econolodge.

Dominic had the keys out in the lobby.

"Back down here at 4 and we weigh in," he said. "Dinner after that."

Growing up, she'd been to the Fairgrounds any number of times but inside the auditorium only once in high school for a model train show she couldn't remember why she attended. It was a vast aluminum shed, high-ceilinged with a concrete floor across which chairs were being set up. The platform of the ring was in place and heavy men on ladders were drilling the cage walls into place. There were banners for a local dojo, CASH NOW! payday lending, Hardee's, Red Bull, and the DeLand Hot Summer Nights Classic Car Drive-in.

After they made weight—all of them, you could see Dominic exhale—they drove to an Olive Garden and ate and laughed. In the parking lot she asked Dominic if he could drop her at her mama's just for like a quick visit.

She found her mother sitting in her easy chair, exactly as Shy had left her months prior.

"Well, well," her mother said, "look what the cat drug in."

"Hey, mama."

"Welcome home, girl," she said, and kissed her forehead.

"Can we sit?"

"If you can spare a minute."

They sat on the back stoop in the gloaming and Shy asked about old friends, people from church. The grass was weedy and uncut, the trash piled. Her mother had left dishes in the sink, as if her dead husband might yet return to clean them.

"Do you think you might come tomorrow?" Shy asked finally. "I put you on the list."

"What, to this fighting thing?"

"You used to always like to come."

Which wasn't true: her mother had spent her life pretending what her daughter loved didn't exist.

"I wish you would," Shy said.

"Why? To see you all oiled up in your birthday suit."

"It's really not like that."

"Two of you tearing each other's hair out like a couple heathens."

"It's not like that at all."

"Fighting somebody you don't even know," she said. "And here I thought I'd raised you Christian."

They sat in silence after that, watched the day gave way to evening, the shadows lengthening and overtaking the house and trees until they sat in the dark with only the sound of the cicadas.

"I wish you'd come, mama," she said eventually.

Her mother slapped at her leg.

"Are you getting bit?" she asked, and pushed herself out of her plastic chair. "I'm getting eat alive."

Her mother walked to the sink and began to run water over the dishes. Shy took the scrub brush but her mother just waved her off.

"Go on. I know you got more important things to do."

Shy left her in the kitchen and walked back to her old room to find it just as she'd left it. More dust on the trophies, maybe. A silt on everything actually.

Her mother was loading the Mr. Coffee when she came back out.

"Your beds made up if you need to turn in early," she said.

"I gotta go back, mama. I've got a curfew."

"You ain't staying the night?"

"I'm sorry. I can't."

"So you're going with them?"

And the way Shy shrugged.

"They're my people."

And the way her mother stood there looking at her

"Your people? I," her mother said, "I am your people."

"I'm sorry but I gotta go."

"Me. Right here."

"I gotta go, mama."

But she didn't, at least not yet, just walked out into the yard and checked her phone. It was dark but not late. She had some time and followed the curve of the road, the chain of intermittent safety lights on the telephone poles, passed the bungalows, the occasional ranch with vinyl siding and a sprinkler system, the occasional wheelchair ramp.

Yard gnomes and bikes, big wheels and above-ground pools.

The left on Amelia took her toward the Church of Life More Abundant in Christ.

Her mother's church—her church, when she'd had such a thing—was a rectangular building in a sandy yard patched with grass. There was nothing on the sign besides the service times—Sunday 10:00 & 6:00, Wed 6:30—and a message in block letters that read: THE LORD IS WATCHING. A single room, a few pews angled toward an altar. Behind it, a baptistery that looked like a kiddie pool framed out with two-by-fours. Christ on the wall. His eyes brown, his hair long and straight. Knocking on a door with no handle because He has to be invited in.

By the time I made it there, the day the Reverend Lonnie Blatts would attempt to drown me in the St. John's River, the church had long since burned to the ground. But seeing photos would remind me of the small mountain church where I'd grown up. Actually not just remind me, it would stagger me.

I knew this world.

I had discarded the evangelical Christianity of my boyhood with such a thoroughness that by my early twenties I had begun to feel the rough grain of my decision. It was difficult for me to believe, and yet it was impossible not to. I felt the necessity of choosing something—anything—on my skin like a rash. I eventually chose books and fighting, writing and going to the gym where I took too seriously Joyce Carol Oates' claim that the first and third Ali-Frazier fights were "boxing's analogues to *King Lear*."

I say all this to convey that while I know what it feels like to kneel at the altar of a church, I also know what it feels like to be hit so squarely and with so much force you feel your skull for the briefest of milliseconds reconstitute itself as light. I know what it feels like to hit someone that way, too. Fighting is a stay against the listless self-pity of living a relatively safe life, a way to remind yourself that the real matters more than the abstract, that—as the sculptor Donald Judd said, things exist, and everything is on their side.

I'm not the first to note that once we sought counsel from priests and parents, from our father and mothers and friends. Then it became therapists and counselors—paid, trained, and clinically indifferent. Not we seek out influencers, or, given some algorithm emanating from a startup in Palo Alto or Williamsburg, they seek us. As if the real has been replaced by the simulacra, as if we can't quite pay attention. It's banal to say as much. But such banality doesn't make it any less true. It's such banality, in fact, that makes the claim valid since, while life is bricked out of many things, the cornerstone is an everyday distraction so common we seldom notice.

I was looking for a different way to be in the world, I suppose. Something if not transcendent, at least more than transactional. You can make money. You can buy things. There is perhaps no other way to be in the world. Or maybe there is, it just requires the sort of focus most of us no longer possess. I was as ill-equipped as anyone and did my best, choosing my books and my fists. Writing and fighting, people liked to say, as if it were a punchline and not my life.

When it was so obviously both.

I'd once done a long retreat at Gethsemane, the Trappist Abbey in Kentucky (*retreat* the word isn't lost on me), and over the course of my time there read the entirety of Dostoevsky's oeuvre. Like all of us, he was built from contradictions, only, perhaps, more so: he wrote Zosima's sermon of love; he sold his wife's clothes and jewelry. He both loved and loathed God.

He was given to prayer and seizures and compulsive gambling. Which makes him a kindred spirit. A far brighter light, certainly, but someone who, as he spat on me, as he dismissed me, might have also understood me. Who might have known me.

As for Shy, she remembered how they were always singing. The Reverend Blatts in short sleeves and Dickies pants., about her dad's age had her dad not died. The rest of the congregation—maybe thirty people—were always older, a room of Wal-Mart greeters with a few grandchildren helplessly underfoot, half of them wispy underfed ghosts, the other half fat on Mountain Dew and Pixie Sticks.

She'd spent much of her childhood here and the memories layered and deep. But standing there she couldn't call any of them up, not really. Flashes—that was all she had. Hands raised and swaying during the altar calls. The clouds of Aqua Net and cigarette smoke in the parking lot. The Sunday dinners on foldout tables: casseroles and fried chicken. Games of whiffle ball and tag in the buggy sand.

She made it back to her mama's house and from the sidewalk summoned an Uber. There was no use going back inside. The lights were off. Her mother was asleep and her daddy wasn't coming home. She could stand barefoot on the gravel till morning, but he still wasn't coming home. She could grind her toes until they bleed, but his heart wasn't restarting, not tonight, not any night.

● ● ●

The next day they wrapped and signed her hands and she sat in the crowded dressing room with Dominic and Kenny and five other girls and their seconds until an official came by and said all men would have to go, folks needed to change, come on, gentlemen, let's move here.

"You be okay?" Kenny asked and she nodded. "We'll be right out here."

She watched them go and went out into the hall to shadowbox.

When they called her fight, she walked out with Dominic and Kenny—the auditorium hot and loud and smelling of Lysol and beer—and saw her opponent. Forty-one seconds later Shy knocked her unconscious with a head kick.

She kissed Kenny by the locker room, showered, and was walking to the van when the man came stumbling toward her, drunk it appeared.

"Shy! Shy!" he was calling, and it took her a moment to realize it was her old coach Rolly, hunched and brown-bagging the sun right out of the sky. He smiled sloppily while she hugged him. "You've made us all so proud," he said, if not drunk-drunk, then punch drunk.

● ● ●

By the end of her first year she was undefeated, seven fights, seven knockouts, so it was no great surprise when Jakob asked if she and Sophia would be interested in setting up shop in Vegas.

"Mr. Roque just opened a new gym out there. You can teach classes. Take all the fights you want. Might be a great opportunity."

Two weeks later she started fighting thousand-dollar undercards in Vegas. 10 and 0. 11 and 0. For a while she fought every Saturday night because when you can win in less than a minute why not? Training was harder.

The burpees with head colds.

The pull-ups with raw palms.

She and Sophia would go out Saturday nights after fighting and drink La Croix at the Chandelier while men hit on them. It was harmless fun. Sophia was seeing a thoracic surgeon back in Coral Gables. Kenny was still in Miami, but Shy was making enough to fly him out every other weekend. He wasn't really fighting anymore, but neither of them seemed to notice. She went to 18 and 0 and was introduced to Stu at a South Beach party. Signed with him the following Monday. *If you think I'm not already ruminating,* he told her, *if you think I'm not already gaming your career out, sister, you'd be wrong, wrong, wrong.* She got an endorsement deal with a third-rate energy drink and a spot on the undercard of a UFC event where she won in the third round with a sudden overhand right to the jaw of a red-haired Oklahoman, a woman who looked built from the scraps of oil derricks, and went down like a felled tree. Flew back to my Miami for some local commercials, a Chevy dealership, a Rug & Carpet outlet. Won a ten-thousand dollar purse and flew back to Vegas business class, the lobster ravioli paired to the chardonnay.

By her second UFC card she was name, she was somebody.

By her third she was a champion.

There's a word for it, even if Rolly could never quite come up with it.

That word is meteoric.

• ● •

Thanksgiving came and it was a small house. Kenny's sister Joan arrived with her husband and son who went into the living room to play *Call of Duty* and never came out so that it was six around the table, or five and Joan's husband's wheelchair edged as close as possible. He'd had a stroke back in August. There'd already been a whole thing with lifting the chair up the front two steps during which Joan had said to her brother, "I thought y'all were going to do something about this."

"Like what?" Kenny asked.

"Like build a ramp or something."

"We just got here."

"*Just?*"

They carved the bird in the dining room, served the dressing, the creamed corn. Said the blessing to the sound of gunfire coming through the Samsung flatscreen. His mother kept her Kools where the fork would otherwise have been.

They were doing the dishes when Joan asked Shy if she could borrow ten-thousand dollars for medical bills.

"Our insurance has pretty much run out," she said.

"I'm so sorry," Shy said, "of course, I didn't know."

And she hadn't—but how could that be? There had been the vague awareness that Kenny's brother-in-law was no longer teaching high school physics, his brain as slurred as his speech, but that was all she'd known. Still, how could that be? she thought. But it was simple: she'd been in training. She hadn't asked, and Kenny hadn't said.

"His therapy," Joan said.

"Of course."

"He's seeing three different ladies."

"Of course. Let me just write you a check."

Which was when Kenny came through the swinging door with a dish of sweet potato casserole to say *a check for what?* His sister kept her back to him, hands in the suds.

"A check for what, Joan?"

"We're having a private conversation, Kenny."

"I figured that. A check for what?"

"For Chuck if you have to know," she said, turning fast enough to spray the window with bubbles. "He's got speech therapy, occupational. He's doing this whole thing with his legs."

"You're asking her for money?"

"It's okay," Shy said.

"You're seriously asking her for money?"

"Yes, actually. Yes, I most certainly am."

"It's okay," Shy said quieter still.

"You have no right to ask her for anything."

"I'm asking because you never offered, either of you. I'm sitting around trying to stretch an unemployment check to cover forty thousand dollars of medical bills and neither of you ever once offered to help."

"You might consider getting a job," Kenny said.

"Fuck you, Kenny. I've got a job. It's called taking care of my husband."

Their mother came into the kitchen.

"What's all this yelling?"

"What do the two of you even do?" Joan asked. "She kicks people in the head. She beats people up. I'm sorry, Shy, but you beat people up for a living."

Their mother's head seemed to vibrate.

"I won't have all this yelling in my house."

"What's does hitting someone in the face add to society, Kenny?"

"Fuck you, Joan."

"Tell me cause I honestly want to know. What's does kicking people do to make the world better? Chuck taught science. Chuck did something."

"Well, what do you do?" Kenny said. "Huh, Joan, tell me that?"

"I try to stretch six hundred dollars of unemployment is what I do."

"Let me just write a check," Shy said.

"I spend my days arguing with our HMO. I spend my days trying to stretch six hundred dollars into a life."

Their mother kept shaking her head.

His sister was crying.

"She kicks people in the head."

"I hear they're hiring at the Dollar General," Kenny said.

"Please just let me just go to the ATM," Shy said.

• • •

Her phone had remained off, but Kenny's wasn't. Kenny seemed to be in touch with everyone. She wondered who he thought he was, speaking for her. But she was grateful, too. At times she was wildly grateful.

"We need to talk to the media, babe."

But she didn't want to talk to the media.

"This dude from *Rolling Stone* keeps texting. Then there's this other cat from FOX Sports. Stu said…"

But she didn't want to talk to Stu, she didn't want to talk to anyone. At night, lying in bed, she found herself circling, edging into the center of the ring. She knew she was contractually obligated to reenter the world, but for the moment all she wanted to do was lay on Kenny's bed beneath his poster of Troy Aikman, Roku remote balanced on her stomach. If she kept her eyes open and remained still, the circling stopped.

"I reckon y'all will be in a hurry to head back," his mother said that evening from her glider, "now that the holiday's passed."

"What's that, mama?"

She thought of the way roundhouse had seemed to appear, to materialize out of the noise and light. Like she never could have seen it. But also like she had seen it so long she had grown bored with it. When she first started fighting, she would sometimes take a single intentional blow. Something to clear her head, to make plain the stakes. But it wasn't like that. Or maybe it was.

His mother was smoking Kools and watching *Dancing with the Stars*.

"Y'all probably getting restless," she said. "I know I would be."

She went back to Kenny's room and tried to meditate.

• ● •

It was Dominic who'd taught her to meditate in that year between the fight in Volusia and the move to Vegas. But it was the ex-Marine who taught her about sin.

"I need to learn to strike," she'd said to Dominic on the bus after her first official fight.

"You need to learn to breathe."

And she had, sitting on the mat after an evening of rolling, the cleaning fluid sharp enough to make her eyes water even when they were closed. You just followed your breath, that was all. Feel your stomach expand, feel it empty. It was hard to sit for two minutes at first but she did it every morning and every evening and soon enough she was sitting for forty minutes though she had no real sense of such, her perception of time having collapsed like so much else. Memories, accusations, thoughts of her father—at times she'd sit with tears running down her face and not a single idea why. She knew it troubled people, that folks stared but...

"I'm worried about your self-esteem," Jakob said to her the day he called her into his office.

"I haven't lost a fight."

"I'm not worried about your fighting, and honestly I feel a bit ridiculous just saying this..."

That sense of worthlessness, what a cliché, Shy. That sense that she justified her existence in three-minute increments of extreme violence—you really want to carry that shit around? She thought she didn't, but was equally sure she did. Things were fine with Kenny, things were good. Most evenings they ended the day watching Honey Boo Boo or *Survivor Philippines* on the couch, eating carrot sticks and drinking protein shakes, the sex quiet and slow; the parties dry since no one drank in the run up to a fight.

But then sometimes she did.

Kenny didn't know, but yeah, sometimes she did and it was usually bad.

It had started after her third fight when the ex-Marine she'd met on the bus ride had asked if she wanted to go see some sort of tough guy contest and Shy being in one of those places she sometimes got in had said yes. It turned out to be in the same Liberty City warehouse where she'd fought months prior and she'd worried briefly someone might remember her but they hadn't stayed long. Just sat in his truck smoking Jamaican Red and then making out on the rubberized matting in the bed.

It was summer when they drove all the way to Lake Lanier, Georgia to rent a cabin. She'd lied to not only Kenny but Sophia and Domi and the lie, she understood the lie. What she couldn't make sense of was the truth. Which was that she'd actually wanted to go even if she had no idea why. She didn't love him. She didn't even particularly like him.

Yet she went.

They rode and rode until somewhere in middle Georgia—which, she learned, is what they call it, like it's a kingdom or an era—they got behind a giant articulated dump truck, the sort of thing you'd never expect to see on a two-lane, yet there it was. The bed was full, mounded beneath a tarp, and it took probably five miles before either realized that what was blowing off were chicken feathers. The truck was full of chicken carcasses, what must have been tens of thousands of them, little snowflake tufts matting against the windshield.

That evening they got their cabin and walked down to the roped-and-buoyed swimming area, the Round-the–World miniature golf course with its Eiffel Tower and Onion-domed Kremlin, a red windmill, its latticed wings as fine as lace. When it started to rain the world took on a sudden shimmer and then, just as quickly, reassumed its dull gloss.

They went inside, took their wet clothes off and got on the bed.

"There's so much sin in this world." He was looking out the window where a magnolia tree stood, big leaves bright with rain. "I was in Herat not six months ago."

"That's in Afghanistan?"

"So much evil," he said. "I look at people and I think: children. Sheep, you know? Because they've just never seen it. They've just never fucking seen."

●　●　●

It was a solid twenty-hour drive back to Vegas and Kenny was on the phone with first Stu and then the guy from the *Rolling Stone* so she had time to think.

Too much time.

And what she was thinking of was him, of how she'd seen him just before the fight, the ex-Marine. First time in years, first time since that night in Georgia after which he'd disappeared, leaving behind even the Cremo spray cologne in his locker, and it was seeing him maybe that had turned herself back toward what she had almost forgotten she was, what she'd fooled herself into thinking she'd evolved past.

Two days prior to the fight she'd been contractually obligated to spend sixty minutes at a meet-and-greet for which folks had paid $175 per person to pick at the buffet of herb grilled chicken and steamed vegetables from which Shy could neither eat nor drink. She was supposed to mingle, smile for photos—nothing more.

It was fine.

She'd done it before and this was no different: two hundred people in a banquet hall overlooking the floor of the casino. Thirty-something guys in cargo shorts, overweight and smirking. Dads with sons. Wealthy men with their second wives who weren't exactly sure what it was they were doing there by the roast beef station, they simply were.

She signed autographs, posed for a few selfies, and eventually looked up to see him waiting for her just beyond a circle of fans. He'd gained forty pounds and lost most of his hair but she knew him immediately, even with the boy at this knee he introduced as his son David, six years old, say hello, David.

"I didn't know you had a son," she said.

"His mom's in Atlanta. Is there someplace we could talk?"

She looked across the room where Stu and Kenny stood with a clutch of well-dressed UFC business drones. "You mean besides here?"

They wound up standing in the stairwell, the boy left inside with a hot dog and a Coke.

"I get the feeling you're not exactly happy to see me," he said.

"I need to be back out there in like sixty seconds."

"I get the feeling you'd rather I was elsewhere."

"I'm 'contractually obligated.'"

"I'm sure you are."

He'd lived all over, Georgia, Texas, now Arizona where he'd bought tickets for the fight for he and his son. His son lived with him now. He was seventeen months clean and sober. She was glad, but what did he want from her? What did he come from?

"I don't know," he said, "confirmation maybe."

"Of what?"

He shook his head.

"I guess I wanted to know if it's was really you."

"Who else would I be?"

But she knew who else: her old self, the person she was and would be again.

There's so much sin in this world.

• ● •

I never knew her, of course, and though I'd seen her at Rolly's clinic and have watched countless clips online, I saw her fight in person only once, at the Daytona Civic Center where she had worked as a teenager parking cars. She won the fight, naturally—she won all her fights until the last one. But that isn't what sticks. What sticks happened in the immediate aftermath of her landing a big overhand right to the jaw of a wiry girl with red cornrows and hooded eyes. What sticks is the moment Siobhan Walsh looked back over her shoulder, gleaming and bloody—though it wasn't her blood. I was sitting just behind her corner and when she looked it seemed she was staring almost directly at me, and I remember thinking, my God, I remember thinking it so clearly: Vermeer would have painted her just like that.

Just. Like. That.

• ● •

Vegas.

The stitches in her tongue had dissolved. The paparazzi were long gone. Otherwise, they could have gotten a pic of her entering The Sands, the great purple slug of her lower lip, the crescent moon of bruise that mapped the left side of her face. They could have gotten Kenny on the phone with the guy from FOX Sports. She didn't know what to think of it all, but suspected if she could get kicked just one more time she would. There would be sudden clarity. It would solve something. But she wasn't going to get kicked again, not now and not ever. She was finished fighting and told Kenny.

There was a scene in the room, inevitable, but not as bad as she'd feared.

"I can't believe this bullshit." Kenny saying this. "After all we've goddamn been through, to have come this far."

He pulled out his phone to call Stu or Jakob or Dominic or someone, put it away, took it back out to throw across the room. This was Kenny irate, Kenny screaming, but then recalibrating: Kenny all conciliatory, all "Look, I get it, babe. Take some time off, collect yourself. You relax, get your shit together, come back when you're ready."

But there would be no coming back. There would be no ready.

She called her mama and said I'm on Delta Flight 36 if you want to track it.

She called her mama and said I land at 4:50.

Her mama picked her up at Orlando International and they said mostly nothing. Stopped at a Pollo Tropical off I-4 where she tried to eat the chicken but couldn't. She did manage to gum the rice, her teeth a little more stable, a little more secure.

Her mama motioning at her face.

"You're getting like your daddy. Too much like him."

"How so?"

"Like you can't see it. Like you can't walk to the ladies and see it right there on your face."

Shy lifted a fork of rice.

"It'll get better, mama. You should have seen me right after."

"I wouldn't have wanted such."

"I'm already so much better."

It was her mama who looked bad, who looked sick. She had been for a while though with great focus Shy had managed to mostly not think about it. But there was no ignoring it now: her mother was dying, even then, right there by the window with the interstate just beyond the frontage road.

"You need eat," her mama said.

Instead, Shy walked to the bathroom and washed her face

beneath the automatic faucet. When she looked up a woman was staring at her in the mirror, a black girl with nails that alternated red and silver.

"You don't have to let him treat you like that," the woman said.

Shy thought she was about the same age, late twenties, maybe thirty.

"Don't nobody qualify for that sort of bullshit," the woman said.

"I'm okay."

The woman checked her lipstick in the mirror. "Don't nobody need a man like that."

She took the keys from her mother in the parking lot and was almost to the car when the man and a teenager who was maybe his son came up to her. The boy already had his phone out, filming.

"Hey," the man was saying, "hey, excuse me. I know who you are. Excuse me. Get her face," he said to the teenager who was maybe his son. "Get her like, right there, her eyes and shit."

They kept walking, Shy and her mother.

"Hey, Shy," the man called. "I just want to talk you."

"Please leave me alone."

"What?"

"Please just leave me alone."

"Film her face," the man said. "Look at that shit. We're in Maitland, Florida," the man narrated to the camera, "and this is Siobhan Walsh who just like a week ago—"

"Please—"

"Like maybe not even a week or whatever."

It was online in minutes, on TV that night.

Shy didn't care, told herself she didn't care, told herself even if she did care what did it matter, crying like that, looking like that? She went back to her old room, her old dreams, all of it sitting on the plastic Judo trophies like dust. Like what was left after the things that were realized and the things that weren't had both come and gone.

The next morning her mother didn't wake until after ten and even then looked tired.

Shy couldn't deny her mama's failing health any longer and deposited $30K in an account set up with automatic bill pay: power, water, cable.

"What are you doing on that thing?"

And Shy not even looking up from her laptop.

"Nothing, mama."

That first day was awkward and mostly silent but they got through it, and then the one after that. Sitting together in the mornings, her mother in a housecoat, hair uncombed, the day not yet begun. It got better, settled into something like a routine. I can live like this, Shy would sometimes think, we both can. Then she'd catch herself. You think there will be a million mornings, day after day in the carpeted heat. But there can't be. You tell yourself you'll get chance after chance. But you know you won't.

She kept her phone off, didn't check her email.

She did think about going to see her old coach Rolly. Actually went so far as to take Highway 40 and pass the lurking hulk of the Daytona Speedway. Rolly's gym was on Beach Street, two blocks from the ocean. She parked by a surf shop and walked down. The building windowless, constructed from once-white cinder blocks, the silhouette of a fighter crouched beside cursive script that read *Rolly's Boxing & Fitness Emporium.*

She thought for a long time about just walking in, putting on the headgear, hitting the heavy bag. She couldn't think of what to do and then did: it was after midnight when she found Kenny's sister's address online and wrote a check for 40K.

• ● •

It would have been around this time that Doc took the call from Dwyane out by the pool.

"You're a fascist, aren't you, dad?"

"It's very possible."

"Perfect. I've got a proposition for you then."

Doc drove up the next day and that was when Dwayne told him *you don't have to live like that, dad. In fact, I've got a little shit stirring I could use some help with.* Dwyane was working with a guy named Craig, a shaman, he said, who was running Mexican Rail from the southwest. Had a next-door kid named Twitch making local deliveries on a moped but distribution, dad. That's where we need to put our big fat brains together.

I don't know if Doc thought immediately of Dante. Maybe it took some time. Maybe he thought he might yet go straight.

But what is straight in this world?

I'm asking an actual question.

Though its one I failed to ask of Doc's father.

A few weeks after he called I flew to Fort Lauderdale and—otherwise unannounced—called him from the sidewalk outside his home on Sunrise Key. It was a massive house—three stories vaulted above sidewalk shrubs of beach elder and the leafy stalks of banana plants behind them, vaulted above even the skinny palms half-ticked by the breeze—and I think he had no intention of inviting me inside until he parted a third-floor curtain and saw me standing outside, waving like a fool.

"I'm here," I told him on the phone.

The curtain was pulled back, his large figure barely visible against the late morning glare.

"Yes, that certainly appears to be the case."

He led me upstairs with as much resignation as regret, apologized for his wife's absence, offered me something to drink. We sat in the living room where I would later learn he had last seen Doc and Shy and Dante Henry. That incident, he would call it. That awful goddamn night.

"I didn't know you were in town," he said.

"No. I should have called. I just sort of…"

"You just sort of came."

"Yeah."

The room was vast and dim but for a band of brilliant light bisecting the curtain. Dust motes, the sort of heavy furniture that belonged in a colder clime.

"So," he said, and let it hang there between us.

I heard the air shudder on, heard the ice maker dump. A piano sat against the back wall.

"You're down here for what?" he said finally. "Looking for clues."

"Something like that."

"Looking for answers."

"Something to help me sleep at night," I said, and watched his face set into something hard.

"I won't say I regret calling you," he said. "I won't say that."

"But you do."

"I've just come to question the efficacy of it all."

"I understand."

That hard face then, giving way to something in his chest that was almost a laugh. He put a hand on a stiff couch cushion decorated with eyes, almond and iridescent, the pupils black and cocked at angles, as if watching.

"No actually," he said, "you couldn't possibly understand, Mr. Powers. You couldn't possibly."

"I guess not."

"You guess, do you?"

That was when he told me about Doc's last visit over a year ago, the visit he had mentioned when he first called. Doc's father yelling, his mother crying. He told the story and then he told it a second time, not so angry this time, slower. The argument, the giant brown man I knew to be Dante Henry sitting placidly at the table, the girlfriend I knew to be Siobhan Walsh sitting silently on the couch. I think he was on the verge of telling it a third time when we heard something in the back room and he did something, Doc's father. He began, perhaps, to sob into his fist, or maybe he only coughed. Either way, he stopped as quickly as he started and his lips smiled bitterly. By the then the light from the part in the curtains had spread over us and we sat in a band of blinding sunlight. The room had an aura. Doc's father had an aura. Both of us on the migraine edge of falling apart.

We heard the sound again and he excused himself.

He left me there on the couch where I sat until I heard him in the other room, speaking, whispering, cooing. Though I couldn't hear what exactly he was saying, I knew it was something soft and loving, and I felt something break inside me, some tightly held thing that released so suddenly I only then became aware of its presence. I sat on the couch and took several deep breaths, the first painless breaths I had taken in I couldn't say how long, only that whatever had wrapped itself around me was gone. I shut my eyes when I heard him speaking again. It was intelligible now. He was saying *yes, honey, it's okay, son, come here, honey.*

I walked to the door frame.

It seemed like something I shouldn't do but I did it anyway.

From the hall I could see him lifting his son from his wheelchair. This very large, very old man lifting someone who must have been about my age.

I took another step.

I stood on the threshold of a bedroom but no one looked up.

He was breathing heavily, Doc's father, straining, lifting.

Then he was changing his son, changing his adult diaper, still whispering, still cooing.

There we go, he said, *there we go.*

I was down the stairs before I realized my eyes were crying, before I realized I was crying, silently, relentlessly. I let myself out and stood for a moment in the blinding December light. I thought perhaps I'd go straight back to the airport and try to get on an evening flight, and stood there for some time with my phone in my hand, the Lyft app open and flashing. Then I remembered the one other person I'd thought to see: Shy's old agent, Stuart Pérez.

I walked to a coffeeshop and watched the folks go by outside the glass.

When I felt calmer I made some calls.

Left a message and sat there thinking

Yes, honey, come here, honey.

Stu liked to do it all in person, liked the individual touch, liked to get up early and drive what he thought of as a circuit of his little empire. His three gyms (he managed for Pitr Roque), seven fast food joints (Kentucky Fried franchises, owned by his father but you know), and one (singular) gentleman's club (The Race Horse, owned outright but currently in economic freefall) and what the fuck if that meant he'd spend the day in the car, bobbing and weaving in traffic, the Catholic Channel on SiriusXM? What was he supposed to do, poor put-upon Stu? He had people counting on him and at least it was just greater Miami, Kendale Lakes up to Hollywood then bring it back through Hialeah, one stop, two stops, you found a rhythm, you had to. They expected it, his people, and while he had done many things in his forty-seven years on this earth disappoint his people wasn't one of them.

The last day he saw Shy he woke adrift on the sea of his waterbed, last inflatable bladder in Coral Gables he liked to think. Left Gloria asleep on her stomach.

"There I was," he would tell me when we finally met, "in the very midst of my winter bulk."

He drank his coffee black and listened to a meditation app while he waited on the piss to come, the woman's voice soothingly narcotic for what should have been ten minutes but Stu could never take past five. Anxious. Busy.

Let's move already.

Things to do, people to see, and so on.

He brushed his teeth while he checked his phone.

"That morning," he said. "Mother of Mercy, that morning. Relentless. I don't know what else to say."

Eleven texts, a voicemail, who knew how many emails and still he'd need to squeeze in a phone call to his papi somewhere in the mix so—again—what was he supposed to do? He had a smoothie that took twenty minutes to mix. No joke. Kale and blueberries, almonds and ice. A mushroom powder you don't even ask about, a greens powder, a protein powder—half his life was powder. Blast it with Greek yogurt and raw milk. Pour the whole thing into a sixty-four-ounce mixer cup.

He found his slippers back under the edge of the bed.

Let the dogs out while he said his prayers. Attentive to his prayers, Stu was. Mother Mary while his three pit-bulls shat in the backyard beneath the saw palms or on the glossy tile around the pool. He prayed for his papi even if he acted like he was overseeing US Sugar's operations and not playing Sudoku in a senior living center outside Orlando. Prayed for his mamá's dead soul. Prayed for himself, for the family back in Cuba he didn't meet until he was past forty, and this against his father's wishes, the trip back to the promised land, his luggage packed with soft-ply toilet paper and 2-in-1 shampoo and conditioner. His heart swollen with hope.

He called the dogs.

This was on his mind today, Cuba.

His parents had fled the revolution as children, Stu born years later in a Florida City hospital. The shock of flight, the shock of losing their home, the four thousand hectares of sugar cane his grandfather had managed. There had been no more children for his parents, Stu cursed to walk the planet alone which is maybe why he was so intent on seeing his people in the flesh. That was what Castro had taken from them: not just their house and their livelihood, but the brothers and sisters Stu would never have. Now this new this pendejo Obama was gonna make peace, sit down and play patty-cake with Raoul or whoever the fuck. Supposedly the Pope was involved, supposedly. Stu couldn't believe it, being a religious man, a praying man, a man who daily injected an ampoule of testosterone into his non-existent belly fat—no, the Pope, this isn't possible.

This was very much on his mind.

He shut the sliding glass door and began the process of doling out breakfast, three bowls of beef, broiled lightly, still bloody. You think it's cheap, being a responsible man? You think you don't pay a price for such attentiveness? He had two freezers and a guy in LaBelle bringing him a side of beef every six weeks—this costs American dollars, this takes time. Twenty minutes to feed the dogs. His vitamin routine alone took another fifteen. A multi, CoQ10, turmeric and an NAD+ cell regenerator. You got your Tongkat Ali and your AMPK metabolic activator and Obama wants to sit down and act like none of it happened? Wants the Pope to bless it? Are you fucking kidding me?

He put on a Reiss Joey tracksuit, a new Colourblock Zip Through Jumper, heather gray with the horizontal stripe. Gloria asleep on her side now, one long leg extended.

More coffee.

More prayers.

Shaker cup on the passenger seat by his weight belt and a Glock 19.

In his Lexus by 8:03 which, okay, a little late but that's fine.

He rolled up Granada and hit the traffic on 41 just as his phone went off.

It was Kenny What-the-fuck's-his name, Shy Walsh's remarkably pedestrian boyfriend.

To what did Stu owe the pleasure?

"She's gone home, Stu."

"Home. Shy?"

"She isn't answering her phone. She's ignoring texts."

"Home like here?"

"She's crying in a parking lot on fucking TMZ."

"Home like Miami? Because you think she might have said."

"No, home like Daytona Beach. Like her mom's house."

Stu wedged the phone against his shoulder and started unscrewing his thermos.

"So she's needs her mom. Give her some space."

"Crying on *Entertainment Tonight*. You didn't see this?"

"Well, look, okay—she lost. What's the problem here?"

"It's not like that. Fucking listen, man. She's giving away her money."

"She's what?"

"Like she just wrote a check to my sister. She's just giving it away."

"She lost, Kenneth. She's searching. Give her a minute."

"It's not like that. You gotta talk to her."

"Look, okay. I gotta run right now."

"Stu—"

"Let me call you back."

The first gym was off Coral Way, very plush, very luxe, knockout girl at the reception he didn't knows name. She didn't recognize him and he had to do a little song and dance, keep his temper down, this wasn't the day for such.

Nevertheless.

Be that as it may.

He stripped to his skivvies and cranked the weight belt down two notches past reasonable. The call had him out of sorts but he was dead lifting and that was that. Could dead 700 in his prime, back like a slab of beef, so much prime real estate he'd wound up with Reagan tattooed on one shoulder blade and Nixon on the other. Danny-D was pulling 495 for reps but dropped the bar when he saw Stu walk in.

"Just the man I'm looking for."

"Not today, D."

"Just the man and here he walks right in."

"Not fucking today, D. Today I'm deads and out."

"Okay, man, but I still want to talk…" Stu waved him off. Danny-D had this idea for transgender workout wear, had market studies, numbers. Wanted Stu as an investor and like he had time for this. He worked his way up to five reps at 405 and then went looking for Danny-D who was on the incline bench staring at 225.

"Now Obama wants to sit down and play patty-cake like none of it happened."

"What's this?"

"Fucking Obama in Havana," Stu said, "and now they're telling me the Pope."

"What are you saying? Like the *Pope* Pope?"

"Yeah, the fucking *Pope* Pope. Who else would it be?"

He walked back to the platform and did three reps at 455, two at 475.

Panting, clapping his hands.

"You get down in the rhythm of the thing," he told the woman he caught watching in the mirror, "the vascularity if you will. Feel your heart beating in your neck."

The tattoos were black and white, intricate shading, he forgave people for staring but today, what the actual fuck?

He drank his smoothie in the locker room, showered, the girl at reception an absolute knockout and all Danny-D can talk about is his workout line.

He collapsed into his Lexus.

Fifteen minutes just to take his vitamins and people want to act like he doesn't care?

• • •

He was back in the car when his phone went off. It was Jakob De Lomme, head coach of Hammerhead MMA but more than that Pitr Roque's whatever you want to call him—assistant, chief of staff. Jesus. Day of days. To what did he owe this incomparable pleasure?

"He wants you to go see her, Stu."

"Shy we're talking about? I was planning a call."

"Kenny's got him in a fix. Says Shy's gone dark. She's a big fish and if she's gone off the rails."

"You mean the hook."

"What?"

"If she's a big fish gone off the hook, not rails."

Jakob sighed.

"Pitr said—"

"Tell Pitr to relax. Tell him I'll call her today. We'll talk."

"Not talk. Go see her."

"I'm driving a circuit here, Jackob. I'm in the midst of things."

"It's two, three hours. Drive up, Stu."

"I'm in motion you understand? And this talk about going off the rails or the hook or whatever—where this is coming from I want someone to tell me."

"If not today, tonight. You have to meet with her."

"There's someone everywhere I have to meet with which is why I just missed the light. Tell him tomorrow."

"Tomorrow's too late. Tonight, Stu."

"I just missed the fucking light is what I'm saying. Right here on 32nd. This is not something I do."

"I'll tell Pitr you'll be there by eight but nine will be fine. Nine he can live with."

He ate steak tips and asparagus at his club. Asparagus in beef fat because it does something to it, doesn't it? Some like transmutation or some such. Delicious. Practically licked the plate which was fine. He was still in the midst of his winter bulk. It was April and not winter, not like winter ever came, but, again, whatever. The waitress brought him two Bud Lights and a bowl of lime wedges he squeezed one by one. The girl on the stage was down to her G-string but it was hitting him wrong, bad lighting, bad mood.

He'd been by another of his gyms and two of his KFCs but his mind was on other things. First the Pope and now Jakob with his bullshit call. *Nine he can live with.* Shy going dark, Shy going off the rails. And still he had to let the dogs out.

He was back on the road when Gloria called to tell him your papi called, cariño. He said somebody named Peter Something called him.

"Pitr Roque," Stu said. "Jesus Christ, these people."

"This is your boss?"

"This is my associate, Gloria. My business partner."

"He didn't sound like a partner, cariño. But he knows your father?"

"Yeah, yeah, geriatric Cold Warriors, united in hate is what they are. Where this is coming from I wish someone would tell me."

"You should listen to your padre, cariño. You have to show respect."

He could barely keep the phone pinned to his shoulder, spilled lukewarm coffee down the leg of his pants. You are twenty-fucking-four, he wanted to say. You sleep till noon, spend all my money, and you want to lecture me about my father?

He bit the left side of his mouth.

"I have to go." He hung up the phone and threw it across his Lexus before he thought to say, "and stop calling me cariño."

Day of fucking days!

He felt his pulse pound in his throat—unbelievable. Imagine the insulin spike, the stress hormones.

He leaned across the street to fish his phone off the floorboard, pulled in into a Wawa to call Gloria back. He knew she had Bikram in a half hour but could she please please please let the dogs out before she left?

● ● ●

He was outside Orlando by seven, northeast on 417, the inside of his mouth a chewed mess.

"You have to understand," he would tell me when we finally met, "I was running on adrenaline at this point. The mind gets cloudy, you maybe say things you might regret later."

"What do you regret?"

He threw his hands in the air.

"Nothing!" he said. "I regret nothing. This is a hypothetical I'm talking now a—what's the word? A scenario I want to call it. I'm saying you might regret later. Emphasis on *might*."

It had been easy to find him. Stuart Pérez was a known entity. By that time he was no longer an agent—"a foray," he called it, "a teensy little might-have-been"—but seemed to have his fingers in everything else. I had gotten him on the phone almost immediately after leaving Doc's father. Meeting him was a different story. He was evasive, vague, hung up on me twice before asking me outright if I was in the employ of any federal and/or state agencies? No? How about the Cuban Intelligence Service, those twisty bastards? I said I was a writer trying to piece together the story of what happened to Shy Walsh and the next day we met in the LIV nightclub at the Fontainebleau. It was early and the place was mostly empty, a few barbacks unpacking bottles of Alizé vodka, a cleaning service spraying glass surfaces with something lemony and harsh. He asked me if I wanted to meet Pit Bull.

I thanked him but did not.

"Because if you think it's a thing for me," he said, "like a consequential effort or what have you, I'm here to assure you now and forever it most certainly is not."

I told him I just wanted to talk about Shy and he pulled at the lapels of his wine-red leather jacket and gave a solemn nod.

"Day of fucking days that was," he told me.

We had walked up to the Scarpetta Bar and ordered cocktails before he asked me where the cameras were. I told him there were no cameras, I was a writer. He nodded as if he'd suspected as much then looked past me as if still searching.

"I drove up that evening," he said. "You have to understand. I was running on adrenaline at this point."

He got Shy's mother's address from Kenny and drove straight there, found her sitting on the couch in pajama pants, eating the Special K with the fucking red berries. He'd tried to calm himself on the ride but seeing her there mawing those nasty dehydrated things knew he had failed. Blowing up was not tactically wise but here was someone throwing away her entire goddamn world all over a loss. Still, he waited till her mother went to bed before exploding. People lose, Shy. Fighters lose. It happens. Did she not know that?

"It has nothing to do with that," she said.

"With what?"

She was infuriatingly calm.

"With losing, Stu. It's not about losing at all."

Could she please then just tell him what the hell it was about?

"I don't know," she said, and lifted yet another spoonful of those goddamn red berries to her mouth. "I don't know if I could or not."

"That's when I lost my shit," he told me that day at the Scarpetta. Got down on his knees in front of her, begging, pleading for an answer. What was happening here, was she morphing into some sort of housewife?

"At some point one begins to think in durable goods," he told her. "Is that what this is? You're wanting to nest? Is that what you're telling me, Shy? Become like some domesticated thing?"

"I'm sorry."

"You want a kitchen and then you want to redo it? I'm asking a question here."

"I don't know what you're talking about."

"All I'm asking, Shy, all my simple basic elementary question amounts to is do you seriously want me to believe you're nesting? I want an answer. Jakob wants an answer. You want the avocado range, huh? Pitr fucking Roque wants an answer, Shy. You want the quartz countertops, the slot for a built-in microwave?"

"I really and truly don't know what you're talking about."

"I think you do. I think you fucking well do. Give me your hands."

"Why?"

"Give me your hands, Shy."

"Why?"

Finally, he got hold, took her palms that felt damp with the heat of his anger.

"Because, goddamn it, I want to pray with you."

He put his hands out, face down, that day at the Scarpetta. "Like this." Head tipped back, eyes closed. "We prayed like this, together."

He hadn't heard from her since.

Kenny was out in bum-fuck Texas somewhere.

He didn't hear much from Pitr, had lost his trust, he supposed, but had gone in as an investor with Danny-D on the whole line of transgender workout clothes.

"If you're looking for a place to park some money," he said.

I wasn't, and thanked him for his time.

He nodded and waved the waitress over for a drink.

"Stay and meet Pitbull," he said.

"I need to get going. But I appreciate your time."

"There's fifty percent chance he shows in like the next half hour."

I put a twenty on the banquette and caught the waitress's eye.

"No camera though?" he asked.

"No camera."

"I would have thought different, you know, for interviewing purposes."

I was by the door when he caught me.

"Where do you think she is?" He was almost panting. "Don't lie to me."

"I don't know."

"You think you'll find her?"

"I don't know that either."

"Well, when you do," he said, "if you do. Tell her…"

"Yeah."

"Tell her…you know."

I told him I did.

I told him I would.

● ● ●

Two weeks after coming home Shy turned her phone back on, but there was nothing from Kenny and certainly not anything from Stu. It made her a little sad. A little angry too, though she knew it was a matter of giving her headspace, as Kenny had put it. She knew that after his failed visit Stu would have called

Kenny and told him to back off, to leave her alone for a bit longer and that was all whatever, that was fine. It all felt behind her. That she had once been something entirely different—it seemed false. That just days ago her agent had kneeled there in front of the couch—had it really happened?

She supposed it had, but also knew it didn't matter.

That world was gone.

There was no going back.

So instead of going back, she went to church with her mama, back to the old hymns, the old God, circling transcendence like horseflies. Walking the four blocks in clear winter light, her mother in her JC Penny dress, leaned on Shy's arm as if for assurance as much as balance. It wasn't hard to fall into that life. Most of the people at the church Shy recognized from a decade ago.

The man with the stoma, the woman in the wheelchair.

It was Sunday and then it was Sunday again.

By Christmas they had fallen into something approaching routine. Shy walked with her mama to church, drove her to her appointments with the cancer doctor. They watched *General Hospital* and Shy filled the bird feeders.

Evenings, they would sit on the back patio and watch the sun bleed its way into the laurel oaks and ragged palms, listen to the birds. Loud, she couldn't believe how loud they were, the chatter, the plaintiveness. It felt like enough.

Most days it felt like enough.

● ● ●

But she must have been the only one to think so.

Just after the New Year, her phone started ringing again and suddenly there were texts and voicemails from Kenny and Stu, each a little more urgent than the one before—like they had planned it, timed it, which she knew they had. Shy listened dutifully and then one day began deleting each without reading or listening. They wanted her to say yes, yes to a return, to a rematch, yes to getting back to training.

Instead of answering, she started meditating again, sitting, trying at first to possess something that wasn't hers to possess. And then letting go of that desire, releasing everything so that everything was a form of dissolution, not just the sitting but Shy herself. The steady deconstruction of the great kingdom of me, the empty arrogance, the false ego, the raging goddamn defiance until all that was left was blood and bone, every bit of it quantifiable on the Periodic table of elements, every bit of it reduced to base matter. Which is the heart of the matter—such reduction, the possibility of becoming purely physical—if the matter even has a heart.

I'm agnostic on the question.

But I do believe that's what Shy was after, first sitting, and later swimming in the dark waters of the St. John's River where a couple of years later Rev. Lonnie Blatts would attempt to drown me.

But forgive me: that was all later.

● ● ●

Meanwhile, her mother's health deteriorated through the holidays and then with the falling of leaves, January, February, Shy out in the yard raking them, sweeping them in wet clumps off the sidewalk. It was one of the things that had never made sense to her, the leaves in Florida. The empty trees like nerve endings.

Meanwhile, her mother slept, woke a little later, hunched a little more. People arrived. The home health nurses with their blood pressure cuffs. Folks from the church with their Bundt cakes. Everyone with their prayers, and while they sat with her, Shy drove around.

Out to Razzles, the dance club with the green hand-stamp where a boy from driver's ed had been stabbed with a steak knife and her friend Sharon got Chlamydia in a bathroom stall. Out to Booth's Bowery where she had bartended, out to the Y where she'd taught aqua-aerobics to seniors. The places she'd gone with boys without really wanting to: beneath the pier where swallows nested, the old Bulow sugar plantation ruins where the Friday night cars would form a long line beneath the water oaks and rock like railcars until the cops showed up to scatter the proud.

She drove and drove.

Dixie Highway past the Popeye's, Gentle Dental, Minglers Social Club, past the Budget Inn and the Royal Inn, the Kingdom Come Family Church of Greater Daytona, the Avenue 12 Women's Recovery Home, the Mount Zion AME. The Express Bail Bonds and the single white ibis in the retaining pond around Tomoka Correctional.

Sometimes her mother rode along, piled into the seat like a sack of laundry.

The voice on the radio said, "Right now at Maitland KIA."

They passed highway memorials with crosses and laminated photographs and wet petals strewn along the shoulder as if ahead of a bride. Two Sandhill cranes were slowing traffic on Highway 44. At the intersection of Woodland and Indiana a protest was going on. Teenagers in sky blue t-shirts passing out tracts and holding signs that read JESUS LOVES YOU and FORGIVENESS IS NEAR while a single older woman in pastels waved the traditional REPENT. They kept driving.

The voice on the radio said, "I am not afraid to reveal my vulnerabilities, brothers and sisters."

One day Shy found what she thought was her mother's old AAA road atlas but realized it must have been her father's, half the routes traced in blue ink disappearing into the fold, trips planned but never made.

"Tell me about daddy," she asked.

And her mama, propped in bed, shaking her papery head. "Your daddy? We weren't never the kind of family to have no coat of arms." Had he really called her Bug? She tried not to think about it. It was enough to consider her mama, to see the hump of her back or the swollen twists of her fingers, the fruit of years spent removing pubic hairs from the toilets of chain motels by day and hauling draft Bud and jalapeno poppers to frat boys in FSU baseball caps by night.

The Reverend stopped by almost every evening in his blue coveralls, name sewn over his heart, clapping his hands and smelling of 3-in-One oil. Short and big handed. Shy left them alone, only gradually realizing they must have once been in love, and maybe were still.

It was one of the things right with her mama.

The problem was there were a million things wrong with her, most especially the bone cancer that was terminal, the bone cancer that had spread.

But more than that, she was old.

She was exhausted.

Tired of life.

"Everything's floating away from everything else," she said one day.

Shy sat on the edge of her bed and petted her hand, the nightstand crowded with old *TV Guides* and wooden nickels from the state fair.

"What, mama?"

"The solar system or the whole whatever you call it." She waved one arthritic hand above her. "The whole universe."

Outside, the birds at the feeder were deafening.

● ● ●

Reverend Blatts came by and sat with Shy in the kitchen, dropped his battered hands on a Formica tabletop the color of river sand.

"You know when someone's sick like your mama is we ask why are we being punished? Of course that's a ridiculous question—we aren't being punished. We have science, medicine to explain death. But sometimes it still feels like we're being punished all the same. And if it feels like it, maybe it's not so ridiculous a question after all."

"I told her you're here."

"That's the whole of Jesus right there: the world is an awful place. Someone had to pay."

"She's waiting on you."

"All right. Let me walk on back before she starts yelling."

"That would be her."

"A pistol, yes, ma'am." He pushed himself up from the table. "But loves the Lord, and loves you. Always tried to do right by both of you. You know that, right?"

"Go on back."

"But life is hard."

"Yes, it is. Go on back, Reverend."

Every day the birds outside got louder and every day she looked at people and thought: children. Sheep, you know? Because they've just never seen it. They've just never fucking seen.

● ● ●

In March she helped her mama into a rented wheelchair, parked it on the back stoop, and prepared the garden. Drove to Walmart one afternoon to buy them both new clothes and came home with a bag of Wendy's to find her mama had made her own way onto the porch and into the warm sunlight where they sat there eating, Shy wondering if she could have had this life all alone, this easy peace. But knowing she couldn't. That she had to go away for it to happen. That certain things had to fall apart in order to reassemble.

She watched her mama eat.

The box fan on high to keep away the mosquitos.

"He always called you bug, your daddy did. Do you remember?"

"I do, sort of. Get a drink here." She stood by her mama, holding a glass of tea. "Or maybe I just remember people telling me. Lift up your head."

"Where's my bug run off to?"

Soon enough she would find out.

Soon enough she would locate her own life, go online or better still drive to the main branch of the Volusia County Library. Newspapers. Microfiche, maybe, because she couldn't bear to read it online. The speculation. The theories and reader comments. The talk that Siobhan Walsh was retired/injured/being held against her will in either a rehab center outside Palm Springs or an ashram in Northern California. It was all speculation, all ridiculous, but seeing it would make it real, the proper nouns taking on a resonance in much the same way the as the names of old friends, names once intimate but unheard in twenty years. Then someone says it and the room alters slightly. You understand what you are reading is not an event or a happening or something on the wire services, but a life forgotten, a life more or less lost to you.

As most lives are.

Spring came and Shy's mother slept more and more and while she slept Shy found herself spending too much time staring into her mother's medicine cabinet. The Elavil and Percocet. Her own leftover Lortab. She found herself thinking too much about her dad out in his pickup with his Dianobol and his blow, his Mexican Dex.

She thought: painkillers. Jesus, the name alone.

She thought: look, but don't touch.

She thought: easy, Shy.

Outside three Hispanic boys wrestled on the lawn and she felt something prickle and walked faster, looked away, went home to find her mama sitting up in bed in one of Shy's old KEEP FIGHTING t-shirts.

The Reverend brought over a plastic bag full of okra from his green house.

"We came here because my daddy died," Shy told him. "Florida, I mean." They were back at the kitchen table, her mama propped in bed with a Yeti of ice water and Great American Country on the TV. "She came to church because she was scared."

"You only enter the church on your knees, Siobhan."

"Scared of everything."

"The suffering are God's people. That's what the cross means."

"She had a *Course in Miracles*. Read that for years."

"Your mama's been a natural born seeker ever minute of her life."

The birds got louder.

• ● •

One day, Dr. Hamad pulled her into the hallway outside the examining room and said, "You need to start thinking about Hospice."

"Hospice?"

"I can have Candace at the front desk get you the information."

She went home, put her mother to bed, and went into the garage where she did pull-ups on the exposed beam, sets of 7 until her hands bled, then sets of 5.

• ● •

By April she was a ring circling the planet of her mother's dying, ice and dust and the micro particles of rock that all appeared solid until you got close enough to really see. One day two women from the church came with their fried apple hand pies and their Sudoku and said, you go on, young lady. Get outside for the day. Cooped up like this. We're going sit with your mama.

"I don't know if I should—"

"Should what? You got your phone?"

"Yes, ma'am."

"We'll call you if we need we," one of the women said.

"But we ain't going call you," said the other. "We're just gonna sit and gossip with your mama here like we used to."

Shy looked at her, the oxygen looped across her upper lip and into her nose.

"Is that okay, mama? If I go out a little?"

"Of course it is," one of the women said, and settled into rocking chair in the corner. "Let's open those blinds, Delores. Get some sun in here. You go on and do something, child."

Only she didn't what to do besides drive around.

The hermit crabs. The shark's teeth and GIRLS RAISED IN THE SOUTH beach towels. The screen-printed tees with their beer and boobs and what seems to be the officer, problem? The gravel lot by the Civic Center where she'd worn a reflective vest and helped park cars for Sandi Patty and Dave Matthews, for a Promisekeepers rally and an Aerosmith tribute band. How the circus marched in through the freight bay, the elephants trunk to tail. How the Gaither Brothers left behind a spread of strawberries and peel-n-eat shrimp she'd carried home in Ziploc bags.

The air full of ozone and a haze of lovebugs that seemed to drift at windshield height. The pastures given over to Charolais cattle and the pastures given over to NITE-TIME HOG HUNTS CALL FOR GROUP RATES. The pastures of ECO-SAFE waste disposal happening beneath a field of black tarps. The palm nurseries of saw and sabal. Windmill, queen, majestic.

Nothing had changed, though actually everything had changed.

Where you are is a place, she told herself.

What is happening to you is your life.

● ● ●

Her mother died on the tenth of May and was buried two days later across town in the great retaining pond that was Memorial Gardens. Shy stayed alone in the house for several days but this was not a good thing. She let her phone die, got distracted and left the refrigerator door open, the lights on and the food she never ate forgotten and dissolving on the shelves.

The walks became longer and she realized there was no one left to pray for her. She realized how narrow she was becoming. 113 pounds. 21 pounds below her fighting weight. A good 30 below her old walking around. Finally, she decided to sell the house, then changed her mind and deeded it to the church.

She hired a moving crew, donated what she could, threw the rest away.

She spent the last night alone in her old bedroom failing to meditate, the room empty now of the trophies and dust, absent the sturdy little physical plant of her ego. The room empty of everything except Shy who lay on the floor inside her childhood sleeping bag with its nylon unicorn and faded rainbow. She'd kept some photographs, a few of her mother's things, that was all. Took what was left of the pain medication. Safe keeping, she told herself.

She was losing herself, shedding her old life like a worn skin, but wasn't that maybe the point?

● ● ●

It was late May when she rented the cabin and started swimming in the outdoor pool of the Family Oaks Campground, the salt water still cool but that just meant she had it to herself. The St. John's River marked the rear of the property. The pool itself was shaped like the state of Florida, which meant she followed the curve of the Gulf north to get her twenty-five meters, and then a quick flip-turn, and she was headed south again. Pensacola to Tallahassee to Tampa to Miami to the Keys. A mile, two miles.

She got calls and emails from Stu and Kenny. They'd heard about her mother. They were sorry. They wanted to tell her how sorry they were. Also, they wanted to talk about the future. But instead of talking about the future she swam, her muscles elongating, strengthening.

After, she would stand by the giant ice cooler—ten-pound bags for two bucks—towel over her shoulders, and shiver. Around her RVs and Rust Belt retirees. Green sawgrass in hummocks, brightening. Time was passing, life organizing itself in disappearing increments.

She didn't know what she was doing.

Only that she'd turn twenty-eight in a few weeks.

Only that her teeth felt stable.

The Reverend came by with a plastic Dollar General bag of carrots one day.

"From your mama's garden," he said.

"How are the birds?"

"What birds?"

"The ones around the feeder. They were always so loud."

Kenny kept leaving voicemails and she listened to them at night, shoulders trembling from her laps. But Kenny didn't get it. No one did. The kind of focus, the kind of single-mindedness that was necessary to do anything important. You staked everything on it. People like to admire perseverance but not really. Perseverance, the real unadulterated thing, scared people. You weren't well-rounded. You didn't know when to quit. Enough was never enough.

Still, the messages kept arriving, signals from another planet.

"Hey, hon," he would say. "Hon, you getting these?"

She liked the way he seemed to be addressing someone she couldn't quite remember, and there were days standing in front of the mirror she'd tacked to the wall she hardly recognized herself.

"Are you out there?"

She was and wasn't.

• • •

Either way, she was served in June. Out by the pool when a man in board shorts and a wolf spider tattooed on his throat walked out all blonde and smiling and said, "Hey, are you Siobhan Walsh?" and she said yes before she could think, and just like that the papers were in her hand: Hammerhead MMA Promotions & Management Inc. was suing her for breach of contract. She put the papers in the kitchen cabinet, did 200 pushups, and walked back to the pool.

The Reverend came by with a bag of okra.

"Shy, I'm sorry about this," Kenny said on her voicemail, "but if you'd just listen a minute."

●　●　●

It was not long after that she met the disgraced doctor who had done seven years for buying 100 Oxys from an informant in the parking lot behind the Maitland Sheraton. She knew these things because Doc told her, talking constantly, shirtless in a chaise longue while he drank vodka tonics and watched her swim. An ER doctor with expensive sunglasses, mid-forties and sunburnt and more or less broke, his wife having cleaned him out while he was awaiting trial "and please believe me, she deserved every penny and more, the poor stupid woman. You've never met a worse husband than me." His name was Thomas Clayton and he was going to work for Médecins sans Frontières shortly but there were issues with his license—which he'd lost—and bankruptcy—which he'd declared. In the meantime, he was living in a houseboat tied to the pylons on the river he'd paid for with a collection of rare books.

He told her she needed to eat.

"Look at you," he'd say. "I see ribs."

She ignored him, smiled at him, indulged him.

"Look how skinny you're getting."

And it was true, how skinny she was getting. Narrow, lean. *Girl, you turn sideways and you disappear.* But that, maybe, had become the point.

You live a life to be rid of it, her mother had said.

Stupid, sure, but what was she supposed to do with her stupid?

Eat it?

Ignore it?

Live with it—that was what you could do.

She went with the doctor back to his boat only a few times, three or four, she counted. But why count? she wondered. She thought he would try to touch her, grab her, but instead he cooked her Campbell's soup on a hot plate while a police scanner played like soft rain.

"I want to take you somewhere," he said. "You like seafood?"

"You like jai alai?"

"You like ballet? I think you'd love ballet."

One day he introduced her to two skeezy looking guys, one in a Juggalos t-shirt who stood over the hot plate stirring a cauldron of fish stew, the other so blonde he appeared translucent.

"You dear old dad's girl?" Juggalos asked.

That was Dwayne Robbins. The blonde one was the shaman named Craig.

"We're business associates," Doc told her. "So to speak."

Eventually, she moved onto the boat with him and if they didn't exactly fall in love they certainly fell into something approaching comfort, approaching normalcy.

Later, at the Golden Lion, he would introduce her to a giant Guatemalan.

"This is Dante, old buddy of mine from back in the day," Doc would say. And it was Dante who after a moment of hard staring said, "Shit, girl. You the one that got knocked out. I knew

I recognized you." Only it wasn't true, or was no longer true, whatever difference that made.

What happens to the body?

Is it the same thing as what happens to you?

The answer is both yes and no.

Who you are is no different but it isn't the same either.

I'm not trying to be cryptic. Her shoulder grinds in the socket. Her ears aren't exactly cauliflowered but aren't exactly not either. At times the world sparkles, glimmers of bright light that are never actually there. Sometimes she's circling again. Sometimes she's back at the Olympics, suffocating beneath the Russian's gi like something deposited on the ocean floor. Sometimes she's sixteen and grappling in a basement grow room, UV lights and marijuana plants pushed to the edge of the mat, someone running to pick up the scattered potting soil. She sees the sandhill cranes blocking traffic, angled imperious things. She hears Dominic say *there's striking, and then there's* striking, *Shy. You feel me?* She does, did, will again because none of it felt like it was going in a straight line anymore, time, her life.

They went to Miami, to the ballet, to see the disgraced doctor's daughter in trailer park outside Ocala, a lonely girl in a seahorse necklace. Meanwhile, Shy kept swimming, made her flip turn, kicked off the wall. Then one day she saw something moving along the tiled bottom, and when that something crawled from the pool she followed it down to the banks of the St. Johns where it had disappeared into the river.

Doc must have watched her go over the top of his Ray-Bans.

"Hey, Shy?" he wanted to know. "What are you doing?"

"Did you see it?" she called.

"See what?"

"The dolphin," she said, already wading into the dark of the river. "It's a dolphin!"

The next day she began to swim off the boat in the river behind the campground.

• • •

The St. John's is the largest north-flowing river in the Northern Hemisphere, its current not unlike life's middle years, the subtle acceleration that comes after the big events, the weddings and births, but before the deaths. It so slow you barely notice, barely care, yet there you are, so many miles beyond where you thought you'd be. You've flowed north without even realizing it.

You've flowed away.

Which is exactly what Shy did. Day after day after day until the church burned and the doctor went alone to a small hotel room in Fort Lauderdale. Siobhan Walsh had signed her money over to Hammerhead by then and wanted only to swim, to pass beneath the bridges of Jacksonville out of the mouth of the harbor and into the Atlantic.

That last day she walked from the houseboat down to the water where the birds were screaming, calling, beckoning, walked down to the water and waited. When she saw it, she entered the water and put her face beneath the surface, and followed.

And following was a glorious thing—her entire life was down here and how had she not known? Along the seafloor she found her old Judo trophies. Swam through her old room at the Sands, past Kenny's mother on the couch and Doc weeping on a sleeper sofa on Siesta Key. Her own mother in prayer. Her father smiling at her before dropping into another set of squats.

She swam a thousand miles, let the current carry her. It was easy, it was nothing. She was so narrow now, out among the fish and tortoises, the giant container ships on the horizon. She watched her arms turn to fins, her legs to a single scaled muscle, and realized she could keep going. Then one day the dolphin told her of the darker places, the places without light, introduced her to the beaked whales diving to seven thousand feet. They welcomed her, the whales, they could take her with them if she wanted.

She could go with them forever, and why shouldn't she?

She swam away, she went.

She kept going until there was nothing left.

Until Siobhan Rae Walsh had disappeared.

It was Doc's daughter who was present.

I want to go back to her, back to the summer Samantha Clayton turned eighteen.

That summer Sam was committed to forty days at the Sanctuary at Healing Pines, a rehab clinic off Highway 11 just south of Bunnel, Florida, the campus fifty gated acres of terra-cotta roofed buildings and walking trails, all of it tasteful and expensive and linked by raised footpaths that wound through the fern and palm, as if even the earth threatened relapse. Let's start with Sam's arrival, two days dopesick, hungry for light and love, for a shower and Suboxone, though none of it in that order.

None of it in any order, actually.

She'd spent the previous forty-eight hours drinking Red Bulls and smoking Newport Lights in the Flagler Super 8, eating (a single slice of) Domino's and getting blazed with three other girls she'd met in a Facebook group who were also bound for the Sanctuary. It had all started fine. The first night they went to a party in Ormond, college boys, soft. A bungalow two blocks off the ocean, the Xbox and black light. Except around midnight something turned, some bad motherfuckers had showed up, or maybe woken up, and there was a fight that overturned a garbage can and left a red fantail of blood on the concrete and then a little while later some crazy chick put her arm down on the grill where not twenty minutes before there had been burgers and dogs.

Sam slept till noon the next day and then went out to spend the last of the large bills her grandparents had given her on a purply-red heart tattooed just right of her navel. She'd gotten her boobs done that spring—her idea though her mom had been surprisingly willing to spring for it, as if plastic surgery was a hobby they might bond over—so the tattoo had felt like a matter of time.

The second night they'd sat on the balcony and traded stories, the filched pills and open liquor cabinets, the indifferent parents. The bullshit bragging and worn clichés that might have embarrassed Sam had she not been too busy unloading. *Oh my god, there was this was one time...* The open Domino's box in front of them, creases zipped through the cardboard by the pizza wheel, and it was all *bitch this* and *bitch that*. All the girls from wealthy families noted for their cosmic dysfunction, all the girls precocious in the mismanagement of their lives, saying things not because they knew they'd remember them the next day but because they knew they wouldn't.

Bitch, please.

Bitch, listen.

Bitch, I was fentanyl when fentanyl wasn't even a thing.

When the shuttle bus arrived to pick them up the next morning they'd lost one—she'd disappeared the night before to eat a sheet of acid with an old boyfriend in his Econoline, Maria might have been her name—but Sam and the two other girls had piled in dutifully, all sunglasses and ibuprofen and the exhausted eyes of the driver that kept flashing in the rear view as they pulled out.

The ride was less than hour but felt longer, sadder too. Inland from where they'd sat and listened to the tide, on past the I-95 interchange, past the factory outlets, the Calvin Klein and Nike, the Yankee Candle and Banana Republic. Sam's eyes hurt. Sam's face hurt. Outside it was impossibly bright, inside impossibly silent. The bus meant for twelve hauling three which meant they each had their own row. Room for our demons, Sam thought, and shook her head, embarrassed at the thought, embarrassed that she'd become what she so clearly was: the poor little rich girl no one loved enough or loved right or some such shit. And demons—seriously?

They passed into the country, the last twenty miles through an arbor of live oak and pine, the asphalt sun-dappled in a way that evoked something Jurassic, something antediluvian that might yet come crawling out of the swampy muck to block the road and wouldn't that have been welcome? A sign or something, Sam must have thought, though who could say of what? She touched her face, the hurt of it, as they passed a palm nursery, a couple of horse stables. A ranger station, finally, marking the edge of this or that wildlife management area.

Now, seriously: where was that Suboxone?

She thought she might vomit if she didn't get it fairly quick.

"Okay, ladies," the driver said, eyes back in the rearview as he made the turn off the highway onto a driveway of crushed shell lined with saw palms, yet another thing expensive and loud. Which, she thought—stepping out of the van into the wet heat—while we're on the topic of my mother…

(She was just hilarious today.)

A man and woman waited to greet them, hands clasped, beaming in a way that seemed to signal a well-intended mindlessness. The man gave a welcome, a blessing, and, Sam, Sam smiled back, pretty Sam, sad Sam who just really *really* wanted a hit of maybe even Librium if that's all they had. She was sweating but everyone was sweating: it was at least ninety, the humidity like wet wool. Still, her heart rate wasn't right. She checked her watch. 144. Just standing there. Sweating. While this asshole hippie went on about healing and self-respect and over eleven miles of trail suitable for walking.

151.

The food was vegan.

157.

The sheets organic cotton.

161.

Just goddamn standing there.

And even Sam knew it wasn't supposed to be like that.

● ● ●

It was supposed to be easy.

It was supposed to be golf course living. Twenty-seven holes of Robert Trent Jones and her part of it, her mother's part of it, thirty-two hundred custom square feet and a giant back deck that overlooked the trim of the seventh fairway and on out to the Atlantic. This was after her father's trial, after—or at least amid—the shock waves of anger and humiliation. Most definitely after the seven months she'd spent watching *Jeopardy* at her grandparents while her mother "got back on her feet," which meant sleeping with a North Florida land developer who "popped the question, honey, he did! he did!" right there on the white sand of St. Bart's. The time at her grandparents had been a reprieve, she supposed. They lived in an over-55 community of "active adults" who drank afternoon margaritas and wrecked their golf carts in great peals of laughter. Sam had the entire upper floor to herself and besides dance classes and her walks on the footpaths over and between the dunes mostly stayed there. Somewhere between her father's arrest, his time in state-mandated rehab, his trial, and, ultimately, his sentencing, Sam had turned thirteen without anyone really noticing. A card from her grandparents, an *oh-my-god we'll celebrate at the*

Melting Pot this weekend from her mom. But then her grandparents were busy, her mom was off with the land developer, and Sam was upstairs.

In a once empty bedroom, her grandparents had installed a ballet bar and three mirrors that covered the length of the wall. The floor was heart-of-pine and pushed in the corner was an iron-framed daybed that had once belonged to her mother. Sam had a bedroom across the hall but this became her de facto home, lying on the bed absently flecking white paint from a curlicue of iron, or moving through her warmup in front of the bar, the pliés and demi pliés and tendus. She enrolled in the Florida Virtual Academy so her schooling was online, and between French and ELA and Math I she spent her time stretching or researching ballet academies. Her morning walks along the boardwalks and along the beach turned into jogs and she lost weight, her classes, her *iron-willed discipline*—as her grandfather called it—threatening to transform itself into something unhealthy, some eating or exercise disorder. But Sam didn't let it. For the first time, she was in control of her life and intended to remain as such. In the ninth grade she could enroll in the St. Petersburg Academy for the Moving Arts and put the (admittedly thin) breadth of Florida between her and her family. So it really was all discipline: she did her schoolwork, did her ballet work, ate her lean proteins and leafy greens. She also refused to consider her father. That was part of the discipline too, and she made it work, she did. Her only link to him, the only thing that implied his existence, the seahorse charm she wore around her neck.

The following year, fourteen years old and emancipated ("not legally," she told everyone, "but in, like, practice") she moved into a dorm, a suite she shared with three other dancers, her living space small and basic but also far away from anything she'd ever known.

The past went into a locked closet.

The seahorse charm went into a zippered pocket of her makeup bag.

• ● •

It wasn't unlike her room at the Sanctuary. A bed, a desk, a dresser—all of it airy, bright, and reduced to necessity. She left her bag unpacked and walked to the orientation. Besides Sam and the two girls she'd met there were a dozen or so others, all ages, all races, all sad. After the orientation there was a urinalysis, a welcome lunch, a tour of the grounds (the aforementioned walking trails, an open air shed with a ping-pong table; from the trees hung the occasional porch swing). It was three before she got back to her room and felt moved to neatly fold her clothes into the dresser, a drawer for socks and underwear, a drawer for shirts, one for shorts and pants. All the way down until she was on her knees stuffing in a hoodie and suddenly she was crying. No awareness of it at first, just the sensation of something warm and viscous against her thighs, and then she fell into it, the sorrow, or it fell out of her. She panted, wept, it felt a little contrived, a little theatrical, but her eyes were sufficiently puffy by the time she made her way to dinner and then group.

Group was fifteen people on cushions in the great expanse of the open shed.

A guy a few years older than her held his porkpie hat and talked about cutting himself down to the white meat just because.

A woman from an accounting firm in Jacksonville spoke of her previous two trips to rehab and how—fingers crossed and raised—third time would be the charm. Sam tried to be generous, to be as open as the group leader implored them to be. But the woman laughed manically and told the third-times-a-charm joke at least once too often and when Sam found herself smirking it seemed like a reasonable response.

Less reasonable was her own breakdown.

When it was her turn to speak Sam didn't mention Doc. She said nothing, in fact, about her father, locked in a Level II facility less than an hour away. Her mother's name came up only in passing. She didn't discuss how she'd spent her childhood distracted and self-absorbed, floating in a pony-tailed galaxy of cartoons and Bratz dolls. The private school, the tutors, the ice cream in a swan boat on Lake Eola. Instead, she talked about her time at the Academy. The grueling practices, the addiction to expensive coffee, finally the pills she began taking that looked like candy hearts. How she would swallow a TICK, a TICK, another TICK—Jesus, where was the BOOM? She told them about how she'd grown thin enough to consider her ankles. The sight of her own pelvic bone. The blue-veined soles of her feet.

She told them how one morning she had taken out a nearly-crushed Tampax box left behind by her previous roommate and from it removed one of the two Hydromorphone suppositories Jillian had left her just in case. It must have been five in the morning, the dorm dark, the dorm silent.

She told them how she had been up for hours; how it was possible she'd never actually slept.

For the previous six or seven weeks she had contained her panic, wanting to feel it, to name it before she set it free. But three days prior she had felt something come loose so that morning found her with two fingers of Vaseline and her underwear around one ankle. She crawled back beneath the sheets and slipped in the suppository. The whimper wasn't about pain. Neither was the way she bit her bottom lip.

She kept two fingers pushed against her anus until she was sure it would stay, and then she shut her eyes and unclenched her hands, the universe perfectly still but for the warm wet spot that steadily flushed outward until her entire body was afloat in Dilaudid, a word she could never quite remember how to pronounce.

This is, of course, the point you get to shit on her.

This is the point you are free to define her as another creamy cliché of the upper-middle class, as yet another melting snow-flake of the meritocratic elite, and you would have grounds. But let me say this to you first, before you judge her, let me relate to you my first time. It was OxyContin—what else, right?—I was twenty-three, and had never yet been who I was supposed to be, having spent my life fighting, dodging, and losing a war with an anxiety so profound I felt like an underinflated pool float. You know the things you used to see teenage girls sunning on? The swell of the headrest, the cup holder that never quite held the Diet Rite or the cordless phone? Only underinflated, which means useless, which means everything sinks except perhaps that bubble of pillow, the thing by which everyone knows you, sees you, defines you while you flounder and kick, the warm plastic twisted around your legs.

But that day, for the first time in my life, I felt myself self-in-flate. I felt full, useful, confident. I felt self-actualized to go all Abraham Maslow. I felt satori to go all Zen. You are still free to shit on her, of course. On me too, and I wouldn't blame you. But you should also be prepared to shit on the two mil-lion Americans who also felt their lives begin the moment the fruits of Purdue Pharma bound to the opiate receptors in their exhausted brains. You should be prepared to shit on the for-ty-two thousand Americans who overdosed in the last year *for which we have available data*. You should be prepared to shit on the very legitimate concerns of failing economies and fail-ing psyches, of lives spent jobless and hopeless and vaping on a plaid couch while someone eats KFC and plays Fortnite for the sixth consecutive hour, our collective suffering scaled appropriately to life in the Anthropocene.

I'm not trying to be dramatic. I'm not trying to tell you what to think. I am simply telling you that less than an hour after her suppository Sam had risen from the bed and became herself.

She told them that. The rest, too.

About her near suspension her second year when she and her roommate were caught with Vicodin and how her mother had visited campus in the expensive car her expensive husband had bought her and somehow it all went away. (She was talking too much.) Told them how she'd been caught the subsequent year with carfentanil which was no joke and she was sent back to her grandparents and online school because her mother just couldn't deal. Harder stuff then. (Why was she saying all this?) Her grandparents big-hearted and naïve so that she spent weekends at parties, that rager on Crescent Beach, or that insane night at an apartment complex she couldn't remember where, only that it was first time she saw EMTs inject someone with naloxone which should have been a sign but wasn't.

(She couldn't believe she was still talking.)

How dancing was a thing of the past—this sense of self, this identity she had built around it, all the hard work and lost toenails only to throw it away. Which meant—didn't it?—throwing away a large part of herself? Like she'd spent the better part of her life pouring herself into some intricate vase only to shatter that vase in a matter of months.

She wasn't crying.

She was calm and dispassionate. She was focused, as if recalling something she'd heard long ago but only now remembered. Part of it was exhaustion, the throb behind her eyes, the heat that radiated from the still-fresh tattoo on her stomach. Part of it was simply being Doc's child. But it was also the two sets of eyes she felt on her, both soft, accepting. The man who had spoken of white meat—when he dared to glance up he seemed to look at her with what she could only describe as love. His eyes glossed. His thin mustache quivering. His name was Dwayne.

The other was the group leader but it would the following day before she caught his name: he was a shaman, he said, and his name was Craig.

● ● ●

It went on from there, the gusts of warm air, the twelve-stepping. The morning yoga and evening Suboxone. Turns out she had a talent for rehab. Turns out it was not unlike the dance academy: the routine, the enlightened self-interest. Her body filled out. Her resting heart rate fell to 55. She took long walks with Dwayne who was from up near Gainesville, kissed him—albeit against the Standards & Behavior Code she'd signed on arrival—beneath a laurel oak on one of the trails. She liked the sense of order, the Cognitive Behavioral Therapy in the morning, the one-on-one session with Craig in the afternoon, group in the evening.

"Have you ever thought of killing yourself?" she asked Craig one afternoon in their one-on-one session.

"Are you being clever or serious?"

"I'm just asking."

"Yes," he said, "I have. Have you?"

She shrugged in a way that embarrassed her. She actually had meant to be clever, to be a little provocative, but realized suddenly such provocation might be misunderstood.

"I don't know," she said. "Maybe. Or not really, I guess. But it does seem like a way to solve things."

"Solve what things?"

"Everything, I guess. Life."

"You think life is a thing to solve?"

That shrug again: "Maybe."

"Like a puzzle."

"Yeah, I guess."

"Where's your dad, Sam?"

"What do you mean?"

"He's in prison."

"Yeah."

"Is that also a thing to solve?" He leaned in. "Are you think-ing of it now?"

"Of suicide? Like this minute?"

"Like in general."

She smiled. She felt clever after all.

"What if I said I was?"

"I would say," and here he leaned forward, "get on with it." He leaned back. "Or get on with living."

She felt small then and not at all clever.

"One of the two," he told her.

It went on like that—testing limits, testing herself, but mostly getting better.

She kept gaining weight which was a good thing, meeting Dwayne to make-out but nothing more. She wrote to her mom, an apology, a note of understanding. Mailed it. Wrote to her grandparents, a thank you. Mailed it. Wrote to her father. She didn't mail that one, but did one day put the seahorse charm back around her neck. Another day her high school diploma came in the mail, sent by her grandparents.

She was a high school graduate. A tiny thing, a thing in her previous life she would have taken for granted. But no longer.

"I got this tattoo, a heart." She was in her one-on-one with Craig, just the two of them in his breezy office.

"Yes?"

"Sort of purply-red, like right before I got here?" She put a finger in her hair, twirled it like she was eight years old. Became conscious of the gesture and stopped but then couldn't help but go back to it. "But the way I'm starting to understand it or think about it or whatever. It's like—I know this is stupid—but it's like I have this permanent reminder now of what I used to be like, what it used to feel like. In case I ever start to forget."

"Do you think you might forget?"

"I don't know." Her finger back in her hair, the mindless twirling. "I mean I don't think I ever could. I feel like I've seen some really bad things and in a way—I know it's like a cliché of group—but in a way I really am lucky to be alive. I don't ever want to live like that again…"

"But?"

"But I've said that before."

"I see." He leaned back and steepled his fingers in a sort knowing way. "Where is it?"

"The tattoo?"

"The sort of purply-red heart, yes."

"It's here," she said, and touched the waist band of her shorts.

"Show it to me."

"It's sort of…"

"It's okay. Show it to me."

And she did. She felt awkward for a moment, as if showing it to her father but ultimately peeled down her shorts and underwear to reveal the heart, maybe three inches long and slipping off her right pelvic.

"Thank you," he said.

She put her finger back in her hair.

● ◉ ●

Three days before they were to graduate they took a field trip to DeLeon Springs State Park, a circular swimming area built around the boil of a spring, the water sea-glass green and a constant 72. The girls she'd arrived with stretched out on towels on the water's grassy apron, bodies glistening with Coppertone, soaking up the lust of the middle-aged men and teenage boys lurking nearby. Come on, they told her. Watch the daddies drool. But Sam walked with Dwayne. They'd still been meeting every day, more than ever, actually, but kissing less and talking more. Her decision, not Dwayne's. Not that she didn't occasionally let him touch her, but more and more it felt brotherly and sisterly, or like what she imagined such must feel. That was certainly how it felt that day as they looped the swimming area past the sugar mill pancake house, past the concrete steps, past the children splashing and families picnicking and teenagers sitting on benches or cannon-balling into the water.

"Been thinking about the future," Dwayne said, "like after, you know?"

She knew. She'd been thinking about the future too, though more as a default state than something you could plan for. The state would pay for them both go to a sober home for 30 days but after that...

"I maybe got a plan," Dwayne said.

Sam nodded and realized he was waiting for her to speak.

"Yeah, um, I was thinking I'd go back to my grandparents and figure things out," she said. "I think I could even go to my mom's maybe, if she could put up with me."

Her laugh was awkward.

Dwayne's smile lopsided.

"No, no," he said. "I maybe got a plan for us both."

● ● ●

They decided to go swimming, a celebratory thing, the happiness, the promise of a future—it seemed to call for some physical act, some acknowledgement beyond the laps they traced.

Sam slid off her coverup and walked with Dwayne to where several boys in their early teens were diving off the concrete apron.

"It's thirty-two feet down to the boil," one of the boys told them.

"What's the boil?" Sam asked.

"It's where the water comes out from the spring. Like the drain in a bathtub only you can feel it coming out instead of going in."

They took turns trying to swim down.

There is a point where your buoyancy reverses, where you are no longer pulled toward the surface but pulled into the deeps, a point where what it is you have always known is no longer the case. But Sam couldn't reach it.

"What am I doing wrong?" she asked the boy. "I blew out my air and kicked."

"Yeah, but you got to let go," he told her, "just totally let yourself go. Watch."

She and Dwayne borrowed masks and put their faces beneath the surface as the boy swam downward, a trail of bubbles strung behind him.

"Easy," he said, back at the surface and panting.

Dwayne went next.

"Holy shit, Sam. You gotta try it. I touched like the limestone or whatever." He had the mask pushed up into his hair and his smile was so wide she couldn't see his mustache. "It feels like a vent or something."

"Okay," Sam said, blew out her air, smiled, inhaled.

"Nervous?" Dwayne asked.

"A little."

"You've already swam down like five or six times."

"But not the right way."

He gave her that smile.

"You got this."

And she did, she really did. She exhaled, dived her head forward, and swam with a gentle motion, hands in front of her as if parting a curtain that kept falling back into place. Down, down, and then she felt it: the pull. She couldn't believe it at first. It was as if someone had taken her hand and in the tenderest of fashions eased her forward. She'd been under no more than ten, maybe fifteen seconds but suddenly the boil was in front of her and she could feel the current nuzzling its way past. Sunlight waved around her and when she looked up the surface appeared a soft quilt patched from the lightest of blues. It wavered and she felt a shiver pass through her, this calmness, this presence. The silence was absolute. She heard the sound of her breathing, the sound of blood pumping through her head, but then not even that. She turned to the boil. It was darker, a small cave just big enough to wiggle into.

She kicked closer.

It appeared darker still and she put her palms flat on the grainy limestone, her hair swept up and back. And then she saw it. It was no more than a flicker but she was certain and kicked lightly so that her face was at the boil's mouth. What she saw there, it was—it couldn't be, but it was a staircase, and she could just touch the railing, the white banisters, the wood-stained steps. It seemed to spiral and she followed it, one flight, two... she was three flights down when she heard the voices. It was hard to place at first, harder still because they were so familiar yet not. It was her mother, her father, it was her, only not quite. When she saw them she understood why. It was her family, only her family as it once had been, and what she saw before her was her childhood room, the toe shoes ribboned to her wall, the American Girl dolls arranged on her bed. And there was Samantha, and there was her father, and there was her mother, and they were talking, just ordinary talk on this ordinary day.

Grainy light.

The hue no longer blue-green but pink.

The ribbons swaying like sea grass.

Her father putting out his hand, but then—

The jerk was hard, something hooking her arm, the bubbles that weren't hers but Dwayne's or one of the boys maybe. She felt this great up-thrust, felt the surface break around her, the way it seemed to fall from her in sheets. More pulling and then they circled above her, a halo of faces and within it a ring of absolute blue. Dwayne was holding her, screaming her name, and she understood she must have vomited, or not vomited but spat up what felt like gallons of water.

"Sam! Sam!" he kept saying, and she saw the lifeguards pushing their way in, the red board shorts, the plastic tube thingy meant, it occurred to her, for mouth-to-mouth, and seeing it she choked again and took a deep breath. Something swam through her vision, that light, those winding stairs, and just before they could put the plastic tube thingy to her mouth she started laughing.

Started laughing and couldn't stop.

● ● ●

She went to a sober home in Clearwater on the Gulf Coast. It had been hard leaving, harder than she'd allowed herself to admit, as if the rickety structure not just of her sobriety but her entire identity was being shifted across the state, and like a kid trying to transport a construction of Legos, she had to move slowly lest it collapse. The home had once been a drive-in motel, an L of rooms a block off the beach and open to the street, the pool poured over with concrete and covered with deck chairs and a plastic owl once meant to keep seabirds away. There was toast and coffee in the old motel office, a twenty-three dollar per diem she mostly spent on almonds and sugar-free RockStars

at the 7-Eleven. She watched E! and scrolled her phone, sometimes lay on the patio chairs and let the sun soak through her
clothes into her skin and muscles and down into her bones. She
felt like a battery, as if she were storing power. Gathering something she couldn't yet name but knew she would need eventually. She could do it for hours which was just as well. It was all
federal money, insurance money, and so long as she submitted
to a urinalysis three times a week no one really cared what she
did.

"Piss farm," a woman named Tara told her one day. "You
know how much they charge the insurance companies?"

They were standing on the second-floor balcony in an August
heat that seemed all the more smothering for it being beneath a
cover of brain-gray clouds.

"I mean not that I give a shit about insurance companies,"
Tara said, "but this place here, they billed something like four
million in claims last year."

"For this shithole?"

"For this shithole! Yes, exactly. For like the shitty donuts and
orange juice, I guess."

Dwayne was in a sober home near Lauderdale and while they
talked on the phone only occasionally she assumed he would
still be picking her up at the end of their 30 days.

"Craig's into helping people all over," he'd told her that day by
DeLeon Springs. "He's got like a Zen set-up near Micanopy and
he needs us."

● ● ●

Which is where Sam went at the end of her time at the piss farm.
She hadn't counted the days. Time had simply slid out beneath
her. She was there, smoking on the balcony or watching folks
walk by on their way to the 7-Eleven and then she wasn't, she

was in Dwayne's giant pickup headed north. Craig was running something called the Dhammaram Temple whose purpose Dwayne seemed to only understand only vaguely and Sam not at all. Still, Craig was offering Dwayne employment and a place to stay and Dwayne was offering to take Sam with him. Which meant she didn't have to go home, however you chose to define the word.

They wound up in a trailer north of Gainesville. Dwayne was in and out, though what he was doing with Craig Sam didn't know. Actually, she did, she just choose not to think about it. *Many lines in the water, my dear,* Craig told her one day before he and Dwayne disappeared again, *many lines.* Instead of asking about those lines, she stayed home, stayed bored, stayed inside. Watched daytime TV, the game shows and talk shows, the families more dysfunctional than her own (but were they?), the commercials for laundry detergent and teeth whitener. Sometimes she watched no more than the rain that fell onto the trailer roof or onto the palm fronds, the way they bent, the way they seemed to vibrate. The way the rain puckered the dust.

The Dhammaram Temple, she learned, was little more than an old church and a brush arbor that consisted of a roof and bamboo floor with six or seven meditation pillows half-circled around a three-foot brass Buddha. It sat in the back corner of the eighteen acres that had once comprised Our Mother of Grace Trappist Monastery, the Temple far from the highway but near the creek that cut along the meadow's edge.

Sometimes she would go there and on the bamboo floor lose herself dancing. Those days she woke inexplicably happy, like she was ten years in the past and it was springtime again and again. The light soft, the day warm—all of it radiant. She would dance and come home to put on her chocolate brown bikini with the gold ring on the hip and sit in a lounge chair in a kiddie pool, a few inches of warm water around her feet. She knew the boy in the facing trailer—his name was Alan and one day he'd sweetly helped her carry in groceries—could see her and she liked the thought of it, of having some power in this life. Those were the good days.

But the good days were rare. Mostly she stayed inside, fingering her past like prayer beads. The *Frozen* dress she'd kept wearing after she was too old for it—Elsa or Anna—she couldn't remember which. The vegan place in Winter Park she'd go with her mom. For a while, she'd gone everywhere with her mom. To her Bikram classes, or Barre classes, the hours side by side on matching Pelotons. It was easy to forget they'd shared that, but they had. She waited for Dwayne and sometimes waited for the cops to show up but it never happened. The cops all out on I-75, busy pulling over black kids, busy making Salvadorian roofers kneel in the rumble strip. Busy tasing migrant workers piled into U-Hauls. It wasn't really a feeling, these thoughts. Sometimes she remembered boys she'd known and felt slick with some unfocused lust and would lie on the bed and touch herself. But that was only momentary. What persisted was her aloneness, even when Dwayne was there, even when she was wandering the aisles of Publix. It was a smell, a form of light that was also a form of dark. It was her shadow and she fell into it, this stillness, this boredom, as if it offered not a way in but a way out, something other than what she felt which was, well, she couldn't say exactly. Though she was certainly aware, as the philosophers and self-helpers remind us, that her life was slipping by her moment by moment, and if she thought about what was before her, well, now there was a little less, and now a little less still.

Eventually, she decided to enroll at the community college.

She had this sort of serious, sort of ridiculous idea that she could maybe transfer to UF and study art so she signed up for the bridge program: freshman comp, calculus, beginning

French, World History with Dora. Dora being the woman she met smoking Pall Malls out beneath the awning. Dora had a boyfriend, and a two-year-old, and a job at the Waffle House on 441. She wore cornrows and had been in a band called Birth Trauma but there had been, like, creative differences. Sam had gone twice to sit with Dora on her break before Dora invited her to a meeting of the Democratic Socialists of America.

"Bring some jeans," Dora told her. "Like an old pair. We're making jorts."

"Jorts?"

"I don't know. It's fun, it's stupid. We cut up old jeans and talk about inequality."

The meeting was in her English classroom. The professor leading the meeting—'facilitating' he called it—was young and had a silver hoop in his left ear and a box of Krispy Kreme he kept urging them to eat. His lapel pin read SAFE SPACE. Sam took a donut, but only touched it with her napkin.

"People hear professor and think ivory tower," the facilitator said. "They think elbow patches and leather-bound books. But most of us work two jobs, not counting summer."

Sam didn't know anyone else besides Dora but thought she might have recognized one of the men. That maybe, years and years ago, he might have painted her parents' bathroom Chantilly Lace.

"...racial disparities in housing," the facilitator said.

Dora poked her leg and smiled.

"...eviction rates..."

Dora winked.

"...the looming specter of student loans..."

"The financial industry is nothing more than a smokescreen for the ultra-rich," Dora whispered, and they both laughed so hard they had to leave.

"Okay," Dora said outside, "that was boring."

"No, it was interesting. It was like—"

"It was boring. Like apocalyptically boring." They watched drunk college boys in cargo shorts stagger out of the Tilted Kilt and into the sun. "But I've got a better idea. Actually like seriously fun this time."

Dora wanted Sam to come to a party with some of her boyfriend's good time buddies.

"I don't know," Sam told her. "Dwayne might not like it."

"Might not like it? What is he, your pimp?"

Sam put a finger in her hair.

"No. He just takes care of me."

"Well, where is good Mr. Dwayne right now? He taking care of you?"

"He's working."

"Working? Shit, honey," Dora said. "I know all about what he's working. You know Craig Munson?"

"A little, yeah."

"Well then you know Craig Munson is the biggest pill pusher in all of north Florida." She patted Sam's inert hand. "You come have a good time. You need away from that business anyhow."

The problem was, it wasn't away from that business, it was closer.

Sam drove over on an ordinary Saturday evening, parked in the yard where a half dozen pickups and cars sat in the sandy yard outside a brick ranch, and walked inside. The living room was crowded with ashtrays and the bench seat of a van. Past it, two giant gaming chairs sat arranged in front of the largest TV Sam had ever seen. She stood marooned in front of the screen where two women were fighting in a cage.

"The Walsh fight," one of the men in a gaming chair said. "Shy Walsh?"

The woman was bleeding from her mouth and Sam stared

at her, mesmerized, as if she were seeing one small part of her future, which, of course, she was.

"Move." The man motioned at Sam.

"What?"

"Fucking move please."

"Oh," Sam said, "sorry."

She found Dora in the kitchen.

"What do you want to drink?"

"Oh, I don't know, just…"

She wound up with a Mich Ultra in her hand, a narrow sleek can she sipped as she wondered through the house. There were people everywhere, in the bedrooms and in the wood-paneled hall, down the basement stairs where she wondered after Dora had told her to *hold on, I need to see somebody* and not come back. If it wasn't the staircase from her near-drowning it was, at least, something, or maybe just somewhere. Somewhere else.

The basement was unfinished, exposed wall studs and an electrical box with its snakes of wire, a thick stand-pipe. Some sort of speed metal was banging off the concrete floor and she took a drink of her beer if only to further dull her senses.

Past the stairs several boys—you couldn't exactly call them men—were gathered around a weight bench yelling and clapping and laughing as someone got pinned beneath his bench press. Sam floated past them, unnoticed, toward a door that led into a dim space, the music no more than muffled noise. She took another drink and walked forward into the darkness. It was beginning to hit her, the beer, the dreamy lucidity that felt like some stray bolt coming loose behind her eyes. The floor was uneven but wait…no—the floor was fine, the floor was solid.

A light flared ahead of her, trembled and steadied, and Sam felt a hand on her arm.

"Goddamn, Samantha," Dora said, "you scared the shit out of me."

The others came into focus slowly, the room not as dim as Sam had first thought.

"It's fine," Dora said. "It's just Sam."

"Who the fuck is Sam?"

"Just go on, Tim."

And Tim did, Tim went on, turned back to the Coleman stove where above its perfect flame he was heating a shot. Dora picked up the rig, an ugly rusted thing Sam had seen but never touched.

"You ever shoot up?" Dora asked her. "Like when Mr. Dwayne ain't around?"

By the time Sam got back upstairs the girl with the bleeding mouth had been knocked out and the boys were out of the gaming chairs yelling *Knocked the fuck out! Oh, shit!* They squared off and began some sort of shadow martial arts, some Karate Kid idiocy it looked like. But, once again, Sam just floated right on by.

She floated by, in fact, for the rest of the school year, mere months but long enough to start dabbling but then dabbling turned to using, like, serious using and she lost weight and got an infection on her arm and one day realized her teeth felt like really brittle. Which is to say she found herself very much on the edge of a cliff.

Then her dad showed up with his remorse and tickets for Boléro and she fell off.

That night, after they'd stood her father up for the ballet, Dwayne had attempted to console her.

"I thought he'd disappeared," Sam had told him.

"Your dad?"

"Yes, my dad." She was in tears, fingering that goddamn seahorse charm she'd only recently taken to wearing again. "I thought I could be done with him. I thought he'd disappeared. I just—"

"I hear you."

Her heart rate was 167.

"I just…"

Her father would be back. She knew it. He'd be back and what would come with him? Shy Walsh would come. Eventually, I would too. Sam didn't know it at the time, but also, she did. On some level she did.

"I just thought…"

"Yeah, I hear you," Dwayne must have told her. "But seriously, babe, it's harder to disappear than you think."

As for me, I suppose part of my interest was my own inability to disappear. My father had died eighteen months prior, two days short of his sixty-fifth birthday, and my mother, displaying not so much the loyalty that defined their relationship as simple resignation, had wasted no time in following him, dying of loneliness—defined for our purposes as a cerebral edema—five months later. The proximity of their deaths should have been sudden enough to shake me from my self-absorption, but in truth they only made things worse.

My girlfriend was gone and I spent every possible moment mourning not just my parents' lives but my own. It was time, I suppose. Sometime in your thirties, maybe your early forties if you are lucky, you come to realize you are being weaned from this world. You come to realize that as the world steadily becomes less recognizable, a loss of orientation that includes a tallying of the gone—people and places—you are slowly being prepared to someday shrug off this life, to slip away with some hesitation, but not too much. You begin, I suppose, to realize how much of this world is no longer in this world. That's how it began for me, and if you're anything like me—around the middle of life's way—I suspect you number your dead, too. I suspect you start to sound like the person you swore you'd never be. You start, as the late country singer Blaze Foley put it, to build "a castle of memories just to have somewhere to go." You spend an inordinate amount of time thinking about that confounding thing the French surrealist Paul Éluard said, "There is another world, and it is this one." And it is that one, the one you touch only through memory, you spend more and more time inhabiting. An entire world gone, not to be returned.

Later, I would think about water, why it was that Shy and Sam both found sought solace there. I would develop (and discard) some theory about birth, about comfort, about returning to the womb and so forth. But that was all in the future. At the time, I was mired on the dry land of self. Parched and exhausted, but maybe not yet tired enough to try to change anything.

Which is where first the public defender and then Doc's father had found me.

As for my interest—maybe I was just tired of grieving.

Maybe I just wanted a reason to wake up.

Either way, I knew I was headed back to Florida, and in late January, weeks after my unannounced visit to Fort Lauderdale, I went.

● ● ●

Had it not been for Dante Henry's size I might not have recognized him, that and his still-gentle voice. I met him through the perforated Plexiglas of the Columbia Correctional visitor's room, nineteen holes punched to form something resembling a circle through which passed something resembling a voice. There was a headset but neither of us picked it up; I simply leaned forward until I could feel the static electricity coming off the shield.

"Jess," he said. "My brother."

My original petition for visitation had been denied— Columbia was a Level V facility and the inmates here were held in, to use the parlance of the system, "closed custody"—and I'd had to call an old chaplain friend at Lawtey who had called someone in Tallahassee who'd eventually called me. I'd been at home in Atlanta at the time, and when I was told I could meet with Dante for thirty minutes the following day I'd nearly declined the offer. It was a four-hour drive but more than that I was in one of the weather-like systems of mild to moderate depression that now and then blow in with the same rapidity with which they blow out. I'd sat for a while wondering if any of this was worthwhile, whether any of it mattered. Then I'd gotten up and got dressed.

By mid-day I was sitting across from Dante.

"Goddamn, Jess," he said. "I never thought."

"I'm sorry it's been so long."

"No, I get it, my brother. The wheels keep like, you know."

"Yeah, for sure."

He looked older, of course. It had been years after all. But the lines appeared deeper than necessary, the damage more signif-icant. He'd had his hair in braids in the booking photo I'd seen online and now his hair had been shaved back to the dark fuzz I remembered from Lawtey. Still, it was hard to place him: he was Dante but not quite. But then again who was I but myself, only not quite? We talked about old acquaintances, the writing class, the little I knew of his family. Eventually, I asked him if he'd heard about Doc. He had. He asked me if I'd heard anything about the whereabouts of Shy Walsh.

"So she really was his girlfriend?"

"Poor Doc," he said. "That motherfucker sure thought so."

"His father had said, but I was never quite sure if it was true or not."

Dante nodded slowly.

"Doc, yeah," he said in that soft voice. "You never knew with Doc. Man was brilliant, kind. Maybe the most generous person

I've ever known. Do anything for you—you know what I'm saying? But just had this cloud around him, always and forever."

"His father said he'd met you once."

"Yeah. I was with Doc and somehow we wound up at his folk's place for like Thanksgiving dinner or some shit. Doc had Shy with him, just pure hearted as ever, and here it was the three of us sitting there with his folks and his brother. You know his brother?"

"I was down there last month. I didn't know before that he even had a brother."

"Yeah. Probably forty-something. Got a bad brain injury at some point. A sad fucked up human we're talking. He lives with them still, I guess. Doc's folks."

"They have these couch cushions with eyes," I said. "Like someone's watching."

"Do what?"

"On the couch."

"Couch cushions you talking about?"

"Yeah, up in the living room."

"No, Jess. I remember," Dante said, "but not eyes. Those are supposed to be like peacocks."

"What?"

"Like the tails or what have you."

"Oh, I had thought…"

"No, brother. Peacocks, not eyes."

"I see."

"You thought somebody was watching?"

"I don't know."

"Nobody's watching."

I looked away for a moment and when I looked back up Dante was staring softly back at me.

"What about Shy?" I asked.

"Nobody's watching, Jess."

"Yeah, I just thought…"

"It' okay, brother. Shy though." He shook his head and slowly brought it to rest in the great soft of one giant hand. "Pure hearted like I say. Devoted. Absolutely devoted to him but Doc had this fucking cloud I'm talking about. But she was sweet, that girl."

"Where is she, D?"

"That I couldn't tell you, my brother. When the shit fell apart—I had warned him, Jess. Told his ass to stay away but you know Doc. That's my girl, he kept saying. That's my baby girl."

"You're talking about his daughter?"

"Sam, yeah. 'My baby girl,' he'd said. But his baby girl was tied to some bad shit, and then that church burned."

"What church?"

"Shit. You don't know this?"

"None of it."

"His daughter and her boyfriend I guess that motherfucker was. Dwayne something. They was dealing. Just nickel and diming until Doc got involved—I put Doc in touch with a colleague I should go ahead and say—and I guess that just put the shit on steroids. I don't know what Shy knew. Just that it was one big fucking mess and then those kids burned her mama's church."

"When?"

"Right before Doc hung hisself it would have been."

He told me what he knew: the houseboat on the St. John's River by the Family Oaks Campground, the trips from Miami to Ocala running pills. Dante had made the introduction. He regretted it, sure, but you know, fate being the motherfucker it is. Then Doc had gone and kicked the shit out of some preacher.

"What happens, happens, my brother. Mischief got its own way a being. You know this."

"Yeah."

"We all know it."

When the guard entered the room behind Dante I thanked him, I told him I'd write. He put his palm to the glass, fingers spread, that giant hand like a starfish, and against it I put mine. I told him I'd put $40 in his commissary account, the most I was allowed, and he thanked me and told me to take care.

In the parking lot I made a quick search with my phone. The articles posted just after the fight had turned up what one would expect: post-fight analysis and speculation of the inevitable rematch giving way by the summer of 2016 to 'where in the world is...' conjecture (the only clue was a lawsuit filed by Hammerhead MMA Promotions & Management Inc. which meant, in effect, that she was AWOL), giving way by the early months of 2017 to silence. I did find a single mention in the October 2016 Family Oaks Campground newsletter: "Siobhan Walsh, resident of cabin 6B and known to all as 'the swimmer,' has lately taken to swimming in the St. John [sic] River. Have fun, Siobhan, and watch out for the gators!" You might have seen the accompanying photo: it's the one I mentioned before, the one where her shoulders appear wider, her body open—the one that would run years later when she was officially declared missing.

I called the manager of the Family Oaks Campground from my car.

He told me that she'd been living in the houseboat but had "vanished" on him back in the spring. When? I asked. He wasn't sure exactly, mid-May probably. What little she'd left he'd packed up and had in storage. Did I want to come pick it up?

"Normally I'd throw it out," he'd told me. "But I liked Shy. Everybody did."

I told him I'd take the stuff, to please hold it for me.

What did it matter if it wasn't mine?

Nobody's watching.

● ● ●

What she had left behind was stored in a coffin-like Rubbermaid container stowed in a garden shed with a mower and weed eater and a number of old life jackets dematerializing on hooks. I walked around the Florida-shaped pool and along the banks of the St. John's; I stood outside her cabin, occupied now by another Rust Belt retiree. The houseboat was gone—where I never discovered, though I suspect it was repossessed. I thanked the manager and put the Rubbermaid in the trunk of my car.

"If you hear from her," he told me and hesitated longer than perhaps he'd intended.

I assured him I would let him know.

I didn't look in the container until I was back home.

There wasn't much. Some clothes, a stack of KEEP FIGHTING t-shirts that appeared unworn. A few photos. A few empty pill bottles, the contents prescribed to both Shy (Lortab) and her mother (Elavil and Percocet). Moldy *TV Guides* and two dozen wooden nickels. I put it in a closet and tried to forget about it.

Knowing I couldn't.

Knowing I was incapable of such.

● ● ●

Doc would have understood.

The time after getting out of the halfway house had been hard, and in the wake of the failed rapprochement with his daughter, in the wake of the three-night bender with which he'd chased it, he had decided to go straight. But Doc didn't understand straight. Doc was made crooked, Doc was all angles. He kept calling the New York office of Médecins sans Frontières, and Médecins sans Frontières kept not calling him back. Then one day Dwayne called and said, *you don't have to live like that, dad. In fact, I've got a little shit stirring I could use some help with.* They went into business together, he and his daughter and Dwayne. Craig the shaman, the kid with the moped everyone called Twitch.

It didn't bother him, the moral side, the rightness or wrongness, because how could it be wrong, objectively wrong, when objectivity was no more than the accepted perspective, the subjective no more than the whim enough of us agreed on?

But not Doc who was no longer a doctor.

And certainly not Sam who was no longer a dancer.

They became dealers because it was easy and the money was good and what else were they supposed to do? It was accepted because it's the way things are, and as a writer far better than me once put it, Satan is the way things are. Eventually, Dante would introduce Doc to his colleague and the small time would evolve into something decidedly larger: the biggest pill operation in north Florida. That was the thing about Dante' friends: they were big time. Like ridiculously expensive eyewear big time. Like kids learning Mandarin while the wives bought Jimmy Choo heels big time. All the money washed and off-shored. The operation as vast as it was byzantine: burner phones and dead drops straight out of 1960s Berlin signaling this place at this hour. It was less trouble getting to an Iranian centrifuge than the pickup location for the three kilos of black tar on which some 'troubled youth' would soon OD.

That didn't bother Doc either, the damage part.

And why should it? The divorced former father living on a houseboat that stank of mold and wood rot. He spent months running stash and drinking by the Family Oaks swimming pool but the day he met Shy something felt different, something that had been teetering finally went on and fell. The result being that he felt lured toward an actual sustainable life. It started simply enough: she would come back to the boat or he would come back to her cabin and therein they tried to create something approaching a relationship. They fed each other. Talked to each other. Held each other. These very human things.

Did she know about the dealing?

I somehow doubt it. Or maybe she knew, but not exactly, not the extent, not the full reach. She knew he drove every week or so up to see his daughter outside Ocala but it was his daughter—of course he would go see her. By this time, Shy had signed away her earnings and was living off the eleven thousand dollars left in the account she had set up for her mama. What Doc was living off wasn't exactly clear—the occasional book he sold to a dealer in Daytona Beach, she supposed. Either way, they were both lonely, and it made a certain amount of sense that she should move onto the boat, carry over the trundle bed, rehang the clothesline. She had some pots and pans and those came. She had the Rubbermaid I would eventually acquire.

She swam every morning, hours, miles it must have been, lap after lap, and after she'd sit on the deck with Doc and watch the river accept the changing light.

"Do you ever feel like God out there?" he asked her one afternoon.

He was sprawled on the chaise longue, the one with the seashell pattern.

She stood at the galley door, half in, half out, waiting for the Ramen to boil on the hot plate. How long had she swam that morning? Three, maybe four hours.

"Of course you do," he said without ever turning. "That's why you keep doing it."

Sometime that fall Reverend Blatts brought the last of her mama's garden's bounty. Sweet potatoes and lima beans.

"Hello, Reverend," Doc said.

Thomas Clayton wasn't exactly sober.

"Hello, doctor."

Lonnie Blatts wasn't exactly charmed.

"Siobhan," he said, "could I talk to you a minute outside?"

They walked up the dirt path beneath the palms and away from the river, the morning a low ceiling of mosquito heat and children's voices.

"What do you know about that man?" he asked. "Cause I looked him up."

"He's had a hard life, Reverend."

"You could surely say that. You surely could."

They walked to the edge of the swimming pool where a child cried and a mother yelled and the manager fished leaves with a long cleaning pole.

"I'm not trying to overstep my bounds," Blatts said. "But I worry."

When Blatts was gone, Doc wanted to know how exactly Shy knew him.

"He was my preacher growing up."

"Yeah, well I don't like him."

"He's a good man."

"I don't trust him."

"With me?"

"With you or anyone. I'm going up to see Sam tomorrow, by the way," he said. "Maybe spend the night."

"Okay."

"You don't mind?"

"Of course not."

And she didn't, because just then she had seen something moving along the bottom of the pool.

But it wasn't until after the ballet that she realized it was a dolphin.

It wasn't until after the ballet that she realized it had come for her.

• • •

The ballet.

Doc took Shy that fall and this part I can only imagine, but I think I'm imagining it right. How the Dr. Phillip's Center for the Performing Arts looked like something she might have seen over those months in Vegas: all bright glass and brushed steel beneath the great sail of its roof. How they sat in front of the orchestra, center right. Shy must have been in the dress Doc had bought her and how long since she was in a dress? How long since she was in anything but sweats or a wet bathing suit? Doc took her hand. He was in a suit he got she didn't know where, the first time she'd seen him in anything other than a t-shirt and shorts.

The ballet was Stravinsky's *The Rite of Spring*.

The company wasn't great, wasn't perfect, but they were certainly very good, and perfection wasn't the point. The point—as I see it—was recognition.

The dancers moved onto the stage from two, no, three directions.

He'd been waiting for this.

She realized she had too.

He'd come for years with his daughter—he'd told her that. His daughter, not his ex-wife who found it if not too boring, too what? Too naked, maybe.

And his ex was right about that, their nakedness, the rawness of the act.

But the nakedness was the point.

The music came up, they began to move, and as they did, Shy must have felt carried by it, she must have felt recognized because here was what she'd been after all those years, here was what she'd been trying to do: to meld mind and body in a movement that doesn't so much relate to the self as embody it. To so precisely trace the outlines the very lines disappear. To move as one thing that is in fact everything. Did that sound ridiculous? It didn't matter. She wasn't thinking like that; she wasn't trapped in that logic from which we so often fail to divine a life. She watched the dancers and heard the music and felt them as one, felt herself leaning forward, her body straight and alive. It was everything at once and it was overwhelming, so much so that what can you do with it but offer it up? move, dance, make of it an act of devotion, a form of worship but worship without object.

Gratitude without referent.

Joy without source.

To be alive and stripped bare, living nakedly on stage as the dancers were, living nakedly in the cage as she had been. *Everything's floating away from everything else,* her mother had said, only it wasn't true: everything was bound, everything was intimately connected, if only you realized it was so.

Did she think this?

Maybe, though in truth I don't think she was thinking in that moment. It must have been deeper than that, it must have been more elemental, an experience that we might debase by calling *mystical* when it was really no more than the careful moment-by-moment act of paying attention. You feel it a few times in life, you feel it in the big moments of joy and grief—births, death, love. Those moments where the truth arrives in blows. But it's more available; it is the actual living definition of *available*. It is *there*, and she'd known it every time she'd stepped in the cage much as Doc must have known it every time he felt the first sudden flush of opiate joy. I'm not a mystic, I'm not an adept, but believe me when I tell you it is real, this transcendence, and believe me when I tell you that once you live with it, to live without is worse than death. That's a terrible cliché but I will say it again: to live without it is worse than death.

Sometime in my early-thirties, I went back to the church I'd grown up in. I'd always thought I never wanted to see it again and a part of me didn't. Yet I went back. I had a weight-lifting buddy with me, a training partner who was going through some shit with his wife. I knew he was searching and I suggested we go. I told him it was anthropology. I told him we were about to engage in time travel, about to teleport back to the old Appalachia of fire and brimstone. I made a joke out of it. But I wanted badly to go and we did.

The service started.

There was singing and prayers and an offering.

Eventually, the Reverend spoke, wept, thundered, and at the end, when they gave the altar call, when *softly and tenderly Jesus is calling* began on the piano my friend walked forward, unsteadily, as if he were intoxicated, one hand moving from pew to pew until he stood before the altar.

They surrounded him, the Reverend, the elders, men and women.

They laid on hands and my friend, my friend collapsed. My friend was slain in the spirit and, as he buckled toward the burnt orange of the carpet, was caught by the aging and arthritic arms of the believers. After, we stood back in our pew and the Reverend asked him if all was well with his soul.

My friend said it was.

He said, *the Holy Spirit, it just hunted me down relentless.*

Much later, I sat alone in my car behind a bowling alley.

I needed to drive home but I couldn't stop shaking.

I couldn't stop thinking *it just hunted me down relentless.*

● ● ●

Meanwhile, one year folded into the next and suddenly it was hurricane season. Not the named storms of history—not that season, at least—but a time of anonymous, near constant squalls. Flooded streets. Overflowing retaining ponds. Doc's trips to see his daughter became more frequent and the Reverend came around more and more.

That man, Reverend Blatts would say, *I'm worried. I don't like that man.*

That man, Doc would say, *I think that motherfucker's following me.*

Shy tried not to think about either, and not long after the ballet went with Doc to the Golden Lion, an old beachside motel and bar overlooking the red shells of Cinnamon Beach for what Doc called a little getaway. It was a ramshackle place with eight rooms and a tiki bar wrapping three sides of the pool.

"Kerouac drank here," Doc told her. "Back when he was drinking himself to death."

"Is that what you're doing?" she asked.

They were sitting at a wooden table beneath a giant umbrella marked BUDWEISER, sand everywhere, sand on the decking, sand in the air and in the grooves of the planking.

"I'm actually trying to cool out a little," he said, and touched her hand. "Attempting a little respite, I suppose."

A little respite seemed like a good thing, and she felt herself relax into the day, into the sun. It was something she had returned to only lately: that ability to let go of her vigilance. It reminded her of the beautiful exhaustion that had drawn her to fighting in the first place: you hit the weights, you spar, you spend an hour on nothing but takedowns, one after another until your knees bruise and your fingers swell, and that night, when it's over, when it's done, you don't so much fall asleep as feel sleep drift over you like ground fog. Your body aches with careless happiness. The caution had come only later, when fighting was about money, about her position in the larger universe. Had she let herself get kicked? The thought still emerged now and then, though not as often. She thought it possible, though she couldn't be sure. One thing was clear though: if she had, it was the only thing she'd ever done for herself. They could come for her money—they had. They could take her fame—it was gone, wasn't it? But she alone controlled the workings of her body, at least that night in Vegas she had.

So yes: calm.

Only Doc didn't look quite so calm.

"Kerouac," he repeated. "Did I say this already? Shit, I know I did."

He kept getting looks, detecting the hard stares, the whole world angry, the whole world pissed off. They sat beneath the umbrella's shade with a water and lemon for Shy and a pitcher of rum punch for Doc but then the sun shifted and even the air felt predatory.

"Fuck," he said. "Fuck, fuck, fuck, fuck."

She put her hand on his.

"Easy."

But it isn't paranoia if they really are out to get you.

"Pay phones," she thought he said.

"What, honey?"

"Like we're there pay phones before?"

She looked up and smiled.

"Before what?"

"Like a decade ago. Were there still payphones in, say, 2006?"

"I don't remember. Maybe."

"Yeah," he said. "Maybe."

In bed that night, naked beneath the scratchy thin blanket with its fading reef fish, the window AC rattling the panes, she whispered to him, without really meaning to: "there's so much sin in the world."

"Yes," he agreed, suddenly alert, suddenly sober. "There is. The man does not weep because he is sad."

She was silent. She knew she'd made a mistake.

"The man," he said solemnly, "is sad because he weeps."

They spent two nights there, talking by the pool, talking by the beach. Trying to build that life together, that thing that was there but not. Or maybe just trying to cohere their own resurrected lives into something visible, and sometimes it was almost there. Sometimes she saw a spangled brilliance around objects which was maybe the future or maybe damage to her left orbital. So perhaps possibility, but just as likely a frayed nerve and the first intimations of CTE. Those times she scared herself and it seemed her mother had been right: you lived a life to be rid of it. Other times, life felt like a fragile gift. Either way, on the last morning Shy walked out to the pool to find a giant brown man drinking coffee with Doc while past them the red eye of the sun came up the horizon.

"Shy," Doc said, "this is Dante, an old friend of mine."

Around Thanksgiving, the three of them drove down to Fort Lauderdale where Doc's parents lived and where I would later sit. Why this was happening, this trip, why the three of them, wasn't made clear to Shy. Yet that evening the six of them—Doc's mother and father and the brother with the traumatic brain injury about whose existence Shy had not been informed—sat around the heavy table three floors above where the Rio Barcelona Canal opens onto the Intracoastal Waterway before opening again onto the Atlantic. The house was large and weighed with damask and teak, embroidered curtains and an ancient projection TV that covered an entire wall. The piano was not in tune.

"Here they are," his mother said at the door, "so tan and so pretty and so—my, my—so large!"

The food was catered and came in eco-friendly pouches.

"You're welcoming me like a king, mother," Doc said.

"I know you got used to a certain cuisine when you were

inside. You would say that, wouldn't you?" his mother asked. "*Inside.* That's the term?"

Doc looked at her, a sleeve of green beans held before him.

"Yes, mother. That would be the term."

She shook her head at him, almost smiling, certainly drunk.

"Oh, Tommy, what happened to that vaunted sense of humor?"

"Is that what it was?"

"Wicked," his father said.

"I said vaunted."

"And we all heard you, dear. We all heard you."

Shy ate in silence. Kept her head down and thought of her childhood: the translucent retainer. The hair ties and jelly shoes and jumpers. Just inside her daddy's gym was a cooler full of Isopure and an old cigarette machine whose knobs she'd pull as if already in Vegas.

There was wine.

There were cocktails.

Dessert was a strawberry galette.

"How thrilled we are," his mother said, "how absolutely thrilled to have a Mexican with us to celebrate the season."

"He's Guatemalan," Doc said.

"What do they speak in Mexico?" his mother asked, turning to Dante.

"They speak Spanish in Mexico, mother."

"It's cool," Dante said.

"But he's goddamn Guatemalan-American turns out."

"It's cool, Doc."

"Guatemalan, darling. They also speak Spanish," his father said calmly, and then turned to his son. "And you watch your tone with your mother, young man." He arranged his napkin by his plate. "So tell us, what is it you do, Dante?"

"We're in a business venture together," Doc said.

"Lovely, but I'll bet he can answer for himself," his father said, "if you let him."

That must have been the point Dante told them about the class they'd been in together, my class, about the stories they had written. That must have been the point Doc's father determined his son was loaded.

Meanwhile, Shy thought of her mother: the Diet Coke at the McDonald's drive-thru. The fervent prayers and paisley pedal pushers, three for two at K-Mart. The smell of Lysol Pine on her fingertips.

Later, there was coffee.

Later, there was yelling. There was Dr. Clayton père screaming about *the goddamn disappointments in my life* and his son screaming back *your life? are you kidding me—your goddamn life?* There was his mother crying her lipstick onto her front teeth. There was the sound of something breaking in the kitchen, a plate, a dish. There's no record of the brother: the brother must have fled, must have wheeled himself into one of the house's more distant reaches. For her part, Shy simply sat through it, tucked her chin, found a place in the corner. Why this was happening—this trip, this dinner—wasn't made clear until later that evening when Dante introduced them to his colleague in Little Haiti and they drove back with 3000 Roxanol pills tucked beneath the spare tire well. Shy cried but took care to do it silently, Doc in no mood for further theatrics.

"Let me jump on the bat phone," he said when they were back.

"We're gonna up the shit out of this operation," Dwayne said when he came on the line. "Three-thousand of those little bitches? You serious?"

"May our reach always exceed our grasp."

"Fuck yes, may it always. We're going semi-global, dad."

And then Doc left to go see his daughter, to go semi-global.

It got quick after that, it got rough.

Doc started shooting up, started turning mean—the shortest distance between good and bad being the length of a needle. He felt time start to accelerate, which must have lent a sort of desperate air to what he saw racing toward him.

The amphetamines, the end.

Shy swimming in the river, at night. Which is not something you do.

I told you from the start: this is not the story I wanted to tell. And yet.

● ● ●

And yet in January he said it was time to celebrate, time to put on the good dress I bought you for—don't you remember—for the ballet? Time to have some goddamn fun for once in this life.

"Pack up," Doc told Shy. "I'm back by noon."

Weeks had passed since the trip to Lauderdale and in the meantime he'd been gone more than he'd been around. He'd bought her some clothes, paid cash for a BMW. She couldn't make sense of him. So it was no surprise when he disappeared to return at midday with Dwayne and Sam, no surprise when he left the car running and trotted down the path to stand on the dock.

"You aren't packed? Jesus, Shy. Pack. Let's go. We're burning daylight."

By late afternoon, they were at the Seminole Hard Rock Casino in Hollywood, Florida, a white monolith that at dusk was revealed to be lit in the softest of purples, five hundred rooms the shade of a preteen's lip gloss. From their balcony on the ninth floor, the pool area looked like a flooded village, tiki huts rising above the shallow water and skinny palms. A Pacific island an hour after abandonment, underwater lights still burning. Doc said they were having dinner downstairs at seven and here, take these.

"What are these?" Shy asked, two pills in her cupped hand.

"Dexamyl. Black Beauties you call them."

"I don't want these, Tommy."

"You think I do?" He shook his head. "I assure you I don't either but you are intolerable without them. Ever think of that?"

"I'm sorry. I'll take them."

"Give me one."

"I'll take them both. I promise."

"Give me one. I hate the fact you make me like this."

"No, no," she said, "I'll take them."

And she did.

Later, they were in a restaurant that looked like the bridge of a spacecraft, console chairs and flat screen TVs, the servers in silver jumpsuits. Piled in the corner was what Shy understood to be an octopus sculpture, not an actual living octopus, not an actual tentacled thing crawling toward her, despite all evidence to the contrary.

● ● ●

Later still, Doc was in the casino. This much was evident. The dim spaces and old women in white gloves, the sound of the slot machines—yes, he thought, definitely a casino. As for Dwayne, Doc suspected he might be nearby, possibly as close as directly beside him, but it was the dealer with the dark vest and nose stud who had captured his attention. Pencil skirt, hair up in a bun, all secretarial. Saying not a word, but looking, nevertheless, invitingly ergonomic in way that made him aware of his hands, of what he was and wasn't doing with them.

He looked around.

He didn't know where Shy was.

As for those fuckers at Médecins sans Frontières, as for those limp dick Frenchmen with their surgical theaters and Nigerian prostitutes…enough of this *turgid introspection* as Shawn had put it. He needed a drink and wandered into the Tequila Ranch where all the bar stools were saddles and all the bartenders were done up like outlaws with cleavage, above them a giant wagon wheel of colored lights.

He had two shots of Patrón and wandered back to the casino.

He felt good, he felt alive, and after he won his second $100 hand at blackjack, it came to him that he was smarter than anyone around him, possibly the smartest person alive. Certainly the smartest person in the room. Then he lost two hands and the world turned.

The world was against him.

The world had always been against him.

The world had always sought to—

"Hey, dad? You hear me?"

He didn't know where the hell Shy was and decided to have another tequila. The bartender was a blonde girl with an ear full of loops and a sleeve of intersecting tattoos. Doc dropped a hundred-dollar bill on the bar and when she smirked felt a hit of slippery lust. The pouting mouth, her complete disregard. The shot went down cold but then caught in him like a hook, the barb in the general area of his heart.

He felt helpless to logic.

Unhappy.

Angry.

He had his daughter, he had his woman, but what the hell was…what he meant was…he wasn't sure of the question or statement or whatever, only the large and vacant space from which it issued. He decided to go back to the table but changed his mind. Decided to find the actual goddamn table but just wandered around. A waitress asked if he needed a drink. A security guard asked if he needed help finding his room. No and no, motherfucker. And don't put your hands on me.

Finally, he decided what he wanted was to go to Miami. South Beach, Miami Beach—whatever. Just get in a car and go. Wasn't he the man after all? The father. The boss. The goddamn unappreciated provider of blessings and munificence? He found Dwayne and Sam out by the slots. In her white dress his daughter looked younger than her years, her eyes enormous, as if only nominally contained within her head. Dwayne wore a feathered headdress that reached the middle of his back.

"They got your sort of souvenir-type shop I'd call it," Dwayne said. "Tried to get Sam in a little squaw get up but you know your daughter."

"I want to go down to Miami," Doc said.

"All right."

"Like a club or whatever."

"I saw it coming the moment you walked over."

"Where's Shy?"

Dwayne had his phone out.

"You ain't sprung nothing on me, dad," he said. "I have yet to encounter genuine surprise."

"I think she's about by the pool," Sam said.

"Number one place on Yelp," Dwayne said. "$ET UP. Like with a dollar sign. I'll get us a car."

"Let me find Shy first."

"By the sort of lazy river or whatever," Sam said.

●　◉　●

By the sort of lazy river beneath the electronic sign that scrolled 24/7/365…24/7/365… over and over. By the tangle of swimming pools, barefoot in her new dress, just partaking of the visual world, its brightness, its radiance, remembering—strangely—the way her mother's nose ran and ran when she cried. "Shy?" She didn't hear it. "Hey, Shy?" Just standing there with her heels hooked, one to a finger, the pills she'd taken earlier having opened inside her like a night-blooming flower, not just her sinuses but the greater wonder which at the moment was focused on the giant glass guitar, its neck severed, that rose just beyond the pool. When he took her by the arm she didn't move.

"Are there people in there?" she asked.

"What?"

"In the guitar."

"What, that? That's part of the hotel."

"I see."

"Those are rooms, baby. That's what the lights are: people."

"I see," she said.

But actually didn't.

"We're thinking of going to Miami," he said.

"What?"

"A club."

"I want to go back to the room."

"Then go."

And even stoned she sensed him stiffen.

She put one hand on his chest.

"With you," she said. "I'd prefer with you."

"Well that just doesn't strike me as a reasonable."

"It doesn't?" She couldn't take her eyes off the great glass guitar.

"Come on." He began to move her. "As fucking usual everybody's waiting."

They moved downhill—downstairs, she meant. Stairs, not a hill, Jesus. She was maybe confused. Downstairs to where the roulette wheels and blackjack tables sat on the worn geometrics of the carpet and Dwayne and Sam stood in the lobby.

When he pulled her toward them she decided to cry for a minute; it seemed reasonable.

"Oh, Jesus Christ," Doc said.

Dwayne motioned to the door. "Car's waiting."

"You want to cry," Doc whispered. "I'll tell you when to cry."

• ● •

The driver had one impossibly yellowed fingernail that appeared to be more a callus, more an accretion of flesh than a deposit of keratin. You don't want that place, he was telling Dwayne, tapping that nail on the seatback, that place is homey bullshit, like rapper bullshit and all. You don't want that place. You want you a spotes-bah.

Shy put her head back against the seat.

"I can take you to a spotes-bah I know," the driver said. "Got 27 color TV in there and not a lick of that homey bullshit."

Doc turned to Shy.

"Hey," he said. "You okay?"

"Yeah."

"I'm sorry about before."

"Okay."

"Okay?"

She shut her eyes and thought of her mother. She must have believed Shy had been handed back to her, unburdened by God of fame and ambition and back in her bedroom with her toe-spacers and nail polish. She must have believed it was a sort of blessing, but one about which she was wary. Lucifer himself had been kicked out of heaven, bathed in a dazzling brilliance.

"Hey," Doc said. "Here we are."

The driver hung his arm over the seat.

"It's your homey funeral," he said.

The club was noise and light and a DJ behind a Plexiglas

shield. Beside him a blower sent giant bubbles over the crowd. They got a booth and a bottle of Patrón and watched a woman on a platform have tiger stripes airbrushed over her otherwise naked body.

"This is the shit, dad," Dwayne said.

Sam wilted into the banquette, her dress sliding up, a glass of cherry slush by one bare leg.

Shy thought the noise deafening, not unlike the noise at her mama's bird feeders.

"This is the absolute be all end all," Dwayne said.

The bubbles drifted over them, large, sinking, and blindingly iridescent in the moment just before they burst. Shy watched Doc disappear into the strobing crowd. When he was gone, Dwayne slid beside her and put his arm on the seatback, his fingers grazing her neck.

"You think I'm some dirt bag piece of shit, don't you?" He'd grown out his sideburns in what could only be understood as ironic pork chops, a Civil War quartermaster given to graft and betrayal. "You think I'm some white trash dealer, small time, uneducated. I get it, sure. But let me tell you something: this is all part of the master plan. I got doings is what I'm saying. Real estate. These Brazilians looking to move money. Russians looking to hide rubles. I went with Craig to a seminar on mindful investing up in Tallahassee."

"Who's Craig?"

"I'm gonna get Sam dancing again. Did you know she was like a serious ballet dancer? Sam was." He kicked her foot. "Hey, Sam?"

Sam's eyes fluttered.

"Hey, baby?"

She seemed not to recognize Dwayne.

She seemed not to recognize anyone.

Past them, the mass shook like people afraid of something

only they could see, hands up, mouths open. Shy saw Doc float by and for a moment missed Kenny, not that she remembered him exactly.

"Watch him," Dwayne said. "Or I mean don't. Either way, you know? He's got this predilection for crystal like he's in some time warp and it's 2007 or something."

"Crystal like crystal meth?"

"Hey, you are awake in there," he said, and touched her neck. "I thought like the aperture might have closed."

"I thought he just took pills now and then, like random."

"No you didn't."

"I thought just, you know."

"Yeah, well that was one level and now this is another. Imagine it like a number set."

"I don't know what that means."

"Both of them, daddy and daughter. I understand mama's on a golf course, praying for them."

"He's taking meth?"

"You think he'd run like that on unleaded? Yeah, daddy and daughter, both showboating. Both spoiled as a motherfucker." He nudged Samantha's foot. "She had braces as a child, you know? Orthodontia. Her own room. Her own phone. Wouldn't surprise me if she had her own pony. Daddy's girl," he said, almost like he meant it. "Daddy's fucking girl."

Shy's throat felt dry and tight. She felt the edge of panic. It was a trashy cheap world for which you paid a great deal.

"I think I might be sick," she said.

"Sure, Shy."

"My throat."

"Sure, babe."

• • •

They were outside the club waiting on their Uber when the man approached them. What exactly he wanted was unclear, only that Dwayne, Sam slumped against him, kept saying *da fuck, da fuck you talking about?*

Her, her, the man said, possibly referring to Shy, possibly recognizing her and demanding a photograph *with the chick standing right there, little miss knockout* and then the man was grabbing at them, grabbing at Dwayne and then Doc and it was more than a misunderstanding, more than confusion and Shy was moving without thought.

"I ain't asking again," the man was saying, and he didn't have to because he was on the ground, Shy standing over him filled with a certain righteousness, filled with the clear purity of having felt his cheek fracture beneath her right first.

"Holy shit," Doc said.

She hadn't even thought, it hadn't even occurred to her, she just—

"Holy shit. I think you fractured his skull," Doc said, and she felt holy, upright and quick. She felt absolutely possessed by the spirit.

And who are you to say she wasn't?

● ● ●

She didn't sleep that night and at dawn took Doc's car south on a whim, or not a whim maybe: a homing instinct. *These are my people, Ma.* But they weren't, not anymore. And maybe had never been. Her old Miami neighborhood seemed no different, a sleepy noontime quiet of bicycles on porches and trashcans and recycling bins rolled beneath streetlights. Chain-link fences. Duplexes for rent, their louvered windows down-drawn like batting eyes. The houses seemed to be only considering colors, painted in splotches, or painted so long ago they'd faded to something pale and indeterminate, like an unripe peach.

Shabby hedges, untended yards.

She drove past all of it, and parked outside Hammerhead MMA. Didn't enter, just sat in the street and thought of those nights with Sophia and Romi, drinking the tart cherry juice they pretended was wine while listening to Shakira and Amy Winehouse, how easy it had been. Sophia was married to her surgeon. Domi had gone back to Israel. They had all exchanged a few emails, a few Facebook likes and Memories and then lost touch. She didn't know about any of the others. Dominic was still around, she felt certain. Jakob and Mr. Wizard.

She knew they had her money, of course.

Knew, but didn't care.

The rest was much as she remembered it.

She sat there and thought of finding the ex-Marine on her phone, calling him, texting him, something. But instead simply drove on, south past the Santeria shrines and roadside crosses to Florida City with its fast food and motorcourts and billboards for airboat rides. She wanted Largo, because it was somewhere in the backwater there that she'd snorkeled, that she touched that dolphin—a moment that in hindsight seemed the moment from which all others had followed. The magic, the possibility. That thing everywhere evident but nowhere seen.

It would have been late morning by the time she pulled into Pennekamp State Park which wasn't exactly the place but would have to do. But do for what? *God can't cease to exist*—who had said this? Reverend Blatts, of course, who else?—*God can't cease to exist—I mean the old understanding of God, God as everything, the very ground of being—but to reconcile Himself to the world, to his creation, he has to taste death, to taste suffering. Be betrayed. Left alone to die. The world is an awful place, Siobhan.* She stood in the parking lot while families came and went, picnicking, swimming, and then walked down to the beach where there were dive boats and lifeguards and a catamaran moving sleekly along the horizon. But not a dolphin in sight.

The world is an awful place. Someone had to pay.

She was back in the car before she realized her hand was probably broken.

• ● •

She made it to the hotel in time for the inauguration of Donald J. Trump, Doc on the edge of the bed, a room service tray across his lap.

"Why are you watching this?" Shy asked.

"My duty," he said through a mouthful of waffle.

She watched him swallow.

"The world's on fire," he said. "If you aren't burning, it's your duty to watch."

"I thought you hated him."

He smiled broadly, gestured around him at the room, the food, at, maybe, the general benevolence of the world.

"Actually, I'm just waiting for someone to shoot him."

The President said, *The American carnage stops.*

Shy went to the bathroom and held her right hand under the cold water.

You want to cry, she thought.

The President said, *The American carnage stops right here and stops right now.*

She looked at her hand beneath the water, the sliver of bruise like a broken water main.

I'll tell you when to cry, she told the woman staring back at her.

● ● ●

In February, Doc made two more trips south to meet Dante's associate in Little Haiti and two more trips north to meet his daughter. Running ninety up the interstate, seventy on the backroads, the miles never registering because he was flying, floating, gliding on that amphetamine wind and why shouldn't he be? Shy didn't want to talk to him. All Shy wanted to do was swim in the goddamn river where, wait and see, Shy, a gator is doing to gnaw you to the bone, just wait and goddamn see. But she didn't wait or see, she wouldn't, so he kept going, northbound, southbound, hauling pills one way and cash the other. FLDOT on electronic billboards. Amber Alerts, Silver Alerts. The 2009 Audi with Mississippi plates. The nine-year-old girl with green eyes last seen headed west on I-4 with the father who had lost custody. It was background, noise, because the actual world was:

Pills.

Money.

Needle.

Pills.

Money.

Needle.

Until one day what appeared in Doc's eyes as the head of a match flickered and died and she found him crying over the bathroom sink.

"Tommy?" she said, and approached him as you'd approach a wounded animal because what else was he? His mind wouldn't still. All the patience, all the focus he'd acquired in prison—it was like a flight of birds, something that scatters at the merest approach. He knew he was ruining what he had with Shy, what he might yet have, but felt helpless to stop himself, not hungry for the turbulence so much as made out of it. He'd run a three-day bender, red-lined and panting, and then get straight, perform the one or two acts of kindness that kept her in his life, and then make the Miami to Ocala run. When he got back to the boat it was like he was one giant itch and he scratched himself with heroin and Jack Daniels so fast he'd be high before the engine fan of his BMW quit ticking.

"Tommy," she'd said, "don't."

He loved her.

He hated her.

He watched her sleep.

He was a living, breathing cliché, insisting on exhuming psychic graves, wrongs never righted, grievances dating to childhood. He wanted to be tender with her but couldn't, set out in the direction of kindness but never quite arrived. He thought it must have been the air, the water maybe, the goddamn light. Something that placed itself most precisely between who he was and who he'd never be. He blamed Florida: the chalky rock, the sinkholes, the entire peninsula an accumulation of exoskeletons.

He lashed out. She took it.

Her patience was limitless.

"We are together," she would tell him. "We're in this together, Tommy."

When she spoke to him, it was like she was making a series of deposits, steadily handing over her innermost for safekeeping, her I-haven't-told-anyone-this, giving him her spiritual life just so he could have one. And what did he do but make promises and then break them, apologize, shoot up between the toes, beg for forgiveness and mean it but not?

"Tommy, please."

Still, what does anyone want but to have their ashes scatted by a hand that cares? He kept coming back to that, waking with the gentle passing of a boat, standing uncertainly on his two legs, moving, walking, walking away, almost walking away. But then not, then looking back to see her sleeping, defenseless and full of what could only be identified as love. It was a manic season, but not one without hope.

I'm learning something, he would sometimes tell himself, thinking about Shy or maybe Sam.

I'm learning something, though he was afraid to say what.

Sometime in March, they drove to Siesta Key where Shy could swim in the warm lap pool that is the Gulf. Doc had his Arvo Pärt and the last of the books he hadn't yet sold. What were they doing you ask? Trying to hold onto something maybe. More likely trying to make something that, if it wasn't love exactly, wasn't to be dismissed either. Comfort, maybe. Possibly peace. For months his edges had been jagged and angry but all at once he was exhausted and sorry. It came to him that he understood regret. He understood disappointment. He thought of the way his poor father had lost hope, his children monsters, his wife a fool.

"Your mama was crazy," he told Shy in the car.

She kept her eyes forward.

"She was a seeker, that's true."

"She was crazy from what I've heard, and so are you," he said, but she knew he didn't really mean it.

They got a cottage on the beach and she went out and swam past the breakers for what must have been hours. When she came back he was watching the highlights of a fight on ESPN+. *Look at this*, he told her, but she couldn't, or could, but only for a second. They were lean and muscled, but neither appeared to be fighters, neither appeared to be anything beyond what they were: poor kids trying not to die.

"You don't miss it?" he asked.

"Miss what?" she said, and left the room to shower, but then came back, damp and suddenly cold in the air-conditioned room.

"Are you really on meth?" she wanted to know, "or heroin or whatever?"

"Who told you that? Dwayne told you that, didn't he?" He looked away from her at some indeterminate point. "I wonder what it's like for Dwayne, to view the world through the lens of absolute trivial bullshit."

"Are you though?"

"Am I what?"

"Are you using, Tommy?"

"I'm cooling out is what I'm doing. I'm trying to say I'm sorry."

"For what exactly?"

He started to speak but didn't, just gestured around him: this room, this place, this life.

"All right," she said. "All right then."

She went into the bathroom, turned on the extraction fan, and did 200 pushups.

She knew he was trying, but then he must have stopped trying.

He must have gone back to who he was.

(Given enough time, we all go back to who we are.)

There's more, of course. There's so much I'm not telling you about Shy and Doc, about their life together, because I simply can't: I don't know, and worse yet, I can't imagine. Yet I know it existed, this thing they shared. I know they ate meals together, cooked in that tiny galley kitchen, slept at night on that narrow bed as the boat bumped against the pylons of the dock. They must have talked, they must have whispered.

I do know that there were more trips throughout the spring, Miami to Ocala, pills, money, needle, and it was on the last of these that the Reverend showed up with his oils and prayers. It was May by then, the azaleas already wilting, already dropping their petals, and here stands this man on fire with God and anger and a squirt bottle of anointed olive oil.

What that was like—I can only speculate.

What I do know is that Doc wanted to get straight, wanted so badly to do better. Went to bed every night knowing he'd done something unforgivable. Went to bed vowing to do better the next day but the next day just folded into the last, and the one after that, mistake after mistake. That different better life like snowmelt, watching it dissolve, watching it make a mess of things.

I think a lot about Doc.

I think of Shy too, Shy on the beach at night, the expectant sounds, a halo around the moon. Slipping into water warm and viscous as oil in a machine. I imagine what must have been the good times, those days they lingered in bed while rain lashed the windows and the hull settled deeper into the river, deeper and somehow more certain, as if it wasn't just the boat moored safely but their lives.

When Doc's father first called me, I'll admit one of my first thoughts was: how do I write about this? I thought *think piece.* I thought *sprawling essay* that is half-philosophical reflection, half-reportage. I would posit that Siobhan Walsh was a sort of American Saint, or at least an American Martyr, sacrificed on an altar built in equal parts from male expectations and the slaughter bench that is Late Capitalism in the Dying West. Her loss would be an act of autonomy: she got kicked and began to move under her own power. But we are all of us constrained by larger forces—market, cultural, political—and her motions were useless, pointless, absolutely in vain: a character in a novel by Camus.

I wrote a little.

It was even more pretentious than it sounds here.

But it was all I had.

If I wanted anything more, if I wanted to know what happened that May, once again I would have to go back to Florida. Yet I kept not going. I kept thinking: *not yet, not yet.*

• • •

Yet I did go in the end.

I went to see the Reverend Lonnie Blatts several months after my visit to Dante at Colombia Correctional, the Rubbermaid of Shy Walsh's possessions still in my apartment closet, not exactly forgotten, though not exactly acknowledged either.

It was spring and I was full of hope.

In March I'd gone to Gethsemane, the Trappist retreat in Kentucky made famous by Thomas Merton. Five days of silence which I knew might be four-and-a-half too many but I was willing to chance it. I'd made the trip before. Years prior, and in the wake of my publication of my first book, I'd made arrangements to stay for six weeks—forty days, actually, though admitting the exact number had felt embarrassing in a way that's still difficult to admit. At the time, the guest master had been a man about my age, shaved head, ears that were—I almost believe—slightly cauliflowered. His knuckles were blue-inked with what looked like Cyrillic lettering, and when he caught me looking at them he made no effort to hide them. He was a fighter, or had been.

"It's just another form of longing," he'd said, and he led me to my room: bed, desk, chair, A crucifix on the wall.

"Is there anything else you need?"

But of course there wasn't. Here were the essentials and it was the essentials I had come for. More accurately: it was the absence of the nonessentials that had sent me. For the next six weeks I didn't speak to a soul. I attended the offices and services. I ate in the refectory. I read Dostoevsky and ran the trails that wound through the green hills. It was simply me and Fyodor and, when

I ran out of books, something I came to understood might be called the presence of God. I'd sit praying the Jesus prayer after vespers and then untangle myself to make these monumental training runs, eighteen, twenty miles winding through the wet heat, breathing Lord Jesus Christ with one stride, have mercy on me with the next. When I came back from running, I would shower and read my Dostoevsky until sext. It was a recipe for crazy, and I suppose crazy was what I had become. But with the crazy came clarity: I went back home, I got back to work.

It was that clarity, I suppose, that had sent me back. I'd had a slip up but it was behind me—three days of winter depression nursed with Jack Daniels. But my second trip to Gethsemane, though much shorter, had been an equal success: I cleared the toxins both spiritual and physical and left ready to renter life.

At least that was what I was thinking the day Dr. Clayton called a second time.

"I'm formally retracting my request," he said.

"I'm digging around," I told him, which was mostly a lie: I'd done nothing since returning from seeing Dante.

"That's fine," he said, "do what you want. I just don't want to hear about it. More than that, I don't want to look out my window and see you back on my lawn."

"Dr. Clayton—"

"I've thought about this and I cannot—I *will not* forgive what he did to his daughter."

"To Samantha?"

"I've thought about this ever since I called you which I knew immediately was a mistake. The way he chose to die, trying to inflict the maximum amount of pain. Resourceful to the end, the clever son of a bitch."

"What happened to his daughter?"

"You see!" he said. "You see! A complete and goddamn terrible mistake."

And then he hung up, as if I had really had seen.

A quick online search revealed Samantha Clayton and Dwayne Robbins had been arrested the previous year on charges of Possession with Intent to Distribute a Schedule II drug—her dad's old charge. The raid on the Lake Jemike trailer park had come on May 17th, the day before her father had hanged himself with a set of jumper cables tied to a floor joist at the Red Carpet Inn in Fort Lauderdale. A bit more research and I determined the arrests happened the same night the Church of Life More Abundant in Christ burned to its foundation. Arrested at the scene of the fire were Benjamin Franklin Cook, 21, known as "Twitch," and a 17 year old whose name was not made public but I learned was Alan Holman.

● ● ●

I drove down late the following Friday and spent the night at a Motel 6 beneath the palm trees and power lines. LPGA written in crushed shells on a grassy embankment. I'd lived here for eight years and knew this world. Saturday morning I drove past the souvenir shops with their T-SHIRTS 3 FOR $10 and SHARKS TEETH, past the dive shops and the seafood buffets, the gas stations and billboards for eco-tours. The fish camp, the rifle range, the Jewish Community Center.

I found Kenny Walter's online: he'd stayed out west where he ran a gym near Six Flags over Texas. He answered the phone and I identified myself as a writer interested in combat sports. He was engaged and talking until I asked about Shy. He shut up then. He had regrets, sure. More than that he'd signed an NDA. He couldn't talk about any moneys he may or may not have received. *Lawyer told me I can't talk about shit actually.* When he hung up I drove out to Rolly's Boxing & Fitness Emporium in Daytona Beach and sat in his office with the old sweat smells and empty tubes of IcyHot while he told me about the gym—it was not so popular anymore—about his health—Parkinson's, a real bitch—and finally about Shy.

"Three goddamn jobs," he told me.

"I went to see her first fight," he told me. "Out by the fairgrounds."

He shook a sky blue Sinemet out of the pill bottle on his desk and trapped it under one shaking hand.

"You want to get a workout in?" he asked me as I made to leave. "I see you're dressed for success." He motioned at my sweat pants and a BOONEDOCKS MMA t-shirt with a hand that couldn't quite shake it's tremor.

"No, thanks."

"I could hold the mitts for you. You want to strike a little, work off the rust?"

"I really do appreciate you talking to me."

"You want I can wrap your hands, let you have a go at the heavy bag."

I thanked him again and went out to my old gym but found it closed, its storefront now divided between a nail salon and a New China Buffet. I wound up paying $10 to use a Planet Fitness, a sleek and sniveling place of expensive machines and remixes of old pop songs. Celine Dion was playing when I dropped a power clean and was asked to leave, the attendant nineteen and incredulous, his ears gauged, his heart—it appeared—broken.

The next day, Sunday, I drove to the Church of Life More Abundant in Christ. It hadn't occurred to me that it had been just over a year since the church had burned: the new structure had opened only the previous week and streamers faded to the blue of morning still hung from the sign. The church itself appeared as a pre-fab house, all vinyl-siding and fresh mulch, all built atop the foundation of the old. There were maybe a dozen cars nosed into the sandy parking lot. Rolls of sod sat in long stripes. The morning was warm.

I waited until the service started and slipped in while the choir sang *oh what a friend we have in Jesus*. The offering plates were passed. Prayer requests were taken. There were maybe fifty people in attendance and when we were asked to greet each in the fellowship of Christ they all seemed to know each other. I waited for Lonnie Blatts to take to the pulpit and eventually he did. He was in Dickies pants and a short sleeve shirt with pearl snaps and a geometric print. He took his message from the 24th Psalm.

> *Lift up your heads, and the King of glory shall come in.*
> *Who is this King of glory? The Lord strong and mighty, the*
> *Lord mighty in battle.*
> *Lift up your heads, and the King of glory shall come in.*
> And again, the question:
> *Who is this King of glory?*

Who indeed?

I hung back while the congregation filed past the Reverend, out of the church, and into the noon sun, blinking, smiling, meandering their way back to the cars and pickups that slowly left. When I introduced myself Blatts said he knew who I was. He'd seen me there on the back pew and knew right then. He was friends with the manager I'd met at the Family Oaks Campground. He'd figured it was just a matter of time before I came around.

I asked if we could talk and he said he needed to lock up first.

I stood by my car while he turned off the lights and checked the doors. When he walked back out his mood seemed to have changed. He smiled. He seemed less standoffish.

"Why don't we take us a walk," he said, "day like this."

I agreed but when I turned toward the sidewalk I found he had turned the other way and was walking around the church into the field behind it. The grass here was uncut, halfway to my knees, and by the time we stopped at the treeline my feet and the bottom of my cuffs were damp.

"You were Siobhan's friend?" he asked me.

"I didn't know her actually," I said. "I was Thomas Clayton's friend."

"Clayton?"

"I met him in a class I taught. Years ago at Lawtey."

"Clayton?" he said again, as if he hadn't heard right. And then he stepped into the forest and into shadow. The moment he did the low humming noise I hadn't fully registered stopped. It felt like restless jungle, like rainforest. It was swamp, actually, and I realized or maybe just remembered it was still wild here. It was also silent. The insects, the birds, whatever it was I had almost heard had gone quiet. I followed a step behind Blatts, never beside him. The ground was soft and rich, a dark cake that bubbled as we threaded our way past the pines that slowly gave way to palms and oaks.

"Clayton," he said again at one point, though not to me.

I was sweating and could see the sweat on the back of Blatts' neck.

For those not born here, there is a certain wildness to Florida that never quite goes away. The smell of gardenias and night-blooming jasmine. The sheer abundance of chlorophyll— how the world is green and breathing. I ran on the beach once, just before dawn, just south of St. Augustine, and felt that wildness all around me, the way the tide broke and washed and receded, the way I could hear things tucking into the dune grass as I approached. Even the wind felt feral. That was what I felt that day following the Reverend: not just that the world was alive, that everything around me was breathing and buzzing, but that it was untamed too, all of it, myself included.

The ground had been sloping for a while, though it wasn't until Blatts slashed through the foliage of a low-hanging limb that I realized we had walked down to the muddy bank of the St. John's River. The water was blurred with the night's rain, the sun a great rust-colored smear.

"She said it was a dolphin," he said.

Farther down the bank were three Hispanic boys with a single Zebco rod. They saw us and tucked back into the bush, dark and silent and gone.

"A dolphin," he said again. "But that can't be."

"Reverend Blatts?" I said.

I eased my way down to the bank where just below me he had taken up a palm frond and was systematically tearing it, the current taking the fibers as he dropped them. Strangler vines hung around my head.

"Reverend Blatts? What happened to the church?"

"Them boys burned it," he said. "You knew Clayton?"

"Why did they burn it?"

"Why did they burn it?" He looked up at me then, and all at once I was afraid. "Why did they burn a house of the Lord you're asking? Because of him, your friend."

"Because of Thomas Clayton?"

"I went up there," he said. "I knew what was happening. Drugs—it's just another sin. Just another instrument of Him."

"Of who?"

He shook his head and tossed what was left of the frond into the river.

"Sin is just our distance from God, Mr. Powers. 'Your iniquities have made a separation between you and your God.' That's Isiah 59.2. It's probably a joke to you, but it isn't to me."

"It isn't," I said.

"I saw you from the start as one of them piss-and-moan intellectuals. So busy thinking. So busy filling yourself up with your own malarkey. But I tell you this, I knew what was happening. I took up my oil and cast out the demons, so the demons fled. They came here and burned the church. They went with your friend Thomas Clayton down to where he strung himself up in that hotel room of his."

"It isn't a joke to me."

He looked up again, his eyes flat and shining with a light I envied.

"Come down here, Mr. Powers," he said. "Come here."

I did, I came, slipped down the bank, one shoe digging into the soft fluff.

"'Blessed is the man that walketh not in the counsel of the ungodly, nor standeth in the way of sinners, nor sitteth in the seat of the scornful,'" he said. "Come closer."

He smelled of English Leather, a smell I knew from my father.

"Closer."

When he put his hand behind my head I could see a small forest of stubble on his throat, coarse silver hairs. We stumbled out into the river, shin-deep, knee-deep. When it came to my waist I felt the current encircle me like a rope. I felt my feet settle into the soft silt, helpless to stop.

"These are living water," he said. "These are healing waters," he said. "If you believe. Do you believe in these waters, Mr. Powers?"

"I do."

"Do you believe in the power of Jesus Christ the Son of Man and Prince of Peace to wash these sins from your immortal soul?"

"I do," I said.

"Louder, Mr. Powers."

"I said I do."

"Then I baptize thee in the name of the Father, and the Son, and Holy Ghost," he said, and I went back into the water, one hand on the back of my skull, the other across my mouth. It felt like falling into another better life, the way it woke me, and when I opened my eyes I saw the world through amber. I saw the rippling quilt of the surface. I saw the way he had set his feet, wide and firm. He held me there and when I went to rise I felt him push me back down, one of his thumbs going into a nostril, his fingers clawing for my eyes. I thrashed for a moment, feeling him lean into me. It took a moment to realize what was happening, but when it did I struck hard and quick, the base of my left palm into his wrist. He staggered back and I broke free to rise gasping. He had almost fallen and stood cradling his arm.

"I should leave you here," he said through his tears.

I was still gasping, streaming water. I could still feel the way his thin wrist had cracked beneath my hand and it came to me that when Christ died on the cross it was said not a bone was broken.

"I got a mind to leave you right here in this water," he shouted.

I began the slow process of climbing out, the soft riverbed, the gummy bank. I stood beneath the limb he'd knocked aside and panted, the reverend still in the river, waist-deep and weeping.

"You killed her," he said. "All of you did. You people who didn't love her, you godless people who didn't care, who didn't even see her as a human being. You took her money. You took her life. Now you'll go and write a book about her, make her into whatever you want her to be. You are responsible," he said, as I turned and began the long climb back to my car.

"You," he called after me, and I felt it like an arrow.

"You," he said, and I felt it like the truth.

* * *

And here it was, the truth at last.

I learned it, finally, from Alan Holman in the IHOP on Highway 200 outside Ocala just after leaving Reverend Blatts. Alan sat over a glass of OJ and told me how a little over a year before the Church of Life More Abundant in Christ would burn and two vans of FDLE agents would descend on the trailer park, he had met Twitch. Alan and his mom Sandra had just moved in with his grandma in one of the three trailers at the end of Lake Jemike Road, having spent the previous three years in Gainesville where his mother bedded down with a man who owned a string of Money Mike check-cashing franchises while Alan slept in the room above the garage.

"But Twitch?" I asked.

Alan ran a finger around the rim of his OJ.

"He was Dwayne's delivery boy I guess you'd call it."

Alan had been sitting beneath a Thomas Kinkade print when a scrawny boy not much older than him stepped out of a trailer, hiked the crotch of his jeans, and walked over. He was sunburned and wiry with a fuzz of red hair on his head and the Batman emblem tattooed across his back. Alan watched him step delicately across the washed out clearing and stop with one hand on the rail of his grandma's steps.

"She your granny?"

Alan nodded that she was.

"She's all right by me. Miss Carter, I mean," the boy said. "I got pneumonia last year and she pretty much nursed me back to life. Where'd you live before this?"

"Gainesville."

"Well, you ever burn one in Gainesville?"

Which is how Alan wound up back in Twitch's trailer smoking a spliff and listening to Wu-Tang clan. Alan was stoned in a matter of minutes—it wasn't his first time smoking pot, he told me, but it wasn't far from it, either—so later, when he tried to unbend the bullshit biography Twitch had narrated, it was difficult to separate the semi-plausible from the simply ridiculous. There was the back injury in Tallahassee that ended Twitch's season-long winning streak in motocross. Or was it the pneumonia that undid his riding career and the bar fight when he was head of security for Marshall Mathers that cut short his foray into professional bull riding? Maybe it was his time living with grizzlies on the Sitka peninsula in Alaska. Regardless, the Marines were waiting on him. They wanted him as a sniper, train him up, send him to Syria or some shit. He was just waiting on his call-up. Alan smiled, smoked, and eventually passed out.

"The very next day I see him and ask if he's got anymore," Alan told me. "He says he does but it's too late. Says he's just been called up. Says this time next week I'll probably be rolling with some killer up at Quantico. Like he was just some sort of badass commando or whatever."

Alan sat sideways in a booth, skinny with bad skin, somehow both defiant and submissive while the waitress brought out the strawberry pancakes he'd ordered.

"You want more coffee?" I asked.

He appeared both sweet and cynical as he shook his head.

"Maybe just some more juice," he said.

I'd driven up the day before to walk around the trailer where narcotics agents from the Florida Department of Law Enforcement had arrested Samantha Clayton and her boyfriend Dwayne a year prior. Eventually, Alan's grandma had come out to tell me to get the hell on before she called the sheriff, did I not know this was private property? I did, and was in my car and about to leave when Alan came out to say he'd meet me the following day at the IHOP out near the Walmart.

"Maybe just one more glass," he said.

I signaled the waitress and looked at Alan.

"But he didn't go anywhere?"

"Twitch? Hell no."

Twitch was always around, and soon enough they were getting stoned daily, Twitch drinking Four Lokos while Alan slumped in a beach chair and thumbed through his Instagram feed. Twitch had a moped but never went anywhere and Alan thought that a product of the loneliness. Loneliness was everywhere.

His mom had found a Buddhist Temple in Micanopy and his grandma worked to the bone cleaning the lake houses of trial lawyers and periodontists retired to horse country. Both were gone all day and his mother was gone most of the night as well. So Twitch and Alan were always alone, it seemed, and all always high.

It was months later when Sandra brought a man home. She'd been talking about him for weeks: Craig the shaman who had left Taos to study at the Cassadaga Spiritualist Camp before working at a rehab center and eventually stumbling upon Sandra at the Dhammaram Temple. That night, they ate Winn-Dixie fried chicken while Craig explained how what Gaia desired most was our internal harmony.

Dinner was fine, but it all went to shit later that evening when Alan asked about Craig.

"What is he, your dealer? Or are you just sleeping with him?"

He'd at least waited for Craig to leave, but regretted the words before they were even out of his mouth. Sandra looked stunned and he watched her face go wide in confusion before it scrunched with anger.

He started to get up—he had a vision of himself slinking off to bed, indignant, the sight of his back filling his mom with remorse—but she was standing over him, blocking his way.

"I happen to know Craig," she said, "I happen to know Craig from the actual real existing outside world. The world outside this little redneck shit-hole that you would have some vague consciousness of if you ever got balls enough to leave it."

He told me that day at the IHOP he wanted to yell at her, he wanted to have it all out. Look at me, he wanted to say. Look at both of us. This is our life. This is our goddamn existence, mom. Beyond the slinking away fantasy was another, more powerful image: he saw her holding him, both of them crying, but a good cry, the kind of tears that bind. But instead he watched her face harden. Her eyes were dry and her mouth drawn in an ugly hard slot. For the first time since Gainesville, she looked her age.

"I can't talk to you," she said. "I'm sorry. I simply cannot."

Yet when he woke the next morning his mother was sitting cross-legged in the floor, smiling.

"Hey, you," she said. "I was wondering whether you'd want to spend the day with your old mom?"

* * *

The Dhammaram Temple had an air of obsolescence but the grounds remained lovely: a squared-off cemetery and white-washed church, a long sloping meadow and several copses of laurel oaks. It appeared empty the morning Alan and his mother arrived.

"So what do we do?" Alan asked.

"Oh, we do whatever," she said, "we just like, pitch in."

He found a push mower in an aluminum shed and mowed the area down around the Temple and on around the church and graveyard, long sweeping rows that paled the dark grass. It took a couple of hours, and by the end he was soaked in sweat and realized how good it felt to sweat from exertion and not simply from the heat. His mom was raking the walk that led down to the arbor.

"You cut it all?"

"What else can I do?"

She wiped one forearm across her head.

"Oh, baby, take a break. You'll have a heat stroke out here. I think there's a water cooler up near the temple."

He found it around back, a yellow Igloo jug sitting on a discarded pew, a sleeve of paper cones beside it. He fixed a cup and looked out at the lawn. He knew he shouldn't necessarily be proud, but what had been several acres of unruly grass was now as lined and trimmed as an outfield. It wasn't much, really, but he had done a good job and it occurred to him that sometimes that was all that mattered. Do your work. Do it right.

He drank three cones of water and was turning to leave when he saw the two women inside the temple, moving barefoot and silent. It was the younger of the two that held him. She was maybe twenty, he guessed, her hair feathered, her breasts fake, yet unmistakably beautiful.

But more than her beauty, it was the sense of wildness that drew him. There looked to be something feral about her, the thin arms wired with blue veins, the tattooed heart—at least he thought it was a heart—that floated on her brown stomach. She looked twitchy, her body animated by the long-limbed hunger of someone who had survived an extended siege and never lost the habit of nerves. He didn't know who she was but stood watching her until his mother called him.

• • •

"But what about Samantha Clayton?" I asked.

The strawberry pancakes were gone by now.

"That's who I was talking about," Alan said. "That's who I saw."

"Saw where?"

"In the temple like I said, barefoot and all. I didn't realize they'd moved in."

"Samantha and Dwayne?"

"Into the empty trailer, yeah."

• • •

Later that week, Alan was staring at the television—some shit on the Discovery Channel about termites, they didn't have decent cable—and looked out just in time to see Twitch and Dwayne crowded onto the seat and headed up the dirt road. It happened a lot after that, Dwayne and Twitch disappearing together. Craig was around more and Alan spent his evenings and Alan with the TV blaring so that he couldn't hear the headboard knocking against the thin wood-paneled walls. Craig was always gone in the morning, but one day Alan woke to find him at the kitchen table, drinking coffee.

"Day off," his mother told him.

Craig saluted with his cup.

"Lap of luxury, young son. Lap of luxury."

Alan decided to walk to town, whatever there was of it. Craig offered his car but Alan refused it: the point was escape, the point was erasure.

"Well, if you insist," his mother said, "bring us back some beer. Just whatever's cheap, Bud or something."

She gave him a twenty and he started up the highway. It was the time of year crab apples fell and the heat was winey with rot. He hated the smell. Somewhere some kid was growing up with sweet memories about pitching apples in the gloam of evening, dad grilling steaks, mom calling them in to supper. The air full of chlorine and cut grass. But Alan hated it.

The trailers were barely out of sight when he gave up and started for home, sweaty and pissed off, his nose full of death. A moment later the big Dodge barreled down the road, a fan of dust behind it like a rooster's tail. He stepped into the woods but instead of passing the truck slowed. When the window came down he saw that it was Samantha.

"Hey," she said. "You live in the first trailer, don't you?"

"Yeah."

"I thought I'd seen you around. I'm Sam. What's your name?"

"Alan."

"Well, you want a ride or something, Alan?"

Two bags of groceries sat in the passenger seat and she told him to just push them over.

"This is Dwayne's daddy's truck," she said. She looked too small for the driver's seat, skinnier, but prettier too, a seahorse charm against her throat. He could see her knuckles on the wheel, bony thumbs, an onyx ring. The tips of her fingernails were ivory. "I've been after him to get us something but I guess he's too lazy to do anything besides ask his daddy for a handout."

When they passed his mom's trailer he spotted Craig through the front window. He was on the couch. The look of concentration on his face meant he was probably watching Animal Planet, drunk.

"You don't mind walking, do you?" Samantha asked. "I just need to get this stuff in before it melts."

He didn't mind. It was no more than thirty steps, and why didn't he just help her with these bags? He hadn't believed he said it, but she smiled and might have even blushed.

"You are such a gentleman," she said.

He carried the bags up the front steps, stopping by the pool just long enough to look back at the window where he had spent so many days watching this exact spot. Inside, he felt a moment of panic. But Samantha was already unloading the bags. She offered him a Coke but he could tell she was only being polite, her mind wasting on worry, her boyfriend, her isolated life. Whatever it was she spent her days thinking about. He let himself out and trudged back to face Craig and Sandra.

It went on for weeks, Alan watching the trailer all day and only occasionally catching sight of Samantha, Dwayne and Twitch disappearing up the road each evening in the Dodge. Alan would hear them return but was never certain of the time, two, three in the morning. Sometimes another man was there too.

"Thomas Clayton," I said.

"Yeah, Sam's dad. That preacher told me he was the devil. We all just called him Doc."

"You met him?"

"Doc? Twitch was working for him and Dwayne, just like a runner or whatever."

"Did you know what they were doing?"

"I mean no. I mean sort of," he said and took up his orange juice. "I mean it wasn't hard to guess. I think Twitch thought it was some sort of big complicated cartel thing when really it was just Doc middle-manning pills from Miami or wherever up to Dwayne."

"Dwayne was the one selling?"

"To pretty much everyone from Gainesville south to Leesburg. It was a tight thing they had going. Then that preacher came. Blatts or whatever."

"What was he doing?"

"Nothing. Which was the thing. Just walking around not even knocking on a door. Spying, I guess it was. But that wasn't for a while."

Alan's mother wanted him to return to the Temple but Craig was back in the picture and Alan preferred solitude to bullshit. He quit getting up to sit with his grandma in the morning. He quit doing anything beyond watching for Sam.

● ● ●

All the while, the days passed into an even deeper monotony of boredom and routine, one after the next. School started. Christmas came and went. The preacher had started poking around by then, but it didn't affect Alan. His mom and Craig mostly stayed in the trailer, drinking Bud Light and watching CMT. Craig would disappear a couple of days a week only to return with random gifts, costume jewelry, second-hand t-shirts, once a Cleopatra headdress Sandra wore while she danced to Kenny Chesney.

One day Twitch came looking for him, fidgeting on the stoop and drinking one of his sacred Four Lokos. It had been weeks since Alan had seen him and Twitch appeared to have gained some weight.

"I was in the mother-flipping jailhouse," he said. They had shaved his head in jail and his hair had grown out unevenly. A tooth was broken. "Did you not know?" Dwayne had called the cops when Twitch, running on Ivory Snow bath salts, had taken his truck out joyriding. "Criminal god-dang mischief, but you know what? It was all to the good cause I found Jesus in the lockup." They were back by the front stoop, Alan just inside the door, Twitch on the bottom step. "Reverend Blatts, he came to see me. Got me on the straight and narrow now, brother."

"What about Dwayne?"

"I done forgiven Dwayne." Then added, as if he'd almost forgotten: "As Christ has forgiven me."

"So you aren't working for him anymore?"

"Man, come on. I done told you: I'm on the straight and narrow."

But that night Alan heard the moped whine by.

● ● ●

The Reverend showed back up the next morning. He'd come a couple of times before but Alan hadn't seen him lately. His plates said Volusia County which meant a two-hour ride past horse farms and pastures and chicken houses with giant ventilation fans. Churches everywhere. Picnic shelters and big two-by-four crosses with towels dyed purple and hung over the arms.

He didn't care how long it took.

"I figure he thought he was on some sort of mission," Alan told me.

When he'd come before it always the day after Doc had visited, "which meant he was following him, I guess," Alan said. The Reverend hadn't spoken since his first visit. Didn't knock on any doors or attempt to talk to anyone. Just walked around looking, "like he was memorizing the place or something. The whole time waving that Bible around."

But that day was different.

How long he was there before Alan heard him speaking he didn't know, only that he parted the blinds to find the man standing on the gravel road with his arms spread, a Bible in one hand, something Alan couldn't make out in the other.

"But it was oil," he told me, "in like a little squirt water bottle. He was yelling about the Word of God and demons and sin and all. The whole time spraying that little squirt bottle everywhere. About that time Dwayne and Doc come out.

"They were yelling," Alan told me. "I couldn't tell what exactly. Then they just commenced to kicking the shit out of him. They left him there and after a while he just got in his car and left. The preacher, I mean."

● ● ●

It was early evening when Twitch knocked. A storm had blown up in the afternoon, big thunderheads and a startling wind that approached from a reckless angle, but no rain had fallen.

"Your mama not home?" he asked. "She ain't with Craig is she? You ain't seen that son of a bitch, have you?"

"I don't know anything about it."

"Well, all right," he said. "I don't mean to get worked up about it. Real reason I stopped was to see if you'd go out with me." He held up a bottle of Mad Dog 20/20. "Celebrate my release on my own personal recognizance."

They took Craig's car and drove all the way to Volusia County—*just anywhere I don't know a soul, all right?*—but it wasn't just anywhere and they wound up drinking the Mad Dog behind the Church of Life More Abundant in Christ.

"This is his church," Twitch said. "That preacher that come to see me."

"What was it like in jail?" Alan asked.

"It wasn't all that. You had to fight your first day. That was about the worst part." He took a packet of Ivory Wave from his pocket. "You want to go halfs on this?"

Alan shook his head.

"Man, that's the same shit that got you locked up in the first place."

"Not really," Twitch said. He looked dejected though. "It was a lot a shit preceding it, but I know what you're saying. Fuck it. You know what we should do? We should burn this shit, like ceremonially?" He climbed to the edge of the green Dumpster, lit the edge of the packet and held it aloft.

"I don't know, man," said Alan.

"I gotta commit it to the flames."

"I don't know. It's full of cardboard, you know?"

And it was: old boxes pressed flat and piled above the metal lip, the wind lifting them so that they flapped like loose shingles. Twitch looked like he was reconsidering then the packet caught and almost exploded in his hands *oh fuck* and he dropped it. A span of cardboard lit almost immediately.

"Stomp it out," Alan called.

But it was burning wildly now, popping and cracking. Twitch jumped down just as the metal expanded with a dull boom. A flaming box lifted and skittered across the parking lot, then another.

"We need to get out of here," Alan said to himself, and then louder: "We need to get out of here, Twitch."

Cardboard was everywhere now, lifted by the wind, lifted by the turning thermal of the fire, floating in hand-sized triangles of burning ash.

"We need to go," Alan said.

But Twitch wasn't listening. Instead his eyes were fixed on what Alan thought for a brief moment might be an opening in the sky, Twitch's new-found savior come to claim him, but was instead the roof of the church, burning.

He grabbed Twitch by the elbow.

"We gotta go, man. Come on. We gotta run."

"No," Twitch said. There was light enough to see he was

crying. "No," he said. "I've got to stay. I've fucked up every second of my life but I've got to stay."

"Man—"

"Jesus didn't run," he said. "Jesus didn't tap." He turned to Alan. "You go on, though."

But Alan had known from the moment the fire caught that he wasn't going anywhere, and he didn't.

• ● •

"The arson guy from the state police or whatever said we couldn't have started it like that if we'd meant to which is how I got off so light," Alan told me. "Twitch though..."

"He had his prior."

"Yeah. Poor Twitch."

"And that was the same night they arrested Sam and Dwayne?"

Alan nodded. "I mean not that I knew it at the time."

"You think the preacher had called them?"

"No," he said. "I think Twitch did. I think he called them and then came over to get me out."

• ● •

It took two days to track down Sandra and Craig—they were on their way back from Taos, a four day drive they made in two, swallowing White Crosses and taking turns at the wheel of a new Navigator, three kilos of Mexican Rail in Craig's Patagonia bag. Alan's grandma had no idea what to do so Alan spent three days alone in a holding cell at the city jail where he met the public defender, an angry little man with dandruff. But then Craig showed up with a pot of money and soon enough Alan had a lawyer that ran commercials during *The Montel Williams Show*. Twitch went to the state for a year and a day and Alan was sentenced to three months at the Canebrake Wilderness School for At-Risk Youth.

When he got out, he got out. It wasn't a big thing.

Sandra and Craig had split for Taos and Twitch's trailer appeared empty. Dirt daubers had built nests along the siding and the gutter was clogged by a nest of swallows. Alan found the moped down in the scrub pine. Someone had walked it down to the creek and slit the tires. His grandma seemed exhausted beyond recognition, a gray hulk washed up on the shores of her sixty-third year. When she knelt to pray for the cast of *General Hospital* Alan could hear her jaw work, her knees. Her teeth were gray, as leaned and ticked as the garden gnomes in the yard.

He didn't know what had happened to Thomas Clayton until I told him.

"That was the next day?" he asked. "After the fire and all?"

"It was."

"Jesus. That was some bad shit, I guess."

"Did you ever meet Doc's girlfriend? Look here." I took out my phone, brought up a photo of Shy Walsh, and showed him.

"The fighter?" he asked. "That's was Doc's girlfriend?"

"You heard of her?

"Everybody has. The one who disappeared, right?"

"The same."

"Holy shit. I just realized something." He leaned forward in the booth. "That was the other woman, the one I saw that day in the temple with Sam."

"Shy?"

"It had to be. They were both barefoot. Holy shit. I thought they were sisters or something."

"What were they doing?"

He leaned back then, as if the realization was an actual thing there the on table between us, something alive, something possibly dangerous.

"They were." He cleared his throat. "They were dancing."

• • •

How Doc heard about the fire I don't know. He must have got back to the boat that evening, the Reverend's blood still dried on his hands, the blood he told Shy wasn't his. Maybe he heard something that night on the police scanner, but I doubt it. More likely, it was the news the following morning. Whatever it was, I wonder what he felt then? Panic, perhaps. But more than that, I think shame. The shame of having twice ruined his daughter's life. The shame of having wrecked his own. *There's so much sin in the world.* And it's true, there is. There's goodness too, but sin—we make it every second.

Doc must have seen it on the galley TV on the houseboat.

It must have been early: Shy was still swimming.

Doc didn't wait.

I see that shame welling up in him, and with it, that need to get away before Shy returned. I see him grabbing some things, clothes, money, a small stash of pills, shoving it all into his old gym bag before pulling on the same Ariat boots he'd worn that night to the fundraiser for Daniel Garnett. Did he take his books? It's possible, of course. They weren't found after on the boat. They weren't found at the Red Carpet Inn either. He might have already sold the last of them, his Hemingway, his Fitzgerald, but I don't think he had.

I'll tell you what I think.

I think he gathered his books, I think he gathered the useless correspondence with Médecins sans Frontières—

(And what if they had taken him? What if instead of

dealing in North Florida he'd been tending to breech births in Nicaragua? What if he'd never encountered Monica Garnett that night in the ER? How might life have been different? Did he think of this? Did he consider the awful process by which a simple poppy came to bind with the dopamine receptors in his brain? Did he measure it chemically, or geopolitically, how about personally? Did he give thought to a different life, one without the needles and pills and suppositories? I doubt it. *Can you draw out Leviathan with a hook, Or snare his tongue with a line which you lower?*)

—I think he simply gathered his books, gathered the letters, and walked into the river.

How far did he wade out?

Far enough to scare himself, had he still been capable of fear. Waist-deep I think. Deeper, perhaps, as far out as the Reverend Lonnie Blatts had dragged me. And then he sank it all, held it under, forced it under. The books must have frustrated him, their insistent rise, the papers too, like autumn leaves, turning, drifting. But he was vigilant; he stayed until they sank. Then he got in his car and drove away.

It doesn't matter where.

But in the end it does.

In the end, he gets a room in Fort Lauderdale only a few miles from where his parents sit in their dim living room. He calls Shy on his cell. *If you get this—when you get this—hey, please call me, Shy, okay?* Calls her from where he sits on the balcony, the plastic lounge chair tipped against the block wall, perfectly still. His daughter is being held at the Marion County Sheriff's office and by now they must be looking for Doc too. But he doesn't get up, just sits, thinks. Maybe he picks the Reverend's blood from his hands—what he hadn't managed to wash clean the night before. At some point he calls Shy a second time. *Shy, you there?* But beyond that he does nothing except sit through the day, drinking, waiting, the phone in his lap like this thing that might yet wake, this thing that might yet save him.

When he calls her a third time he doesn't leave a message. It's dark now and though the night is beginning to cool it's still warm, the asphalt holding the day's heat, the dried palm fronds swishing, and he thinks for a moment that perhaps he can live like this, alone, adrift. There's a narcotic undertow to it all, to disappear into interstate motels, into movement, the sink baths in truck stop restrooms. Wiping your underarms with brown paper towels. Sticking your wet toothbrush beneath the hand-dryer. He had tried. That's what he'd been doing in that room on Siesta Key: trying. But it hadn't work, nothing had. Still, if she calls back, maybe he can go on. If she calls back, he knows he can.

Does he wish for prison?

For the routine?

For the certainty?

Maybe he doesn't wish for anything at all. Maybe he swallows two Xanax and checks his phone. That must be when he finds his daughter's mugshot on the website of WOGX out of Ocala. He lets that hit him. He lets that settle in him like the single weight he can't bear to carry. He must think of his daughter for a while, maybe remembers that night he came home to sit by her bed, remembers the day he left the little seahorse charm on her pillow. I don't know if he thinks of Shy or not. I hope that he does.

I hope he imagines Shy and Sam together.

I hope that before he goes out and takes those jumper cables from his car, before he pushes up the drop ceiling to find the floor joist (*clever son of a bitch*), I hope that before he plays Arvo Pärt's *Da Pacem Domine* from his phone, before his eyes assume some final color, some last permutation we will all come to know, I hope that he imagines Shy and Sam together.

I hope that he imagines them dancing.

● ● ●

But Shy wasn't dancing, not that day.

She wouldn't have heard about the church burning until late morning.

Let's suppose she came back from her swim and turned on the news and there it was: arson, two males, one a minor, arrested at the scene. The Reverend Lonnie Blatts badly beaten in a separate incident. *My God, Tommy*—but Tommy wasn't around.

Doc was gone and where was he?

Why wasn't he here?

But at least that much must have been clear: Doc was gone because Doc was somehow responsible.

Maybe at first she thought he might explain himself.

Maybe she called for him, walked back around the pool and putt-putt course looking for him. But maybe not. Maybe just she thought: you want to cry?

At some point she must have heard of the narcotics raid, and on hearing, there must have been some spark of knowing, some spark of connection. She must have seen the missed calls from Doc. But she wasn't thinking of Doc anymore. She wasn't thinking at all: it was ritual now, muscle memory, involuntary response. She put on her swimsuit, still damp from the morning swim, and took the trashcan from by the manager's office. Filled it with ice from the cooler by the pool and ran the hose. Lowering her body, it all came back, the way it burned, the way it flipped some internal switch so that suddenly it was not unlike that morning in Texas when she and Kenny had started running and for a moment, as brief as it had been, she had thought they would never stop. They had, of course, but this felt different. This felt like the world for which she'd been intended.

Where you are is a place.

She walked to the river where even at this hour the light was still brilliant, still silver and charged and not yet beginning to fail.

Where you are is a place.

What is happening to you is your life.

She stopped when she heard the birds. The path was a shadowed thread tunneled beneath the palm and oak and when she pushed through the last of the sawgrass the birds were deafening: white ibises, roseate spoonbills, herons, Sandhill cranes—a flotilla of wings folded atop the water and along the riverbank.

She must have gasped, something approaching wonder stillborn in her throat.

At the sound of her, they lifted as one, and she stood on the bank, barefoot and swinging her arms as they rose into the dusk in pinks and whites and the iridescent blue-green of bottle glass. She followed them until they were gone, until the water was still again, until the water was an unbroken mirror in which she saw herself.

She must have realized she could step right into it.

She must have realized she could she swim forever, far enough to leave herself behind. The night Kenny had unwired her jaw she had realized that her body, this body, was just an appendage, something that hung on her, weighed her with sorrow, and she could survive without it. She could. The way she had waited for that roundhouse, knowing it was coming and then letting it come all the same—what was that but renunciation, an acknowledgment that while her life was many things, it wasn't hers? What was getting kicked but the single thing she'd done for herself?

She watched. She waited. She knew it would come for her

and didn't move until she saw its silver gleam, the dorsal fin, the tail. What had her mother said: you live a life to be rid of it.

And it was true, to a certain extent it was true.

She put her face into the water.

It was surely true, everything her mother had said.

Still, what is a dolphin but a blessing?

What is a dolphin but a holy spirit?

I think it just hunted her down relentless.

After seeing Lonnie Blatts and then Alan Holman, I didn't drive straight home to Atlanta but instead decided to stop for the night at the Golden Lion where Doc and Shy had once stayed.

It was late May, not yet tourist season, and the place was mostly empty. I got a room, took off my shoes, and went out to the tiki bar overlooking the shell beach and the tide breaking over it.

I needed a suspension of sorts.

I needed some dividing line, I think, some border greater than the St. Mary's River between the old life I was leaving and the new one, the current one, to which I was returning. Nobody's watching. But that didn't make things any easier.

Maybe I finally understood as much.

Or maybe I simply didn't know what else to do.

I wasn't burning Doc's pages. I lied about that, though I did consider it.

I never wrote the *think piece* I had intended either, Siobhan Walsh as American Martyr and so forth (the line about Vermeer—it embarrasses me now), and sitting there by the beach I knew I never would. I never even went to see Samantha Clayton. It would have made sense: she was serving three years at FCI Tallahassee, low security, and I could have just gone, I could have just shown up, followed her down whatever staircase she had descended. But I didn't want to do that. I didn't, in fact, want to do anything more. I had lived in the northeast for a while and it occurred to me I could go back. Maybe what I needed was a place where fewer things were so obviously and immediately alive, a place with less light. Or maybe I'd go back to Gethsemane, find the old guest master, take up residence in a place with no more than a bed and a desk and Christ on the wall. Maybe this time I would stay.

I considered this sitting there that night, the ocean spread before me. The moon had risen and it was bright enough to see to the horizon, and I thought of Shy swimming through those waters. I was maudlin and maybe a little drunk, a state I've come to recognize as two parts nostalgia and one part bullshit, a state I've come to inhabit more and more lately. Yet I meant it. I hoped for it. That she kept swimming, that she never stopped, that's she's still out there, still moving.

That was my wish.

That was my—

I almost said prayer.

Either way, I wished her Godspeed.

I wanted her to go on forever, happy and blessed and free.

Or maybe I'm talking about my own heart.

ACKNOWLEDGMENTS

This is wholly and completely a work of fiction, but, as with so much of life, it isn't quite that simple. I did live in Florida and teach at Lawtey Correctional Institute, but I am most certainly not the narrator. And while I did know a man known as Doc who very tragically took his own life after his release, that Doc is not the Doc of these pages. Besides a few superficial details about his life before incarceration, the Doc presented herein is imaginary. In fact, while I've drawn on stories, anecdotes, memories, and hearsay, none of the men found in this novel represent men I actually knew. What I have tried to portray accurately is the difficulties faced by so many after incarceration.

My thanks to Ron Earl Phillips and the Shotgun Honey Hive; the Lost Mountain Adventure Club; the Monday Night Sewanee Crew; Katy Abrams; Clint Bentley; Frank Bill; Pete Duval; Caleb Johnson; Jim Steel; Steve Weiss; and Zack Vernon. To Alex Phillips of Evolve Krav Maga, Michael Denner, Daniel Ham, the folks at Boonedocks MMA, and everyone else who ever knocked me around.

This novel began as the short story "Narrowing" in Hunger Mountain. Portions also appeared in the Oxford American and PANK.

My heart to Denise, Silas, and Merritt. This book is in Doc's memory, and dedicated to Dave and Reggie, two brilliant men I met at Lawtey who—like Doc—should in no way be confused with any of the characters here.

Mark Powell is the author of seven previous novels including *Small Treasons* (2017, Gallery/Simon and Schuster), and *Lioness* (2022, WVU Press). He has received fellowships from the National Endowment for the Arts, the Breadloaf and Sewanee Writers' Conferences, and twice from the Fulbright Foundation to Slovakia and Romania. He directs the creative writing program at Appalachian State University in Boone, NC. Prior to ASU, he lived in Florida for eight years where he taught at Stetson University while running a prison writing program.

ABOUT
SHOTGUN HONEY BOOKS

Thank you for reading *Hurricane Season* by Mark Powell.

Shotgun Honey began as a crime genre flash fiction webzine in 2011 created as a venue for new and established writers to experiment in the confines of a mere 700 words. More than a decade later, Shotgun Honey still challenges writers with that storytelling task, but also provides opportunities to expand beyond through our book imprint and has since published anthologies, collections, novellas and novels by new and emerging authors.

We hope you have enjoyed this book. That you will share your experience, review and rate this title positively on your favorite book review sites and with your social media family and friends.

Visit ShotgunHoneyBooks.com

FICTION WITH A KICK

shotgunhoneybooks.com